STRANDED HEARTS

by

Kris Bryant, Amanda Radley, *and* Emily Smith

2022

STRANDED HEARTS

ISBN 13: 978-1-63679-182-1

This Trade Paperback Original Is Published By
Bold Strokes Books, Inc.
P.O. Box 249
Valley Falls, NY 12185

First Edition: July 2022

Credits
Editor: Cindy Cresap
Production Design: Stacia Seaman
Cover Design by Tammy Seidick

CONTENTS

EF5

Kris Bryant

CHAPTER ONE

"You're kidding me, right?" I knew Whitney wasn't. The fact that bridezilla went over my head and contacted my boss directly pissed me off.

"They want you there early because the weather is iffy. Looks like it's supposed to storm this afternoon, so they want the photos done before the ceremony," Whitney said, her emphasis on the word "before."

I took a deep breath and pinched the bridge of my nose. "I told her that a million times, but Mandy wanted to keep it traditional and do it after." I breathed out. "When do they want me?"

"They've bumped everything ninety minutes."

"Fuck."

"Are you ready?" she asked.

I looked at my perfectly toasted bagel smothered in cream cheese and my mug of steaming black coffee and sighed. "Almost. At least the car's packed. I need a few minutes to get ready, but I should be there in an hour or so." If I drove at least ten miles above the limit.

"I'll let them know. Good luck."

I couldn't believe the client went behind my back. She called me for every other little thing. "Can you take photos of the bridal shower? What about the bachelorette party? Isn't it all included in the price? We're paying you a fortune." But she knew I'd push back, so that's why she went directly to Whitney. I couldn't wait for this day to be over. I slipped into my black suit and did a five-minute makeup job. My curly mop was easy to pull up in a bun. I did a quick equipment check and was on the road with my coffee in ten minutes. I packed the bagel for later. The last thing I needed was white cream cheese smeared on my black suit.

My travel app put me in Hodges, Missouri, in one hour and twelve minutes. Most of the travel was on country roads and those were sometimes dicey. The one time I drove down early to scout the property, I had to slam on my brakes to keep from running over a dog chasing a family of skunks. Aside from almost wrecking my car, the trip was inspiration. Bridezilla came from money and the Luffs' house was the perfect backdrop for a Midwestern wedding. Even though she was unbelievably entitled, I was looking forward to taking photos in a place that screamed rustic charm.

The bride and groom were an attractive couple and very much into the country life. Most of the weddings I shot were traditional with tuxedos and long, gorgeous wedding dresses. Bridezilla was wearing white, but it was an asymmetrical chiffon lace gown that was tight in the places she wanted and open in the front so she could show off her turquoise and white cowgirl boots. The groom was wearing black jeans, a white and turquoise sawtooth snap pocket Western shirt, and white and turquoise boots similar to hers. Not my taste, but they were sickeningly cute enough to pull it off.

I was turning onto the first of several country roads that would land me in Hodges when my phone rang. I hit the phone button on my steering wheel. "Hi, Mom. What's going on?" My four-lane interstate luxury was reduced to two lanes. God help me if I got behind a tractor or combine harvester on the curvy roads.

"Are you still shooting that wedding today?"

"Yes, why?"

"I just figured with the weather turning they would have rescheduled."

It's like she knew nothing about the stress of planning a wedding. "No, a wedding isn't easily rescheduled, but they did ask me to show up early before it hits. I'm headed there now."

"Honey, I don't like this. The Weather Channel just elevated the storms to severe. It looks like they might be headed down south where you're going."

My anxiety was already at a nine out of ten. I took a deep breath. "Mom, the weather is the least of my worries right now. I'm dealing with an incredibly selfish bride who is livid that I can't be there right now."

"Well, she's being ridiculous. She should have at least put you up for the night if she wanted so much done."

"Right? She picks the cheapest package but wants everything we offer in the big one at no additional charge." My mom wasn't happy that I became a wedding photographer because they were a dime a dozen, but she also knew I was good at my job and kept quiet when I complained about doing a big job for not enough money. I always gave her friends discounts when they wanted me to take birthday party photos or senior class photos. It was sweet that Mom thought she was doing me a favor by sending business my way, but I barely made a profit on her referrals.

"Just be your normal charming self. You'll get through this. I'll let you go, but please be careful and call me when you're done. You know I worry when you travel alone."

"Thanks, Mom, but I have roadside assistance and a fully charged phone." I disconnected the call only for my loud, head-banging music to be interrupted by another call. I snarled when I saw Mandy Luff's name.

"This is Alyssa." I switched to my professional voice.

"Alyssa, where are you? You were supposed to be here by now."

"I told Whitney that I would be there in about an hour." I looked at my estimated time of arrival. "I still show thirty minutes. I can't go any faster." A part of me wanted to slow down because she was so unlikeable, but her parents were cool and the ones paying me, so I kept it steady.

"But we're waiting on you."

I shrugged and flipped off the display knowing full well she couldn't see me but felt better at releasing my immature rage. "I'm sorry, but I can't get there any sooner. I know there's a storm coming and I'm trying to get there as fast as I can." She made a noise that could only be described as pure frustration and hung up. I should have been worried, but nobody else could get out there in the blink of an eye. Plus, I knew weddings were stressful. She wasn't the first bride to completely lose her shit right before she walked down the aisle.

I took a sip of coffee and tried hard to ignore the rumbling in my stomach. I checked my time. Twenty-two minutes. The speed limit was fifty-five, but I set the cruise at sixty-four. Less than ten was excusable. Over, I'd get a ticket. I steered with both hands because I wanted to be prepared if another woodland creature found its way to the asphalt in front of me. One close call was enough. My ringtone blasted through the speakers, startling me. It was bridezilla's mom. I rolled my eyes.

"Hi, Alyssa. It's Peggy. I thought I would check in to see how close you are."

"Eighteen minutes. I jumped in the car as soon as my boss called."

"I know you're doing the best you can. We'll be patient," she said.

I could hear angry voices in the background even though Peggy muffled the phone. I looked in my rearview mirror. The world looked ominous behind me. "I'm in front of the storm so as soon as I get there, I'll jump out and start photographing." I had my Canon on the seat beside me ready to shoot. I always had a camera ready because you never knew when you were going to see the perfect shot.

"Is there anywhere you want us to be?" Peggy asked, drawing me back into the conversation.

"As long as the weather holds and doesn't put you in any danger, I'd love to start at the barn."

"Sounds good. We'll head there and see you in twenty. Be careful."

At least she was nice. I slowed as I was approaching the small town of Bayonet, one town away from Hodges. I smiled at the old gas station with pumps that had nozzles on the side and porcelain signs that lit up stating they had cold beer and the best chicken wings in Missouri. My stomach rumbled again at the thought of food, even gas station snacks, but I couldn't stop. I would have to power through my hunger and make it through the next two hours before I could sneak away and eat. Maybe I could nab a roll or something from the kitchen before the reception.

I rolled past the gas station and the antique store. There were three main streets in the town, and once I blew through the final street, I sped up. Nobody was out. The dark sky behind me was starting to gain ground. My peripheral vision picked up rain to the north, but I was turning south on Highway 57. That would afford me a few minutes. What I didn't predict was the cop who swung out from behind a rickety, aged billboard advertising local honey who flipped on their red and blue lights signaling me to pull over.

"Damn it!" I smacked the steering wheel and turned into a parking lot of an empty diner. My anxiety was now at a ten. I lowered my window and looked behind me.

"Ma'am, stay in the car," a feminine voice yelled from the police cruiser. So many thoughts crossed my mind. Maybe she would be sympathetic and give me an escort or maybe she would give me a warning and let me go so I would only be ten minutes late. Watching her lithe form saunter in the rearview kicked up the dust around my libido. My heart did a little shimmy and not just because I was nervous. She cocked her head and looked at me. I bit my lip for fear that I would trip over my words and say something ridiculous. She was beautiful. I couldn't tell if I liked her copper brown eyes or her full red lips more. Her hair was pulled back in a long French braid that fell over one shoulder. Even the campaign hat perched on the top of her head gave her a sexy authoritative look. She looked at me expectantly and hitched her brow.

"I'm sorry, Officer. I know I was speeding, but I was trying to beat the storm. I'm a photographer and I'm late to a wedding in Hodges. Can you please let me go? I promise to stay at the limit."

"I clocked you going fifty-four in a thirty-five zone. Can I see your license and registration?" Her voice rose only because the wind had picked up and thunder rumbled continuously above us. The rain would fall any moment.

Fuck. There goes the job. "My purse is in the back seat. Can I get out of the car to get it?" I could tell she wasn't happy about that, but fumbling behind me didn't seem like a good idea either and I needed to get this over and done with now. She nodded and took a step back so I could get out of the car. Damn, she was tall. Gorgeous, serious, and wearing a uniform. If I wasn't in such a hurry, I would have flirted and spent more time charming my way out of a ticket. Who knew the smallest blip of a town would have the hottest cop?

"This doesn't feel safe. The weather, I mean. I feel safe with you." My words were awkward, so I clamped my mouth shut and handed her my information. The wind was even louder outside the car. The sudden shift in the weather was frightening. Leaves and dirt picked up and swirled around us. It smelled like earth and freshly mowed grass. Tiny pebbles hit my chest and all I could think was why did I wear a white shirt?

She looked at the sky. "Oh, shit." She grabbed my arm and pushed me toward the closed diner. "We need shelter right now."

I should have been concerned that she was touching me, but I knew something was wrong. If she was scared, then I should be, too. "What's happening?" I shouted even though, deep down, I already knew the answer.

Chapter Two

Daisy, our office manager and dispatcher who retired from Hodges Elementary School before I graduated high school, sent out an "attention all units" about the weather. I studied my surroundings and frowned at the dark storm forming off in the distance. The last thing I needed was the wind to blow down the old billboard I was parked next to and damage my hand-me-down Dodge Durango from the Kansas City police department. It was our department's newest vehicle. We lost two of our four cruisers in a flash flood three months ago, and since I was sheriff of the county, it was now my car.

I radioed Daisy. "How big is this storm?"

"It looks pretty rough, and Doppler has it closing in on all the counties from down in Arkansas all the way up to Jackson County in Missouri. I haven't heard any sirens, but I'm going to lock up and head to the basement anyway," she said. It wasn't out of the ordinary for her. The station had a nice, secure basement with provisions and several cots set up for emergencies. Daisy cleaned it weekly even though nobody had been down there in months.

"Be safe and take the radio with you." It was the fire department's job to sound the whistle if things got bad, followed up with a text message to everyone in the county who had a cell phone.

A white flash of a car sped by, and I looked at my speed gun in amazement. Fifty-four and climbing. Maybe they were trying to beat the storm, but the town's safety and theirs was more important than a storm. It was the weekend, and a warm one, so more kids were out playing, although hopefully they were safely inside at this moment. I flipped on my lights and peeled out onto the road behind the white car. A short burst of my siren made them quickly pull into the parking lot of my parents' diner, the Lunch Box, that sat on the edge of town. It was being renovated so it was empty. Too bad because the entire town would have loved to see this ticket happen. I tried to run the plates, but I couldn't get a solid connection on my laptop because of the storm. With Daisy already downstairs, I was going to have to do this the old-fashioned way. I grabbed my pen and notebook. A woman stuck her head out the driver's window and yelled something I couldn't hear.

"Ma'am, stay in the car." Keep your pants on, Karen. I'm getting there.

I stepped out of the car and tamped down my hat when it threatened to fly away at the sudden upsweep of wind. We were in for a whopper of a storm. I had to be quick.

She explained she was in a hurry and while I found her attractive, I had a job to do.

"I clocked you going fifty-four in a thirty-five zone. Can I see your license and registration?"

"My purse is in the back seat. Can I get out of the car to get it?" she asked.

I nodded and waited not so patiently as she crawled out of the front seat and opened the back door to get her purse.

"This doesn't feel safe. The weather, I mean. I feel safe with you." She handed me her license.

The thunderstorm roared closer and the tiny hairs on the back of my neck stood at attention. I looked at the nearly black sky and the storm barreling toward us. "Oh, shit." Out of instinct, I grabbed her arm and raced over to the diner. "We need shelter right now."

"What's happening?" Even though she was yelling, it was hard to hear her, but I felt her panic in the way she grasped my arm.

I fumbled with my keys. Fuck. Which one was it? My hands were shaking as the sky roared above us. The woman clung to me. I pushed the stubborn door open and slammed it behind us. From the glass doors we could see the storm lurching closer. I raced behind the counter and grabbed matches and a flashlight.

"Get away from the window," I shouted at her.

"Is that the front of the storm? I've never seen one this close."

"That's a tornado." I bit my lip and nodded, trying hard to keep it together. I'd learned from the catastrophic Joplin tornado that they could be as wide as the eye could see. She looked at me with piercing blue eyes and covered her mouth with both hands in shock. "Holy fuck," she said through shaking fingers. I grabbed her hand and quickly led her to the cooler. It was the safest place in the diner. We were sitting ducks in our cars, and trying to outrun a tornado this close was a horrible idea. This one was swallowing everything in its path.

The cooler was off during renovations and a large deep freezer had been pushed in the corner for safekeeping. "Help me slide this over to the door. The door won't lock from inside so we need to cover it in case it flies open." The deep freezer was on wheels, but it was heavy and took all my strength and hers to get it in front of the door.

We huddled in the now vacated corner of the cooler and held one another. The lights went out and she started crying. Fear gripped my throat, but I held back my tears. The roar above us, a runaway trai gaining speed, was deafening. Even though we were inside the coo¹ we could hear things crash above us, glass break, and steel moan.

The woman clutched me and sobbed. "We're going to die. ' going to die."

My shirt was drenched with her tears. "Shh." I tried to s† hair, but I ended up holding her close and shielding her from The diner was being shredded. I didn't know if it had be⸋ seconds, or hours. The cooler shook as the thick steel tw us. Something smashed into the side of it and threw both Out of instinct, I tucked the woman under me and co⸋ with my arms.

The storm had stalled over us. Either that, or tin⸋ the storm was going to last forever. My ears pop⸋ noises from earlier faded. I could still hear, but e⸋ away. I felt something warm on my face and us⸋ away. I couldn't see anything in the dark. I wi⸋ All body parts seemed to be intact.

"Are you okay?" I couldn't tell if I w⸋ to the woman. I felt her nod beneath me, I moved so that I wasn't smashing her ⸋ way until the destructive twister move⸋ in its path.

The silence was quickly replaced with sheets of rain. How we were still alive was a mystery. It was a massive tornado and if it was as big as it looked before we took shelter, we were in for nonstop days of rescue and months of cleanup. We were going to need help from other counties and cities. My heart ached for the towns who were going to be obliterated, including ours.

"Are you okay? You're scaring me," I said.

She sniffed a bit and reached for me. "Yes, I'm okay. A few scratches, but nothing broken."

"Same here, but I think I'm bleeding," I said. Instantly, her hands ran up my arms and over my body.

"Can you tell where?"

"My head. I think something hit me." Now that the adrenaline was leaving my body, the shakes set in. I winced when I felt a cut on my forehead.

"Where's the flashlight? Fuck, I don't even have my phone. It's back in the car."

I checked my duty belt for my tactical flashlight and clicked it on. We both winced at the brightness. She grabbed it and pointed it at my head.

"Yep, you're bleeding. And it looks bad. Is there a first aid kit around here? I mean, I know it's a cooler, but maybe there are rags or something?"

I ignored how soft her fingers felt on my face and how gingerly he inspected the cut near my hairline. "I doubt there's anything in ere. The kit is probably under the counter up front." I shined the light und the cooler looking for anything my parents would have in here elp staunch the flow. The shelves had toppled over like a line of inoes, pouring empty crates everywhere. We were under a vee of es that was being held up by the deep freezer on wheels. That 't safe. "We need to move. This thing could come crashing down cond."

We need to find something to stop that bleeding and get you up. And then figure out how to get out of here. Can you shine t and try to find my shoe? I don't want to step on glass or sharp when I'm barefoot."

ined the light around us and found her shoe wedged under r. I pulled it out and heard the metal shelves creak under my movement. She nodded thanks for her shoe and I shined the light so she could put it on. She was very attractive even under the extreme brightness of my flashlight and after our harrowing ordeal. Her hair was long and curly and falling out of her updo. Her blue eyes showed fright and anger. It occurred to me that I didn't know this woman's name. I had her license somewhere, but I wasn't paying attention because of the storm.

"I'm Katy," I said.

"I'm Alyssa. Now let's get the fuck out of here," she said.

I checked my radio but it was dead. Whatever sliced my forehead, sliced the cord on my shoulder mic. I tried standing but slipped on the slick cooler floor. I felt her hand on my arm.

"Stay here. You're not in any condition to move. You're bleeding all over and I bet you have a concussion," she said.

I hated feeling helpless. I was a sheriff of a small town. I was sworn to protect and serve these people. They needed me now more than ever and I was trapped in a twisted metal box. I couldn't help them. I couldn't even make a call to help them. I wanted to fight Alyssa, but she was probably right. My head was still tender. I couldn't tell if the ringing in my ears was from the possible concussion or the echo of the tornado.

"How long have we been in here?" Alyssa said.

"I lost track of time. Maybe twenty minutes?" I said.

She shined the flashlight on my wound again and winced at what she saw. "Let me crawl around and see what I can find to help your head." She ripped off the rest of her suit jacket sleeve. "This isn't cotton, but it's something you can use to press against your head." She flipped it inside out. "It's cleaner on this side."

I held the flashlight while she scooted around in the small space until she found a spot where she could stand.

"We're going to have to move these shelves in order to move the freezer out of the way," she said. She reached her hand out for the flashlight. "Honestly, the door is so twisted that I don't think we're going to get out that way." She banged on the side of the cooler to no avail.

"Nobody's going to hear us. The diner was shut down for renovations so nobody's going to think to look for us here," I said. It was morbid, but it was the truth. We were on our own.

"How did you know the diner was empty?" She moved around our small space, carefully, looking for anything to help me. "Wait. You had a key. Do you have keys for all the businesses in town?"

"No. This is my parents' diner."

"I guess we got lucky." She reached into a mangled shelf.

"Victory." She held up a pack of tea towels. "Too bad I can't find a first aid kit."

"As soon as we get out of here, I have some superglue in my first aid kit in the Durango," I said and took one of the towels from her. That was assuming the Durango wasn't swept away.

"You're going to use superglue? Isn't that toxic?" Alyssa asked.

"It's not really superglue. It's called Super Stitch or something like that and it works like superglue but it's safe for skin. It'll work for this cut." I pulled the towel away and looked at the blood on it. "It seems to be slowing down." I had a raging headache and wanted to throw up, but I didn't want her to be concerned. We had enough to worry about.

"Can you scooch over here so you're not directly below the wobbly makeshift scaffolding that could fall and smash you? I'd kind of like to get to know the woman who saved me," she said.

"I didn't save you," I grumbled. Had I not stopped her, maybe she could have outrun the storm. Or got to where she was going and hid in a basement safer than a smashed-up cooler that was quickly becoming our tomb. While she was talking, I shined my flashlight around the ten by fourteen area. Even if we cleared the door, we wouldn't be able to open it. It was twisted in the frame and even though I was strong, there was no way I could move a two-hundred-pound door. We needed another way out.

"You definitely did. I probably would have parked my car and let it sweep me away," she said.

"Judging from the way you were driving, I highly doubt that." I changed the subject. "You said you were going to a wedding. Was it Mandy and Jason's?"

"Do you know them? What am I saying, of course you do. There are only so many people around our age in this area, especially ones with a wedding today."

"That's not entirely true," I said. My head was throbbing, and I was trying hard not to panic. I shined the light on the ceiling, looking for a way out. A sliver of gray poked through the corner of the cooler. I shouldn't have been able to see light that wasn't artificial. That meant the diner was gone.

"I didn't mean it like that. I meant that everybody knows everybody in a small town. Are you from here? What town are we in?"

"Bayonet. There are four small towns in our county and we're the largest with a population of almost a thousand."

"Isn't Hodges bigger than that?" she asked.

"It is, but Hodges is in the next county over." Most outsiders didn't realize that Bayonet and Hodges were opposite sides of the county line.

"I didn't realize. I don't know the area very well."

"Are you from Kansas City?"

"Lee's Summit, but the home office is downtown Kansas City. I work wherever they send me."

"Does your family know you're here? I'm sure they're going to be worried about you," I said.

"I talked to my mom about an hour ago and she told me the storm was bad and asked if the bride canceled. I told her I would call her when I was done. She's probably worried sick."

"I'm going to check on my family once we get out of here. They don't live too far from the diner. Just down the street."

"Are you married? Will your partner be worried about you?" she asked.

"Nope. Still single. Only my parents, and I'm more worried about them."

"Single here, too." She cleared her throat. "How bad do you think it is out there? I mean, it sounded horrific and look at what it did to the cooler. I'm so sorry your family's diner got hit."

"I just hope people got to safety. I didn't hear the sirens." I swallowed the lump in my throat when I thought about my family and wondered if they got to the shelter in time. Chances were that the storm knocked down the cell phone towers so not everybody got the message. Going to the storm shelter was a challenge for my dad, who blew out his knee playing football in college. Hopefully, my mother got his stubborn ass out of his chair even though he was glued to it watching baseball on the weekends. "When we get out of here, I'm taking my dad to a Royals game," I said.

Alyssa stopped moving things from one side of the cooler to the other and sat beside me. She turned off the flashlight to preserve the batteries. Nothing was looming over us in this spot so it was safe for a bit. "Are you close with your family?" she asked.

Her leg and shoulder were pressed against mine. It gave me comfort even though I was the one who should be comforting her and promising her I'd find a way out. I needed a few minutes to catch my breath and stop bleeding before we tried to move things. "I am. We have dinner every Sunday. It's nice." I felt her fingers on my hand.

"I think that's sweet. I see my mom once a week. Sometimes it's a quick visit after work, or sometimes we'll just grab a drink and an appetizer out."

"What about your dad? Is he still in the picture?"

Her shoulder moved against mine when she shook her head. "No. He left when I was little. I haven't heard from him since I was in middle school."

"I'm sorry to hear that."

"It's fine. My mom is wonderful."

"My parents are, too. They were always the parents who were around for any kids who needed help." So many of my friends asked for help because my parents were trustworthy and gave sound advice.

Alyssa squeezed my hand. "I'm sure they're fine. If nothing else, most people know what to do when tornadoes are coming."

Every spring I went over the tornado drill with my parents. My dad waved me off saying he already knew what to do, but my mother humored me and listened as we stocked the cellar with fresh bottles of water, soups with expiration dates from a year out, new batteries, protein bars, peanut butter, and powdered milk. There was even a small duffel bag of clothes and shoes. Even though it was pitch-black inside the cooler, I closed my eyes and said a quick prayer that they were safe.

"Have you been in a tornado before?" she asked.

"I've seen plenty, but never this up close and personal. What about you?"

"No and hopefully never again," she said.

The warmth of her body gave me comfort even though I was starting to sweat. The chill of the cooler was seeping out of the small gaps that formed in the bent corners when the tornado twisted overhead. It was still cooler in here than out there, but I hated being trapped in a metal box. We needed to get out. I pressed the towel harder against my forehead and hissed at the pain. There really wasn't time for me to be hurt. I was thankful it wasn't worse. How many people were trapped in toppled houses? How many people were hurt? How many died? I leaned my head back and sighed. This was the worst day ever and I couldn't imagine it was going to improve.

CHAPTER THREE

"The rain picked up," I said.

Katy shined the flashlight into the corner of the cooler. "Rain's going to slide right into that crease. These floors are already slick enough. It's going to make it into a Slip 'N Slide."

"I'm wearing the worst shoes, too. I will never drive anywhere in heels again." My black nondescript shoes with chunky heels were practical, but not for a natural disaster.

"Not meant for climbing out of coolers, but better than stilettos," she said.

"Do you hear that?"

"I still hear ringing from when the tornado hit us." She covered one ear and then the other. "What do you hear?"

"It sounds like a hissing noise." I jumped when I felt water hit my feet. "We have a water break somewhere. It's too much water for just rain."

Katy shined her flashlight until she found an exposed water pipe that had cracked and was pouring cold water into the cooler. "This isn't good. We need to get out now."

Full panic set in when the water reached my ankles. "How's your cut?" I shined the flashlight at Katy's forehead and waited for her to move the towel. It had stopped bleeding but still looked bad. She was in no position to help lift things. Any strain would open the wound again. I needed to get to the ceiling. It was only eight feet high, but I needed something stable to step on and all I had was wire shelving.

"I feel like it's getting better."

"Your head must be pounding," I said. In any other situation, I would keep a wide berth from a bleeding person, but I was all Katy had. "I don't want you to help move things or you'll open your wound. What size shoe do you wear?" I could put on her shoes and get out of there a lot easier and run for help. Wearing mine, I'd probably twist an ankle or break my leg.

"Ten."

Two sizes too big. My sensible shoes for anything but climbing would have to do. "Okay, here's what I'm thinking. I want to upright the shelves and move the deep freezer back to where it was. I can stand on that and see how big the gap is. Maybe it's our way out if we can't push the door open."

"Why don't we try the door first before you climb things?"

I looked at the twisted frame knowing full well it wasn't going to budge. "Okay, sounds like a plan." I put my hand on her shoulder when she moved to help. "I really want you to stay here and let me at least empty the shelves first. Let me make them as light as possible."

I ignored the cold water that now hit my shins. It was going to be hard to move the shelves the higher the water climbed. I was going to need Katy's strength later. Everything on the top shelves was already smashed on the floor. I heard glass crunch under my shoes and prayed they stayed on. I emptied the first shelf and Katy helped me right it. The second shelf had jars of shelf stable condiments, oils, and sauces. I transferred everything from the second shelf to the upright first shelf. I did this process until we reached the freezer. I was going to need her strength now more than ever.

"How's your head?" I shined the flashlight on it, ignoring her smooth skin and stunning eyes. "It looks like the bleeding's stopped."

"It's not throbbing anymore. And head wounds always bleed hard," she said.

"Let's try to move this back." I put my hands on the deep freeze and tried to push. The water was up to my knees. I was shaking from the chill of it and the fact that I hadn't eaten all day.

"Here comes the hard part," Katy said. She turned so that her hips were against the side of the freezer. "I'm going to push like this." It was a good thing I couldn't see her long muscular legs in the dark. She had them up against the wall. "On the count of three?" Katy asked. At three, we pushed with all our might until the wheels gave a little under the water. It was encouraging.

"Again?" I asked. She nodded. We pushed it away from the door, but as predicted, the door wouldn't budge. My hope fizzled. I sat on top of the freezer to get my body out of the cold water. I wanted to get out. The water was rising, and we could only go up. Katy took the leg off one of the shelves and tried squeezing the rod in between the door and frame to crank it open. It remained twisted and stubborn.

"Let's try the ceiling," she said.

"Hopefully, we can push it up and get out that way." I looked up and frowned at the rain pouring in. The crease in the ceiling funneled the rain straight inside.

"I'm going to stand on the freezer and try to pry open the ceiling more."

I stood with her as though I could help in some way. Katy was so tall she had to bend over to fit on the freezer with me. We pushed at the ceiling. It gave a little, but it was obvious we weren't going to be able to just shove it off. Katy threw her shoulders into it and lifted the corner about six inches. Water rushed in, but it also gave us hope.

"I'm going to pry it open with the metal rod." She braced herself and shoved the rod in the opening. The six inches spread to a solid foot. "Can you look out?"

I could only see the gray sky because I was too short. "Why don't you let me hold the rod and you look out? I promise I won't let it go." I tried to look determined.

"Let's see how strong you are first."

I grabbed the rod and pulled it down with all the strength I could muster. The gap opened at least the same amount as it did when she opened it. She looked at me with surprise.

"Do you think you can hold that open for thirty seconds?"

I nodded. "Go." She stuck her head out and I pulled down as long as I could before my arms started shaking. "Okay." I tapped her with my foot.

She slipped back inside and sat on the freezer, dropping her head in her hands. I left the rod sandwiched between the pieces of metal and sat next to her. Even through the rain and thunder, I knew she was crying. I immediately pulled her to me and hugged her.

"There's nothing left." Her voice was muffled as she leaned into me.

I thought she was talking about the diner. "I'm sure your parents can rebuild. It's just going to take time."

She looked at me. "No, you don't understand. Everything is gone. The diner, the trees, the barn, the Millers' house." She wiped her eyes on her shirtsleeve. "We have to get out of here and help people. Alyssa, I can't fit through the opening. Do you think you can slip through and get help?"

Another round of fear rushed through my blood. What if I failed? What if I fell and broke my leg and Katy was stuck inside and drowned? "I don't know."

She cupped my face in her hands and looked at me with vulnerability. "I need your help."

Even though we were in the middle of a natural disaster and I was scared shitless, a warmth spread low in my stomach and radiated in parts of my body that shouldn't be at attention right now. "Okay, I'll do it. Just don't smash me. How are we going to do this?"

"You'll have to stand on my thighs and wiggle through the opening. I'll need both hands to hold the rod in place. You've got this. You can do this."

Was she giving me the pep talk or herself? Either way, I gritted my teeth as determination set in. I took a deep breath. "I'm ready." The water was up to the top of the deep freeze. I waited until she pulled the rod down and squatted so I could step on her thighs and twist my body through the opening.

"Try to turn around so you can hold onto the top and you don't have far to drop," she yelled.

Since the cooler was only eight feet tall, I was able to find footing on a counter that had smashed up against the side of the freezer. I slid down until my foot touched the ground. Even though the rain was blinding, I finally saw what Katy saw. Nothing. There was nothing around except jagged tree trunks, rubble from buildings and barns, and twisted metal from structures that were built somewhere else but landed close by. I covered my mouth and gave a loud sob. Katy yelled something, but I couldn't hear her.

"I'm okay," I yelled shakily.

Where was I supposed to go? Who was going to help us? Where

was my car? Where was hers? Not that I could drive anywhere with this much debris everywhere, but I could at least get my phone and her first aid kit. I saw a white bumper sticking up out of a median about fifty yards away and prayed it was my car. I teared up when I recognized the twisted metal. I crawled down the hill and wiggled through the busted back windshield, careful to avoid broken glass. My phone was nowhere to be found, but I grabbed my gym bag and, out of pure instinct, my camera case. I couldn't find the camera that had been next to me in the front seat, but the one I used for all my professional shoots was still undisturbed in its case.

I searched the car for something to prop the cooler ceiling up. There was a jack somewhere in the trunk. I was sure of it. Wrestling the trunk open took longer than I wanted it to, but I found it. I was soaked to the bone and exhausted, but I was alive and Katy needed my help. Thankfully, the rain had let up. I forced myself to stay focused.

"Katy, can you hear me?" I yelled. The top cranked open and I saw the top of her head. I held up the jack. "I'm going to get this to you. Hang on." I stood on my tippy-toes and handed it to her. It was too dangerous to try to stand on anything. After three tries, she grabbed it and the jack handle.

When I saw that it was working and the gap was opening, I dug into my gym bag and put on my athletic socks and shoes. I took off the suit jacket, the shirt, and put on my T-shirt and sweatshirt. I didn't care if I was getting soaked again. Now I could move. I watched as Katy squeezed through the gap, careful not to jar the jack. It was tense watching her, but I couldn't look away. I held my hands up and guided her down to a solid surface. I ignored her muscular calves and her tight ass.

She hugged me when she reached the ground. "Thank you."

The smile on my face felt foreign, but also wonderful. I doubted I would smile for a long time in the days ahead. "I think I saw your car in the field over there. Mine's in a ditch about fifty yards away." She put her hands on her hips and surveyed the area. By her look of determination, I half expected her to twirl in rapid motion until a superhero with a red cape emerged.

"I need to make sure my family is okay. Let's get to my car and hope the radio works." She checked her phone for a signal but shook her head. She walked in the direction of the field. It was easier to keep up with her because I was wearing sneakers, but her stride was almost twice the length of mine. I didn't know how or when it happened, but she was holding my hand as we maneuvered over a tree that looked like somebody had blown it up with a grenade. Katy pulled me closer. "Walk where I walk." Her SUV looked as if it had rolled several times but landed tires down.

"Yours looks like it's in better shape," I said. She crawled in the smashed opening that was once the driver's window and reached for the radio. I couldn't help but take photos of what I saw. The mass destruction surrounding me, a giant ball of barbed wire that cut deep into the wet earth, and a sheriff who was squatting next to her banged-up car, blood all over her head and face, on her radio asking for help.

CHAPTER FOUR

Six hundred to dispatch. Six hundred to dispatch." Please, please, Daisy, be there. Please pick up. I waited ten seconds before signaling Daisy again. "Six hundred to dispatch. Come in. Daisy, are you okay?"

"Dispatch, go ahead. I'm a bit shaken up, but I seem to be okay." Her voice was shaky, but strong.

"How is it by you?"

"I can't tell how things are, but it's dark down here and something's covering up the windows. Robert is on his way over to collect me. Where are you?"

Robert was a deputy and Daisy's nephew. "I'm on Phelps over by…" I paused to swallow the lump that was full of emotions I couldn't handle. "Over by the Lunch Box. The tornado took everything including the Durango. I'm going over to the Millers' house to check on them. If you can, radio everybody you know from surrounding areas and make sure they're okay, find out if they need help, and ask for help. This thing took out everything on this side of town."

"Katy, I think it took everything on this side, too."

The news was a punch to the gut. I leaned against the black metal door to catch my breath. "My shoulder radio isn't working, but I've got the walkie. Just know I'm going to the Millers' first and then I'll circle back down Main. I'll be in touch."

"Be careful," Daisy said.

"You, too." I was worried about her heart. She was in her seventies and cool as a cucumber, but this was an extreme situation and even my heartbeat was accelerating.

"Okay, now will you sit for a minute so I can put this stuff on your cut?" Alyssa had found my first aid kit while I was summoning dispatch.

"We have to be quick." She held my chin in her hand and made me focus on her. I gasped and automatically pulled out of her grasp when the alcohol pad she used to clean the wound stung.

She folded her arms in front of her. "Give me five minutes. If we don't treat this now, you're going to pass out or it'll get infected. Then you'll be no help to anybody. Okay?"

True to her word, I was ready to go in five. She was thorough and quick. This wasn't the same woman who sobbed in my arms thirty minutes ago. She was strong and determined. I hooked the walkie on my belt and grabbed my backpack. I shoved the first aid kit, a large flashlight, flares, a crowbar, and neon green spray paint. I checked to make sure the safe securing my shotgun was still engaged. The last thing I needed was looters getting ahold of my shotgun. I handed Alyssa an extra poncho and slipped into my safety orange one. "I could use your help, but if you aren't comfortable with that, you can stay here and I can send somebody out to pick you up."

She touched my forearm. "I'm going with you." She looked solemn and determined. And utterly beautiful in the natural light with rain-soaked hair and wet clothes that clung to her slight frame.

"Thank you. Can you lose the case? I'm going to need both your hands."

"Of course." She quickly transferred flashes and other peripherals into her gym bag and slung it over her shoulder. The camera stayed around her neck. "It's okay that I have this, right?"

Documentation was important even if I hated what she would record. I didn't think she was prepared to see the devastation. I nodded. "I want to check the Millers and make sure they're okay. It's two thirty. We have about five hours of solid daylight." I couldn't believe we were in the cooler for over an hour.

I kept my radio turned up so I could hear the calls. We had a staff of four and would need at least ten times that just to deal with lookie-loos, looters, and even town members who wanted to help, but would do more harm than good. Trained volunteers would eventually come, but time was of the essence. Alyssa and I could have drowned in the cooler. One of Robert's friends drowned in their storm shelter because a tree had fallen across the storm door, preventing him from getting out. The air vents were built straight up to the sky and torrential rainfall filled the shelter within minutes. The lessons learned after disasters were devastating. Now air vents curved downward and some shelters had manual pumps if water seeped in. My parents' shelter was well equipped and modified after that accidental death. I just hoped they got to it in time.

"The Millers have three kids. Two teenagers and an eight-year-old. One of the grandmothers lives with them as well." I stopped and waited until Alyssa was right in front of me. Her teeth chattered and her hair was plastered to her face, but she didn't complain. I was strangely proud of her even though I barely knew her. "Please be careful of sharp things like metal and nails. Their storm shelter is by the shed and we have to get around the debris. I don't want you to get hurt."

"I don't want to get hurt either. I'll follow you," she said.

I heard her snap photos behind me, but she was right on my heels. "Bob! Christine! Kids! Can you hear me?" There were several sections of splintered wood and pink insulation across the yard. I moved a section of the roof that covered their storm door and banged my baton on it. "Are you down there?" Shouts erupted from beneath me and I helped lift the door that was now free but twisted and stuck. I used the crowbar and pried it open.

"Damn, Sheriff. I'm so glad to see you," Bob said.

He clasped my hand in his and stood completely still as he surveyed his property. "Oh, my God. Oh, my God," he repeated over and over.

"Christine, come on out. The tornado is gone and the rain has stopped." I reached for her and brought her up to the surface. She immediately started crying. I held her for a moment until the kids surrounded her, needing her strength. "The good news is that you all are okay." Shit, I didn't see the grandmother. "Where's Ellen?"

"She's at the lodge playing bingo. Hopefully, she found shelter," Bob said.

My heart dropped. The lodge didn't have a safe place. The church across the street did. Maybe Jim Rader, who ran afternoon bingo, got everyone over there. It was doubtful, but I needed hope right now. "Listen, I have to go help others. I'll circle back and keep you updated. Bob, do you have a walkie?" He nodded. "I'm channel twelve. I'll keep you posted if I see Ellen."

"Thank you, Sheriff," Christine said.

Bob nodded as he held his family close. I wanted to stay and help him, but I had to make sure other families were safe. I pulled out the spray paint and tagged his house so that volunteers and other first responders would know they were okay and accounted for. It broke my heart knowing they would spend the next several days picking up bits and pieces of their lives scattered all over the property.

"I've never seen anything like this." Alyssa was snapping photos left and right. "Will they be okay?"

"It'll take some time, but yes. This isn't the first time Bayonet has been hit by a tornado but definitely looks like the worst." I had a job to do, but it was hard to figure out what to do first. Daisy said help was on the way. I didn't need her to tell me the town was decimated. I could see it with my own eyes. The buildings filled with small businesses down Main Street were flattened. It was surreal. The road was littered with bricks, glass, and debris. A group of young teenagers that I recognized from the high school hobbled over to us, but I only knew two of their names. "Darby, Ben. What are you doing here? Are you okay?" I could tell they were in shock. One of the boys had a cut on his arm. Another one was missing a shoe. I pointed to his bare foot. "You can't walk around here like that. There are too many sharp, dangerous things on the road. Where did you come from?"

"Darby's house. We were in the basement playing games when we got the message on our phones. My mom's working," Ben said. He looked around stunned. "We had to climb out the basement window."

"I cut my arm on some glass." One of the kids held up his arm. Alyssa quickly waved him over and grabbed my first aid kit.

"Were you the only ones there?" At their nod, I continued. "Where do the rest of you live?" Ben lived one block over on Maple. I could see where his house once stood.

"We live in Hodges. I don't know how to get in touch with my mom. My phone doesn't work." The boy with a bare foot held out his phone as though I could do something about it. He was standing close to another kid with long, shaggy hair. They shared the same wide blue eyes and round faces.

"The cell towers must've gotten hit. Don't worry. They're sending help. Right now, I need you to stay here. I can't have you climbing over things. What's your mom's phone number? I'll see if dispatch can reach your mom to tell her you guys are okay." I called Daisy and gave her their info. She knew how to reach volunteers who did this very thing. The station was on the other side of town. I knew it was gone so it didn't make sense to get the boys over there. "Listen, I have to keep moving, but I want you to stay here. That way when I hear from your parents, I know where to find you. Do you understand? It's very important for you to stay right here." I looked up at the now blue sky and hoped that the storms were gone. "Wait. I have an idea." The hardware store had been smashed, but if I was careful, I could slip inside and find tools, foldable chairs, anything to start a gathering place for survivors. Daisy said Robert was headed my way with a tent after he got her set up in a safe space. I told Alyssa my plan.

"Do you want me to go with you? We make a great team."

I needed her to stay with the boys because they were frightened and overwhelmed, but I selfishly wanted her close to me. "We do. But you have to be careful. Nothing is stable. I'm just going to peek inside and see what we can find."

"I'll walk where you walk."

I crouched and shined my flashlight into the opening. Almost everything was toppled over but I could see things we needed like sledgehammers, saws, and flashlights. "I'm going to go in." I looked over my shoulder at Alyssa. She balled her fists together and took a deep breath.

"Please be careful. Give me your little flashlight so I can see where you are in case something happens," she said.

Before slipping inside, I kicked at the walls to see if they were sturdy enough. Nothing budged. I raised my eyebrows at Alyssa. "Wish me luck." I worked my way through the opening.

Her fingers pressed softly on my back. "You can hand me things and I can make a pile."

There was so much dust that I immediately started coughing. I found a rag and held it over my nose and mouth. I crawled down a shelf. "Is anyone here? Can anyone hear me?"

My questions were greeted with silence. The hardware store shut down at one on Saturdays, so Chase and his grandfather were hopefully home and safe. I told Alyssa to stand back and tossed everything I could through the hole. Three sledgehammers, ten saws, flashlights, several quarts of paint and paintbrushes. It wasn't safe to venture past the first two shelves, but I snagged a bag of dust masks, bags of rags, and anything cotton that could be used as a bandage or tourniquet. I found small collapsible camping chairs and several sweatshirts and T-shirts. I even found a pair of rubber boots. I wasn't sure about the size but the kid missing a shoe could make these work. I started climbing out when I heard a four-wheeler outside.

"Where is she?" Robert's voice boomed and I saw Alyssa flinch.

"I'm coming out," I said.

Robert poked his beet-red face into the opening and stared at me. I knew that if Alyssa wasn't there, he would have given me quite the tongue-lashing. What I did was a no-no on all levels, but people were counting on me to help them and I didn't have the tools to do so. He pulled me up and out of the hole as if I didn't weigh a thing. I was six feet tall and one hundred and sixty-five pounds. I was sure the rush of anger and adrenaline from me doing something so stupid gave him the extra strength it took to get me out.

"Tell me everything," I said.

He put his fists on his hips and looked at me. I could tell he was debating whether to chide me or give me a rundown of what he knew. "The station's gone. I dug Daisy out, but she wanted to stay put to help. The door to the basement is cleared for people who want to go there."

"Did you bring the tent?" I asked.

He nodded. "I couldn't find the orange one, but I found the yellow one."

"That'll work." Even though we practiced what to do in a natural disaster, we were fortunate enough to not have one happen since I took office. "Have the boys set up the tent. It will be good for them to have a task. The three of us can look for survivors." It was the first time I said *survivors* and the look on Alyssa's face told me she hadn't thought that far in advance. Hopefully, we'd find people alive, but if we didn't hear the warning sirens, other people didn't either.

"Dispatch to six hundred. Do you copy?" We were at the church pulling debris away from the basement doors. We heard shouting so we knew people were stuck inside. I stepped away to answer the walkie.

"Six hundred. Go ahead."

"Your parents have been found safe and sound."

I let out half a sob before I pulled it back and cleared my throat. "Thanks, Daisy. Glad to hear." I didn't need details, I just needed to know they were okay.

"Teams are starting to set up. We have crews down from Warrensburg and up from Mount Ellis. I have a cruiser for you. Bart's parked his north of Telly's Bar. He couldn't get any closer because of the debris, but it's there if you need it. He's rounding up volunteers to march down to the winery and check the houses along the way," Daisy said.

"Send some help to the church. It sounds like a lot of people are trapped here and we need manpower to get them out," I said. It was overwhelming. I wanted to be everywhere at once, but I had to stay focused and approach this one place at a time until more people arrived and we could fan out. Alyssa had switched her wet sweatshirt for a dry one that was two sizes too big. Her hair was tied up and somebody had given her gloves to protect her hands. She was just as involved as everyone else. When we finally got one of the doors open, Alyssa stepped back with her camera.

"Thank you, Sheriff."

I barely recognized clergyman Roger Thomas. He was covered in dust and had a head injury like mine. I put my hand on his shoulder. "Are you okay?"

He thumbed behind him. "I'm fine, but there are a few people who need tending to. Mrs. Wilson broke her arm, and Bud and Seymour have pretty deep cuts on their legs."

"How many people are down there?" I asked.

"Thirty-two. We have the bingo players and a few from the insurance company next door."

"Is Ellen Miller with you?"

"Yes, she's fine."

"Okay, let's get everyone who can climb out first, then we'll go in and help those who need it. We don't know how safe the structure is and I want everyone out. We have tents set up and volunteers ready." I helped Roger up and reached inside for more survivors. Each one squeezed my hand and said a prayer that we found them. Once I had Ellen in the clear, I radioed Bob to let him know his mother was okay.

"Thank you so much, Katy. I'll come and get her."

"Bring a wheelchair. We have two at the station. She's fine, but she won't be able to walk back and you can't drive all the way to the church."

Once we got all thirty-two people out, I spray-painted the door to signal that people were out and accounted for. Alyssa handed me water and a granola bar that one of the volunteers gave her. It was almost four in the afternoon, and I had only searched three buildings. It was a frustratingly slow process. Two ambulances had weaved their way through the rubble after Tyson Baker bulldozed several trees that had blocked Highway 57. EMTs were treating people who had minor injuries, and the ambulances were taking the seriously injured up to Lee's Summit and Kansas City.

"I want to take Bart's cruiser and hit some of the houses outside of town." I was exhausted and running on fumes.

"I'll go with you," Alyssa said.

Not going with me wasn't an option. I was responsible for her, plus she was an extra set of eyes that I needed and, truthfully, wanted beside me.

CHAPTER FIVE

W ho knew a stale granola bar could be so tasty? I devoured two at the volunteer tent and downed a full bottle of water. "Thank you so much." I wanted to cry. Not just because I had food, but because I was alive after witnessing and surviving something so gut-wrenching and frightening. I grabbed two more granola bars and a water and found Katy helping the last of the people out from the church's basement. Even covered with dust and dried blood, she commanded attention. I understood why she was sheriff in a small town. I trusted her the moment I saw her.

"I'll go with you," I said when she told a volunteer she was taking Bart's cruiser to hit some of the houses just outside town.

"Thank you," she said.

It was amazing how comforting those two sweet and smooth words sounded falling from her mouth. I grabbed my camera and followed her to where Bart's cruiser was parked. Part of a steel silo and a giant tree blocked the road into town. Several cars were parked along the road behind the cruisers as volunteers began pouring in. Katy barked orders at them as we drove away from town.

"How many houses do you think we'll get to before it gets dark?"

"As many as we can." She checked her watch. "We have three and a half hours of daylight."

"What happens when it gets too dark?" I feared for the people still trapped in their blown-apart homes who were waiting for help.

"We'll still keep looking, but obviously it'll be harder and we'll have to keep looters away."

"People do that? Even out here? I thought small town life was quaint and nice." My faith in humanity was a roller coaster today. Seeing people help others so selflessly was amazing, but just like that, knowing that they had to protect what was left of their belongings made me angry.

"Not necessarily our own. We catch a lot of people who sneak in from other places and take what they want. I bet the National Guard will be here late tonight or tomorrow morning at the latest. They can help with relief efforts, and we can use our resources for policing," Katy said.

Swirls of dust kicked up when she turned off the highway onto a partially gravel road. I stared out the window and took pictures of warlike devastation of destroyed barns, outbuildings, and gnarled fences. "Where are the animals? I remember seeing a bunch of cows on my way in."

She blew out a deep breath. "I'd say they are somewhere safe, but there's a good chance they didn't make it."

That didn't make sense. "What do you mean, they didn't make it? What happened? Where'd they go?"

"The tornado took them."

She shrugged as though it was normal, but I saw how white her knuckles were on the steering wheel. What did I agree to? I should have called my mom or someone from the office to pick me up. I wasn't prepared to see this kind of devastation, but at the same time, I felt obligated to record it. "Stop the car! Stop the car!"

Katy slammed on the brakes. "What's the matter?"

I rolled down the window as she pulled over. "There's something in the field." I zoomed in on my lens. "Katy, it's a child and a dog." She threw the car in park and we ran at top speed until we got within twenty feet of them. It was a small boy who was covered in dirt. His pants and short-sleeved shirt were torn. I could see tiny cuts on his arms and face. He reached out to us, but Katy stopped me.

"That dog is protecting him. We need to show him we mean no harm."

She squatted and spoke in a soothing voice. "It's okay, boy. We're here to help you." The dog circled the toddler and growled at us. I stood a few feet behind her trying to say encouraging words to the child, who only wanted to be held. He was breaking my heart. I grabbed the last granola bar and held it out to the dog. Maybe food would help warm him up to us.

"Come here, sweetie. It's okay." I tossed a piece at him. He gobbled it up and circled the child again but didn't growl. "You want more? Come here." He moved closer and took a piece of the bar from my hand. I spoke in a soothing voice. "It's okay. You're okay now. We're going to help." I carefully reached out and touched his head while giving him the rest of the granola bar. He wagged his tail and didn't mind when Katy picked up the child and held him close.

"We need to check him out. Let's get them both to the car and I can call it in."

I didn't have to tell the dog to come with us as he pranced around her legs. She opened the back door and he jumped into the seat. She was very gentle when she put the little boy next to the dog.

"I know, baby. We're going to find your mommy. Does it hurt anywhere? Do you have an ouchie?" She gently felt his head, smoothing down the soft locks that were caked with dirt. She ran her hands over his tiny little arms and legs, careful to avoid any scratches or obvious bruises. Where did he come from? Was he a year old? Two years? He pointed to his knee where his thin pants were ripped. Katy turned to me slowly so not to frighten either the boy or the dog. "Can you hand me the first aid kit? Or better yet, can you see if there's one in the trunk? We're going to need both. You should be able to pop it open from the driver's side near the floorboard."

I needed something to do besides take photos. I felt worthless. I found the first aid kit, anxious to help. The toddler had finally stopped crying and was focusing hard on what she was doing.

"Can you hand me the speaker on the radio and crank up the air?" she asked very quietly.

The car was still idling. I stretched the mic and cord through the clear partition and got the boy's attention while Katy called it in. I played peekaboo, and while he didn't laugh, it kept his interest.

"Six hundred to dispatch."

"Dispatch, go ahead."

I didn't recognize the voice. Daisy must've gone home or was resting.

"You're not going to believe this, but I have a child, approximately eighteen months old, and a dog in the squad car. We found them in a field off Highway 57 south by Sinclair Road. He has cuts and bruises, but I don't know who he is or where he came from. I need an ambulance sent ASAP. Has anybody called in missing a child and or a pit bull mix?"

I bit my lip and waited anxiously for dispatch's answer. I was sure there were a ton of calls about missing people, but a toddler? My heart ached for his parents, and I said a little prayer that they were okay.

"Negative. Nothing yet, but I'll send a message out and get an ambulance headed to you."

"Ten-four."

She handed the radio to me through the partition and knelt so that she was eye level with him. "Let's get you cleaned up a little."

I dampened a few fast-food napkins I found in the glove compartment with a bottle of water. Katy carefully wiped the dirt off his face.

"Look at how brave you are. All alone in the big field." She turned her attention to the dog. "And you're a brave boy, too, for watching over him." Katy was rewarded with a slobbery kiss. She held a water bottle to the boy's lips while he drank thirstily.

"Should I give the dog something to drink? Do you have anything in here that would work as a bowl or cup?" I asked. I looked in the trunk, under the seat, and again in the glove compartment hoping for better results. This was the cleanest car I'd ever been in.

"See if the cupholder pulls out," Katy said.

I smiled for the first time all day when the plastic cup popped up. The dog lapped up the entire bottle. "Are there any houses around here? Could he have wandered away?" I refused to think the unthinkable.

"There are, but I don't want to leave since dispatch is sending an ambulance," Katy said. She took out her phone and took a photo of the boy and the dog. "When they take him to the hospital, we'll head down the road and see if anybody knows him."

He lifted his tiny arms and she scooped him up without hesitation. She was a hot mess covered in dirt, dust, and dried blood, but neither of them cared. He snuggled in her arms and rested his head on her shoulder.

I'd been taking photos for so much of my life that the only time I realized I had a camera up to my eye was when I knew I'd taken the perfect shot. I felt it when I pressed the button and heard the click of the shutter. It was beautiful and strong and gave me chills. We turned when we heard the sirens. The baby covered his ears and Katy made the signal to cut the sound.

"Sweetie, I want you to go with this nice woman. She's okay," Katy said.

The transfer was too fast. He clutched Katy and wailed. When she moved closer to the ambulance, he reached out for me. I was so worried that I would hurt him, but I held him anyway. He was so small and so scared. "Why don't I go with the ambulance? And just hang around until you find his parents."

"Are you sure?" At my nod, she agreed. We both knew she had a long week ahead of her and she was going to worry about the boy until he was home safe. She trusted me.

"You keep Fido. He might help you. Oh, check to see if he's chipped," I said.

"Great idea. I'll keep in touch with the ambulance." She handed me her business card and scribbled her phone number on the back. "If we ever get service back, here's my number. And when I find his parents, I'll bring them up. Either way, I'll see you soon."

I sat in the back on the gurney and held him on my lap while they cleaned him up. We were both in desperate need of a bath. "What hospital are we going to?"

"Golden Valley Memorial in Clinton. They weren't hit by a tornado. A lot of injured are going there. Maybe we'll find his parents." Jessica, the EMT, pulled up a video of her new puppy and gave him her phone while she tended to the small nicks and cuts on his arm and cheek. He smiled for the first time. She took off his pants and made a makeshift diaper with an adult diaper she cut up.

"I hope they are okay." I heard the pleading in my own voice.

She looked at me. "A lot of these stories don't end well, but I hope so, too." She pulled off his tattered T-shirt and wrapped him in a warm blanket.

I held him against my chest during the twenty-five-minute drive. This area wasn't affected by the tornado. The trees were upright, the soybeans and corn stalks were budding in straight rows. Everything just looked wet. Houses were still standing, water splashed up on cars as we sped to the hospital. It was amazing that just twenty miles south, small towns were annihilated by a huge tornado. I saw weather trucks and news vans headed south. My camera was slung behind me with photos I knew wouldn't show the true devastation of what happened but would give people an idea of how awful it was.

The baby was asleep when we pulled into the driveway near the emergency room.

"We're going to check you in and then head back down," Jessica said.

I followed her into the emergency room where people in the waiting room stared. We were escorted through doors that locked behind us and taken to the pediatric ward on the second floor. He smiled at the cartoon jungle animals painted on bright yellow walls.

"You're in room fourteen." A nurse pointed down the hallway. "I'll send Dr. Lindsey in to evaluate him. I'll bring in some fresh clothes, food, and a better diaper."

"Good luck," Jessica said.

She disappeared before I had a chance to say thank you. I sat in a chair in his room and turned him so that he faced me. Katy guessed he was about eighteen months. "How are you doing, little guy?" I was extremely awkward around children, but with him, I felt responsible. He had the prettiest blue eyes and softest red hair.

I heard a soft knock at the door.

"Hi, there. I'm Dr. Lindsey. Look at this adorable boy." Dr. Lindsey was very attractive. Hazel eyes that looked more green than blue, and shoulder-length brown hair that was pulled back with a clip at her neckline. She wore the cutest kid-friendly coat covered in teddy bears. "I understand you and Katy found him alone in a field down in Willow County?"

I immediately zoned in on her casual reference to the sheriff as Katy. "Yes. Since volunteers and other emergency personnel showed up to help in town, Katy wanted to check on neighbors outside of town. We were driving along and we saw him and a dog in a field. I couldn't believe it."

She let him play with a toy stethoscope while she listened to his vitals. "He sounds good." She checked his eyes, ears, nose, and the rest of him. "He needs a bath and a diaper that fits him, but otherwise this is one lucky boy." He turned his head back into my chest when she reached for him. "I'll have Nurse Cara bring in a portable bathtub and we'll bathe him here with you close."

He fell asleep against me and didn't wake up until the little bathtub was filled and ready for him in the bathroom. Without hesitating, I sat next to the tub and gently lowered him into the water. Cara told me it was the right temperature and he seemed unfazed. We changed the water once because it was so muddy from the dirt that had clumped in his hair. While she put medicine on his scrapes and dressed him with fresh hospital pajamas, I took a fast shower and slipped into scrubs she found for me. He crawled back on my lap and held a sippy cup of Pedialyte while Cara fed him oatmeal. My stomach rumbled and I smiled with embarrassment.

"It's been a long day." The granola bar from earlier gave me a burst of energy, but that disappeared hours ago.

"I can order you something from the cafeteria," she said.

"I lost my purse, my wallet, my phone, even my car in the tornado."

She patted my knee. "My treat. You stay here and keep him comfortable and I'll get you something."

I squeezed her hand. "Thank you."

"Any allergies? Foods you don't eat?"

"No allergies and I can and will eat anything."

"I'll be back in a flash."

The door quietly closing behind her was the last thing I remembered before drifting off to sleep with the little boy tucked safely in my arms.

❖

"Alyssa?"

I heard my name echo in my head but ignored it. I was tired and warm. Really warm. My chest felt heavy. Where was I? I cracked my eyes open to find Cara softly shaking my shoulder and the sweet boy still in my arms.

"Alyssa. Katy is on her way with the little boy's family."

I opened my eyes in shock. "She found them? Oh my God. That's wonderful! Are they okay?"

"The mom has a broken arm and the dad needed stitches, but they are well enough to come up here." She pointed to the tray of food next to me on the table. "I didn't want to wake you, but try to get a few bites down."

"Thank you so much." The cheeseburger was plain and the french fries were cold, but I didn't care. Hospital food was notoriously bad, but this was the best meal. It was hard to eat over a sleeping boy in my arms, but I wasn't going to let him or my food go. I was his safety net until his parents arrived.

"Liam!" A couple walked into the room and the mother rushed over to me.

I smiled when I saw Katy walk in behind them. "He's safe, warm, and healthy except for a few scratches." I carefully handed him to his father, who looked like he'd been through hell and back. Liam woke up and smiled.

"Dada."

That was the proof I needed. Liam was theirs.

"Thank you so much for finding him." Liam's mother was wearing a removable cast that dug into my back when she hugged me.

Samantha and Brian Shoreman were from Mt. Sterling, Illinois, visiting relatives in Bayonet when the tornado hit. Katy found them from the identification chip between Pongo's shoulder blades. The station had a chip reader because so many residents let their animals run free and if the department found them, they read their chip information and either called the owner to pick them up or dropped the dog off with a stern warning.

The Shoremans were trying to find shelter after going on a short walk and getting turned around when the tornado hit. Brian was knocked unconscious, and Liam was ripped from Samantha's arms as they lay flat in a median hoping to survive the tornado. We found Liam almost a mile away, but we weren't sure if the tornado dropped him in the field or if he and Pongo walked there.

"He's a wonderful child. Strong and brave. And looks a lot better than he did when we found him." I grabbed my camera and showed them the photos of Liam that I had taken.

Samantha covered the sob with her hand. "My poor baby." She kissed him all over his face while his dad nuzzled the top of his head. Tears sprang to my eyes at the emotional reunion.

"Are you a journalist?" she asked.

"Photographer. I was on my way to take photos of a wedding when I got caught." I debated on whether or not I should ask, but it couldn't hurt. "Do you mind if I send a few of these photos to the news? His is such a wonderful story, and that's what we need right now after that much devastation."

"You can do anything you want. We owe you both so much."

"Thank you. I'll protect your privacy."

"We don't deserve all the credit. Pongo was amazing and wouldn't let us get near until he trusted us," Katy said.

"He's such a good dog and he really loves Liam."

My heart broke a little when I had to say good-bye. The hospital was keeping him now that his parents were available to sign off on additional testing. "What about Pongo?"

"He's staying with the family at the motel down the street," Katy said. She reached inside her bag and pulled out my phone.

"Oh, my God. You found it. Where was it?" I punched in my code and frowned when it was apparent my texts weren't working and only missed calls showed up. I had several from the same people.

"It was about fifteen feet from your car. I cleaned it up the best I could. It looks like it's somewhat working. Also, you should probably call your mother." She looked at her watch. "Do you need me to take you home? You're about a half an hour away, right?"

I knew she was itching to get back to the search and rescue. I was surprised she left to come up here. "I can catch a ride. My mom isn't far away." I paused when I realized I wasn't done with Katy or the town of Bayonet. I still wanted to help. "But if you need another volunteer, I'm here. I ate and I had a quick nap. I'm good to go."

"Are you serious about the help?"

"Definitely." I touched Katy's arm. "How are you? Do you need a quick break?" I didn't know her well, but I could tell she was tense.

"I'll be fine. I'll probably catch a nap at the station if there's an open cot."

"I can drive us back down there if you want while you get a little shut-eye."

She smirked at me. "Thanks, but no. I've seen the way you drive."

CHAPTER SIX

I was impressed with the photos Alyssa showed the Shoremans even though I was looking at my town in shambles. Today felt like the longest day and it was only seven. I don't know why I said yes when Alyssa offered to help. Her instincts had been good so far, but she wasn't a trained professional. She would probably get in the way and I would worry about her the whole time, but I wanted her with me.

"So, I have your permission to send photos to my friend at the Associated Press? I promise they are good," she said. From what I could tell, they were more than good. Her photos were incredible.

"Yes, you have my permission." I couldn't imagine she had any decent ones of me and for a split second, I wavered. But it didn't matter if I looked good. This would raise awareness so we could get some help.

"My camera has Wi-Fi and since we're still in a relatively populated area with working cell phone towers, I can send them to my phone and email them. It'll only take me a few minutes."

"Technology is wonderful." I watched as her fingers flew across her phone. I didn't use my phone a lot since I had the radio, but people who ran their business from a smartphone always amazed me.

"Done. That was fast, right?"

Her smile warmed me and I realized I wanted her with me because I wanted to get to know her better. My awareness of her was heightened by our horrible ordeal. She made me feel alive, and knowing that death was so close, I wasn't ready to give up the security she gave me. She was attractive and feisty and a city girl. My opposite and I was totally into her. "Amazingly fast."

"And just in time." She waved her phone at me. "No service. But we're not close to Bayonet yet are we?"

"The tornado was on the ground for several miles and the destruction was more than just Bayonet and Hodges."

"Is anything left?"

"Not much of downtown Bayonet. Hodges was hit hard, too, but the tornado slid between several farms so a lot of houses were spared." I didn't tell her that we'd found eight bodies so far. I expected the count to go up.

"I'm so glad you found Liam's parents and that they are alive."

"You saved me tons of time by suggesting that I see if Pongo was chipped. You're good to have in an emergency." She blushed at my words. The navy blue scrubs weren't sexy at all, but cleaned up, she looked even more beautiful. I remembered she caught my eye when I pulled her over. I couldn't believe it was just a few short hours ago. I felt like I knew Alyssa longer than an afternoon.

"You're the only person to ever say that to me. I don't do well when things are falling apart around me."

"Whoever told you that you're bad in a crisis was wrong," I said.

She put her hand on my forearm. "Oh, my God. Katy. How's your house? Was it hit?"

"I have very minimal damage. My parents are there now since their house was smashed. I'll help them once the National Guard arrives. Right now, we're doing our best to find people still stuck and keep outsiders out. We're not even letting the news in because the place isn't secure. Your photos will probably be some of the first ones that people see."

She shivered. "Not the way I want people to know my photography, that's for sure."

I flipped on my lights when traffic started thickening up around the exit we needed to take to get to Bayonet. Most people moved out of our way, but a few sat in the fast lane until I popped short bursts of my siren.

"People are so rude," Alyssa said.

"It's like this all the time now." I didn't have to go into details, and she didn't have to ask. "Now we have people who want to come down and see the destruction the tornado left. While I understand it, I wish they would see that we have a job to do and their presence hinders our progress."

"But sometimes exposure is good. People in Minnesota or Idaho or Ohio will see the devastation here and send money, supplies, volunteers."

She had a point, but I was still raw and angry over the whole thing. I needed Liam as an excuse to step away from the overwhelming pull in every direction. Once the fire departments from nearby towns and FEMA showed up, I took a step back. They were the experts and I was too emotional to take charge. "You're right. It can be helpful as long as they stay out of the way." I don't know why I was arguing. My anxiety was ramping up the closer we got to Bayonet.

"I can't believe we survived this. I'm so sorry for you and everyone in town." Alyssa's face was pressed against the window as though seeing it for the first time. She lowered the window and took photos of crushed silos surrounded by mounds of grains that they once held. A trail of grain followed the path of the tornado until it thinned out. "What got damaged at your place?" she asked.

I waited to answer until we were through the roadblock. I didn't have to flash any credentials. I was in a squad car and still dusty from pulling people out of the rubble. "My garage, part of my shed, my personal car, but the house is solid. The tornado clipped my property, but all of that stuff can be replaced." I parked the car near the center of town and gave Alyssa a headlamp and gloves. "The temperature is going to drop soon. Take my raincoat so that you're warm and we can still see you."

She slipped into the safety orange coat that was too big and put the headlamp around her forehead. Without makeup and fresh from a shower, she looked so much younger than thirty-two. I always noticed driver's licenses when they had the same birth year as me. I didn't even want to think what I looked like. I changed into a long-sleeved shirt I found in the basement of the station when I checked Pongo's chip, but my pants were still covered in dust. I was self-conscious around Alyssa because she was so pretty and I was a hot mess.

"Where do you want me to look?" she asked.

"Let's check in and see where we are needed."

"They already have bulldozers here. How do they know it's safe?"

"They will push debris out of the way until the structural integrity of the buildings can be evaluated. They're just clearing paths for emergency vehicles and a place for FEMA to set up. We have so many farms and asphalt plants around so equipment is easy to find." I hated that I sounded so small-town to Alyssa. She probably moved to the Midwest because of a job. She didn't have an accent and seemed more refined than most of my friends.

A sharp whistle got my attention. Deputy Cameron waved his hand and shouted. "Sheriff, we're getting some people together to cover Gus's. It's not heavily damaged, but there's a lot of interest."

"We'll head there," I yelled back.

"Gus's? What's that?" Alyssa asked.

"It's a liquor store."

"Why would we need to go there when so much help is needed here?"

She was so innocent.

"We're stopping the looters. Liquor and gas are the first things people steal. We have people stationed at the businesses. This town might be leveled, but there are still things of value. Look at what I found in the hardware store in just the ten minutes I was there." I knew insurance would cover the inventory in Chance's store, but guilt still pressed on my chest for jumping in and taking things that I didn't buy.

"This is so incredibly eye-opening. Not just from a photographer's standpoint, but from a human. I would think people would come together to help, not loot."

"Some people take because they can and some people take because they need. I'm just glad FEMA's here now and I can help people instead of arresting or detaining them for stupid shit like stealing ceramic cats or air fresheners at the gas station. Who does that? Who needs that? They take because they can. It's ridiculous." I felt Alyssa's fingers on my arm.

"I have a feeling you're a great sheriff and you really love this town."

My skin jumped when her fingers brushed my arm. "I was born here. This is my home. I went to Kansas State but came back after I graduated." She looked surprised and I didn't know if it was because I had a degree or I returned to Bayonet.

"What's your degree in?"

"Sociology with criminology concentration. We don't get a lot of crime here, but it's nice to have my finger on the pulse of this town. I know people. I know their successes and heartaches."

"I think it's great. That means you have character and love putting down roots," she said.

"What about you? Are you from Kansas City?" I asked. She smiled and the little jolt kickstarted my heart.

"Believe it or not, I, too, am a small-town girl. I grew up in Peony, Illinois. Went to school in Kansas City and never left," she said.

"Did your mom follow you?"

"She did. There was more opportunity in the big city." She air-quoted big city.

The generator outside powered the strong lights that shined on the station. The broken bricks, glass, and concrete had been bulldozed away from the steps leading to the basement, which now served as the sheriff's station entrance.

"What's the latest?" I asked Mac Arnold, the sheriff from the next county over. His entire crew was here. I surveyed the room. Even though we had twenty cots set up, they were all full. Fans were circulating the oppressive, stale air in the room, but it was better than the thick, dusty, humid air outside. Three EMTs were checking out people who had bumps and scrapes.

"Over fifty people were taken to area hospitals and the death count has risen to fourteen." Mac's voice was low enough for only me.

Our town's population was just over a thousand. Fourteen people were going to make a difference in the town's dynamic. How many people would move now that they'd lost everything? I reviewed the list Mac had compiled about injuries and what hospitals people were taken to.

I hoped Alyssa didn't hear Mac's news. "It's getting dark. How many people are still unaccounted for?"

"Well, we're not sure who was in town. And we're still combing some of the houses on the east side. We have over eighty-five percent accounted for."

That sounded positive. This was the weekend of graduations and end-of-school parties, so chances the unaccounted were out of town were high. "Is FEMA still digging?"

"They'll stop if we get any phone calls from people who we haven't reached," he said.

"I'll leave you to it."

❖

"You're falling asleep standing up."

Alyssa looked at me with hooded eyes and stifled a yawn. "I'm here for you, Sheriff."

I touched her face to wipe off dust, but my fingers lingered on her cheek. Her skin was smooth and soft, and for a moment, I forgot about the atrocities of the day. "It's midnight. We both need rest."

"Are we sleeping at the station?"

"No, I'm taking you to my house." She leaned against my shoulder as I walked her to the squad car. The normally five-minute drive was pushed to ten as I drove slowly around piles of bricks, tree limbs, and dumpsters.

I hadn't seen my family yet. The house was eerily dark. I didn't have a generator. When I lost power, I always went to my parents' house. This was a sad reminder that I needed to get one.

"Hey, Alyssa, wake up." I shook her gently. She snuggled against me and made a cute little sighing noise. I smiled and turned off the car. A part of me wanted to lean my head back and fall asleep with Alyssa in my arms, but we both needed solid sleep on a bed.

"What? Where are we?" Alyssa asked. She rubbed her eyes and stretched. It took her about five seconds before her eyes flew open and she slid away from me. "I'm so sorry. I didn't mean to fall asleep on you. I'm just so exhausted."

"Come on. Let's go inside. We have a long day ahead." I turned on my flashlight and grabbed her hand. "Watch where you step."

"You have a nice place," she said.

"I can't tell you how happy I am that it's still standing. Come on. The bedroom is upstairs." I showed Alyssa the bathroom and my bedroom and pulled out a T-shirt and a pair of sweats even though it was warm and stuffy inside. "Get comfortable. I'm going to check on my parents." I made my way back downstairs and knocked on the guest room door before I opened it. My mom slipped out of bed and hugged me. I don't know who started crying first, but we woke up my dad.

"If you keep that up, I'm going to start crying and you know then we'll never stop." His voice was gruff, but I knew he was a softie. My mom lit the candle on the nightstand.

"Dad, I'm really sorry you all lost the house and the diner." I sat on the bed and reached for him.

He held me close. "Insurance will cover the house and our things. I just know it's going to be a hard month ahead for you. We're thankful your house is still standing."

"You can stay here as long as you want."

"I know, kiddo. Thank you. I can finally get around to some of the projects here like fixing the basement door and installing an attic fan."

"You worry about getting a fair deal from your insurance company. That's first. My stuff can wait." I shifted off the bed and kissed them both good night. "Get some sleep. We all have an early start tomorrow." I closed the door behind me and locked up before I headed upstairs.

The full moonlight was a blessing since the entire town was out of power. Alyssa was fully dressed and asleep in my bed. I took off her damp shoes and peeled off her socks. She had small feet with manicured toes. I opened both windows for air. The night was silent. No crickets, no frogs, no humming of the outside lights on my property. It was eerie and a somber reminder that the tornado disrupted everything, including nature.

I grabbed fresh clothes and slipped into the bathroom to clean up the best I could with two gallons of water. I didn't trust the water in the lines. I wasn't nearly as clean as I wanted to be, but it was good to be out of dirty, torn clothes. I stretched out on the couch and thought about the longest day of my life. Bayonet, Missouri, had a real struggle ahead. We were a strong town, but this was surreal. I drifted off to sleep hoping today was just a bad dream and tomorrow everything would be back to normal except somehow I still wanted Alyssa around.

CHAPTER SEVEN

I heard people whispering but I was too tired and sore to realize I wasn't still asleep. I rolled over and reached for my pillow but came up empty-handed.

"Who are you?"

I popped open one eye when I realized they were asking me. I winced at the early morning sunlight. Where the hell was I?

"Who are you?" they asked again. It was an older couple, about my mom's age.

I moved up in the bed until my back was pressed against the headboard. I kept the anger out of my voice because for a few moments, I had no idea where I was. "I'm Alyssa. I came here with the sheriff."

Both of them instantly relaxed. "We thought you were a squatter. We're Katy's parents. I'm Stacy and this is Grant. We're the Emersons."

I squeezed Stacy's hand. "I'm so sorry to hear about your house. And the diner."

"We're just thankful Katy's house wasn't hit. It's probably one of the few in the area still standing. Are you Katy's new girlfriend?"

My heart beat a little faster at their question. I was kind of getting a lesbian vibe from her, but their confirmation gave me hope. Worst timing ever for a possible date, but it was nice to have that information tucked away. "I'm a volunteer. She pulled me over for speeding. We ended up in your diner's parking lot."

"She gave you a ticket during a tornado?"

"The tornado came up out of nowhere. We didn't have time. She pulled me into the diner and we hid in the cooler." I didn't want to talk about our ordeal because I didn't know how much Katy wanted her family to know.

"It's a good thing it was bolted into the floor," Grant said.

Katy poked her head in after knocking. "Did my parents wake you up?" She stood in the doorway wearing a tight khaki T-shirt that showed off her curves and khaki cargo pants. She was wearing a different pair of boots and her hair cascaded over her shoulders and down her back. I swallowed hard. She was magnificent and powerful.

"They thought I was a squatter."

"Like who's been sleeping in my bed from Goldilocks?" she asked. She turned to her parents. "I'm headed out in about five. Dad, do you want a ride over to the house or do you want the Gator?"

"We'll take the Gator and check out the house and the diner," he said.

Katy handed him a radio. "Check in with me and be careful."

I jumped up because I was the only one not ready to start the day. I stifled my groan and straightened out the scrubs. "Just give me a few minutes to get ready."

"I put a new toothbrush and some clothes that might fit you in the bathroom. Your shoes are dry. I put them out last night after you fell asleep."

I patted down my unruly curls, fully aware of how awful I must look. "Thank you for the hospitality. Yesterday was the longest day. I don't know how you are going to do this for the months to come."

"It'll be hard, but we'll get a lot of help. Do you want to come into town with me today? I can take you to your car. I don't know when we'll have a tow truck for it, but maybe you can get some of your personal items out of it." She tucked her hair behind her ear and waited for my answer.

I bit my lip at her intensity when our eyes met. Now was not the time to hit on her. "I would love a ride. Give me five minutes."

"Don't use the water from the faucet. We don't know if it's been contaminated. Use the bottled water instead. I'll see you downstairs."

I slipped into the bathroom, thankful for the clean clothes. I splashed water on my face and brushed my teeth. I ignored the dark circles under my eyes and pinched color into my cheeks. Five minutes later, I entered the kitchen and put on my sneakers that Katy had left by the stairs. She greeted me with a Gatorade that was still somewhat cold from her refrigerator.

"Our options for breakfast are Clif Bars, apples, or dry cereal." Her hair was brushed back in a no-nonsense bun at the back of her neck. Her duty belt was low on her hips. She twirled a sheriff's ball cap in her hand and looked at me expectantly. She was antsy.

I grabbed both a Clif Bar and an apple. "I'm ready."

"Great. Let's go." She grabbed another ball cap that said Willow County Sheriff's Dept. and locked the door behind us. "Here, this will help keep the dust out of your hair and the sun from your eyes."

"And it will keep people from trying to run me off. I'll just say 'I'm with the sheriff.'" I watched as Katy blushed and slipped on a pair of sunglasses before looking at me.

"That'll work, too. Let's swing by your car and see if they have that road cleared."

There were about ten times the number of cars and people as last night. "Are all these people here to help or gawk?"

"If they are this far in, probably to help." Katy parked near the tangled metal mess that once was my car.

My heart still hurt seeing it totaled. That car and I had been through so much. "Is it weird that I'm sad to see my car like this? I mean, it's just a car."

"I get it. I once wrecked a 1969 Camaro and I still tear up thinking about it," she said.

I laughed and it sounded foreign coming out of my mouth. I felt guilty at the sound given that I was standing in a town that wasn't much of anything anymore. I could see the volunteer tents lined down Main Street where, before the tornado, I wouldn't have been able to see. "You know what I mean. People get attached to their cars."

"She was midnight black and smoking hot. My first true love."

I felt her smile all the way down to my toes. "I would say I'm surprised, but I'm not."

She put her hand on her heart. "What? Are you making fun of me?" She was so damn charming. "Come on. Let's see what we can salvage here. Be careful and don't cut yourself."

With her strong arm out to steady me, I climbed through the front windshield. My nose wrinkled at the smell of wet and muddy upholstery. It took a crowbar to get the glove compartment opened. Most of the paperwork was dripping wet. There wasn't anything worth salvaging. I had a small victory when I found my purse wedged under the back seat. Everything else was destroyed. I was glad to have most of my camera equipment. I'd hated paying five hundred dollars for the case, but not so much now that everything was safe and had survived the tornado.

"I'm sorry about your car."

I waved it off like it wasn't a big deal. "I'm sorry about your town. A car can be replaced in a week."

She huffed out a big sigh. "I wish it was that easy here."

"Put me to work and let's see what we can do." I wished I had a pain reliever because my arms felt like wet noodles and my knees felt wobbly. I wasn't cut out to lift concrete blocks and drag large branches long distances. But I wanted to help and I had the sheriff's blessing to be here.

I snapped photos of the volunteers and workers throwing bricks into the back of dump trucks, people making piles of salvageable items from stores, and Willow's Power and Light utility trucks lined up to fix downed power lines. It was hard to believe that less than twenty-four hours ago, it was a scene out of a war-torn town.

"Is everyone accounted for? What about Hodges? Was it wiped out, too?" When I switched out my camera battery, I thought of the Luffs and wondered if their ranch was hit by the tornado. I visualized bridezilla shaking her fist at the twister yelling "not today!" I hoped they were safe even though Mandy was awful.

"We'll find out," Katy said.

I followed her down the stairs to the basement of the station where it was standing room only. All beds were taken as workers who worked through the night caught a few hours of sleep. The room smelled of dust, sweat, and burnt coffee. The generator outside was running power to large fans, but with so many people inside, it was hard to get a good flow around the entire room. I stood by Katy and listened as she was briefed by a soft-spoken young man with a crew cut and a slight lisp.

"We've heard from everyone except the Booker place and the two farms on 10."

"I'll grab Robert and head that way."

"Channel 15 got through," he said.

Katy shook her head. "I'll handle them. Where are they?"

"Down at the winery."

She flipped her wrist and looked at her watch. It was the kind you wound up by turning the tiny knob back and forth until the tension couldn't stand another twist. It was probably a family heirloom. "It's seven oh five now. I'll check in every hour. How long are you at this station?"

"Until eight. Then I'm rotating out with someone down from Clinton."

"Stay connected."

He nodded at her. "Will do, boss."

"Let's take care of the reporters and then grab Robert on our way out to the Booker place," Katy said to me.

I followed her down the street until we saw a sign that said Martha's Vines with an arrow pointing east. "What did you do this weekend, Alyssa? Well, I visited Martha's Vineyard."

Katy laughed. "The owner's name really is Martha. And she brings a lot of tourism to the area, believe it or not."

We sobered up the closer we got to the winery. The only thing standing was a stone firepit. The rows of budding grapes were swept away. There was one thing left standing in the field, and I made it my mission to find out what it was.

"I'll talk to the news crew. Be careful where you walk."

It was hard not watching her do her job. Her demeanor screamed authority. I could hear her bark at them for driving through a roadblock and on private property just to sneak into town. I walked over to see what was still standing in the field and found a stake with two of the smallest grapes still clinging to it. It amazed me what was still standing after a tornado. I took several pictures of them with the leveled town in the background. I met Katy halfway through the vineyard and she didn't look happy.

"What's going on?" I asked.

"They want to talk to you." Her full lips were pressed in a tight, straight line.

"Me? Why? What did I do?" I quickened my step. "Can I help you?"

"Are you Alyssa Bates? I'm Tamryn Swan from News 15 out of Clinton. I wanted to congratulate you on your photos from the tornado."

The reporter looked clean and fresh. I envied everything about her from her pressed clothes to her styled hair and perfect makeup. It reminded me of how dusty and crusty I felt. My confidence was shot standing in front of her. "What are you talking about?"

"You don't know?"

"Uh, no. We're kind of dealing with a natural disaster right now so things outside this town haven't been too important."

"Here, take a look at this."

She handed me her iPad and on the front page of the Associated Press's website were four of my photos. One was Katy with blood on her shirt and the side of her face, crouching down radioing for help; one of her holding Liam; one of a deputy helping somebody out from the church basement; and one of the high school aged boys covered in dust climbing over the debris, his bare foot dirty and cut.

"You also made the Weather Channel, CNN, and a few other major news channels. I'd like to interview you."

"Are you kidding me? Look at this place. Look at me. Now isn't the time."

"It's the perfect time. We'll showcase your photos and tell your story on tonight's news. You were on the front lines. Once we have a quick chat, we'll leave per the sheriff's request."

I suddenly hated reporters. But telling the story of this horrible ordeal was something I wanted, so I found myself nodding in agreement. They wasted no time hooking up a microphone to my dirty scrubs. The old classic Don Henley song "Dirty Laundry" cued up in my head as I spent too much time staring at Tamryn. How she could smile at a time like this seemed surreal. She stood next to me and nodded after the cameraman nodded to her.

"I'm standing in the small town of Bayonet that was literally wiped out by a tornado yesterday. With me is photographer Alyssa Bates, who captured a lot of the early rescue efforts. Thank you, Alyssa, for speaking with us today. What was the ordeal like?"

"It was the worst thing I'd ever experienced. I'm still in shock."

"Do you live here?"

"No, I'm from Lee's Summit. I was on my way to a wedding when I got pulled over by the sheriff. We were close to a diner and hid inside the cooler right before the tornado hit."

"That must have been frightening."

I nodded and tried to block out the moment it hit us and how I thought we were going to die. "The tornado pretty much took this entire town. It's going to take a lot of time and money to rebuild."

"You could have gone home yesterday, but you stayed to help and document the event," she said. I must have given her a look of disbelief at the question, because she backpedaled. "It was very nice of you to stay and volunteer to help. From what I can see, there is so much to do. Thankfully, the National Guard is here to help organize. What has been the most rewarding part?"

I was glad she revamped the question. "Helping people. I can't imagine what losing everything feels like. I've met some wonderful people under the worst circumstances, and I feel like I'll always have a connection here." I quickly looked at Katy, who was standing by waiting for me. Her arms were crossed and she looked irritated at them, but she gave me a quick, small smile.

"You took some incredible photos, which we are putting up on the screen for our viewers to see. What's one thing you want people to know about what happened here?"

I looked into the camera. "The people of Bayonet and Hodges and every other town this massive tornado hit are going to need everything. There is nothing left here. Houses and businesses are going to need to start from scratch, so whatever money you can donate to these towns would be greatly appreciated."

"Thank you, Alyssa, for your time and your photos that really show the horrors of what happened here in Bayonet."

She turned back to the cameraman and closed out the interview. I handed the mic clipped to the neckline of my shirt back to the sound guy and walked over to Katy. "The photo looked better than I thought it did. Also, I hate that they have internet and the rest of us don't. How is that even possible?"

"Swanky news truck. I predict we'll have sketchy service before too long. Are you ready to hit some farms and see if anybody needs us?"

"Definitely. Are they going to leave?" I thumbed back at the news crew, who were taking their sweet time packing up.

"Probably not, but I have more important things to do, and I don't need to waste it chasing after them," Katy said.

CHAPTER EIGHT

I didn't like the quiet. We pulled up in the driveway and I immediately regretted bringing Alyssa. I should have left her in town so she could help there. I gave Robert a look and he gave me a curt nod. He moved ahead of us.

"What's he doing?" she asked.

I pretended to tighten the laces on my boots and pulled my cap down a little tighter. "He's headed to the house, and we'll head over to the barn." The horses in the field probably belonged to the Bookers. After seeing the house split and the barn completely gone, I wasn't sure how that was possible.

"We should probably go with Robert. I don't know if I can stand to see a hurt animal. I mean, people we know how to help, but I don't know the first thing about administering first aid to a cow or goat or horse." Alyssa pointed to the three horses we could see in the distance.

"You're not wrong, but just be prepared," I said. She knew about the fourteen deaths. It was all everyone was talking about. I was surprised the news crew didn't ask her if she knew the victims. I handed her a flashlight and a fresh pair of gloves.

"Boss, I'm going to need you over by the south side of the house. We have a survivor." Robert's excited voice boomed over the walkie. I grabbed Alyssa's hand and ran to where he was.

"What's happening?" I asked.

Robert was moving sections of wood and drywall. "There's somebody down here."

Both Alyssa and I started digging. The sections were too heavy for the three of us to lift so Robert went back to the SUV and returned with two sledgehammers. I grabbed one and started smashing everything. "You're going to have to back up. I don't want anything to hit you." Alyssa stood to the side and watched. She took photos but I knew the second we needed her, she would abandon her job of photographer and slip into volunteer. We peeled back layers of roof and ceilings until we uncovered a clawfoot bathtub that had overturned.

"There's somebody underneath," Robert said. He looked at Alyssa. "Run back to the car and get the jack and crowbar. It's got to be hard to breathe like this."

Alyssa ran to the car while we continued digging through the pile. My heart was ready to explode at the heavy lifting and twisting and turning as we threw debris behind us. "Hello? Can you hear us?" Robert and I stopped for a moment. We heard tapping against the metal tub. As much as I hated how heavy the old-fashioned tub was, it probably saved this person's life. Robert and I climbed down and tried to lift the tub up, but there was still too much weight pressing it down.

"Maybe you can pull some of the heavy stuff off by using the SUV? Don't they come with towing equipment?" Alyssa asked.

"Great idea!" I ran back to the SUV and drove it to a spot Robert pointed to.

"This is part of the frame. If we can move this back a few feet, we should be able to get enough weight off."

I parked and shimmied under the bumper to find the winch. The steel braided cord looked thin, but I knew it could do the job. I gave the hook to Robert, who looped it under a beam and gave me a thumbs-up. Alyssa had backed up out of harm's way, and I cranked the power slowly and steadily until the frame slid off the top with several other layers. Once he yelled "clear" I joined him on the ground and slid the jack into place as he lifted up one of the sides with the crowbar. "This is Sheriff Emerson and Deputy Williams. We're here to help. Can you hear us?" I shined my flashlight and saw an older man curled up inside. He moaned. I grabbed my walkie. "Six hundred to dispatch."

"Dispatch, go ahead."

"I need an ambulance at the Booker place as soon as possible. We have a survivor who needs medical attention." I clipped my walkie back on my belt and grabbed several pieces of wood to stack next to the jack if it failed. By the time we had the tub jacked high enough to see who was under it, the ambulance pulled up beside us. I stood. "Bring the stretcher. We're going to have to slip it underneath him. We can't risk the weight of the debris shifting and knocking the tub over." Robert and I stood back to give the EMTs room. Alyssa stood next to me and grabbed my hand.

"Is there anybody else? Do we need to keep looking?" she asked.

"Eugene. Eugene. Is there anybody else we need to look for?" Robert said.

He moaned something, but we couldn't understand him.

"Eugene, don't try to talk. Can you nod if there's somebody else or shake your head no?"

When he shook his head, the three of us visibly relaxed. While he wasn't in the best shape, he was alive. It took the EMTs five minutes to get him strapped to the gurney and wiggle him away from the tub. His left ankle was crushed, and his foot was bent in an unnatural way. Alyssa walked away from us. One EMT immediately tended to his ankle while the other checked his stats. "Let's get him out of here."

It had taken us over an hour to dig Eugene out. The other two farms on this road had moderate damage but both families were okay. I called dispatch to inform FEMA. I was sore and tired and it wasn't even noon. We headed back into town to check in.

"Hey, I have service."

Alyssa held up her phone victoriously. Robert checked his and shook his head.

"Nothing here."

"Oh, wait. It's gone again." She frowned and shrugged.

I parked the SUV as close as I could to the controlled chaos that was now the center of my town. There were a lot of people here to help. I knew it was a matter of time before more news trucks made their way to the frontlines because people wanted to talk. They needed to share their feelings and experiences.

"What's going on?" I asked Daisy when we found her.

Daisy was sitting at a table, passing out waters as people filed in and out of the makeshift station. "People are trying to get their insurance agents in and the whole town is overwhelmed."

I turned to Alyssa. "Why don't you hang out here and help Daisy for a bit? I'm going to check in." She looked bone tired after the heavy lifting at Eugene's. It was only a matter of time before I had to send her home. She had a life that didn't involve Bayonet's problems. I leaned closer. "Daisy looks tired, but she won't go home. I need eyes on her."

She looked relieved to have a moment to sit. "Sure. Whatever you need." I smiled and headed to the FEMA tents. People were able to make calls to family and friends to let them know they were okay. FEMA said they had restored some cell service, but it would be another day before the towers were fixed. I got more hugs and tears than ever before.

"Sheriff, what are we going to do?" Brenda Mitchell, who owned the Craft & Candle store, hugged me and cried on my shoulder. She and my mother graduated high school the same year. I'd known Brenda my entire life.

"We're going to rebuild, Ms. Mitchell. It might take time, but we'll do it. And I'll be here every step of the way."

She pulled away. "How are your parents? Are they okay?"

I nodded. "They're at my house. Their house was hit. So was the Lunch Box. But they are healthy and safe and we were very fortunate."

Brenda made it over to the church in time because she was working and not home, but her neighbor was one of the fourteen who didn't survive. Most of the victims lived on her street.

"I just don't know what to do." She pointed behind us to the pile of bricks and mortar that was once her business. It was obvious she didn't have a clue on where to start.

"First of all, do you have a place to stay?" I knew that her son had moved to Columbia, Missouri. She was a widow and never remarried when her husband died.

"I'm staying with Linda and Nick Combs." Their house was one of the few still standing. I couldn't imagine Brenda staying in a FEMA tent. Her son was a lawyer and would probably help her deal with the insurance claims, but she hadn't been able to reach him. It had been twenty-four hours since the tornado struck, and it had been nationwide news ever since.

"I'm sure Noah will show up soon. You left a message, right?"

"Yes. On his cell phone and his office voice mail."

"I'm sure it's just a matter of time before he reaches out." Hopefully, sooner rather than later.

I looked at the graying sky. The rain would hinder the cleanup efforts. One of the guardsmen informed me that more dump trucks were arriving in about an hour along with more security. We had three pieces of heavy equipment on site to help remove debris. The shower truck and laundry truck, services offered in Kansas City for the homeless population, were parked near the Lunch Box to give people a chance to clean up. It amazed me how quick the response was to our disaster. At this point, my job was to make people feel safe. We'd get through this, one house at a time, one business at a time.

"Why don't you head to the station and get off your feet for a bit? We'll let you know when we hear from your son."

"Tell your parents I'm glad they're okay," Brenda said.

My parents' house was a brisk five-minute walk from downtown. I wanted to see the damage for myself. Plus, I didn't trust my dad to not do anything stupid. He was notorious for bad decisions, and with a knee that buckled, I worried about him digging through the destruction. I radioed dispatch to let them know what I was doing.

"Sheriff, we have a woman over here who wants to speak with you." A deputy stopped me. I recognized him from previous events, but he wasn't from my county and I couldn't remember his name.

"What can I do for you?" The woman was in her mid-fifties, very well put together, and clean. It was obvious she just arrived. Great. The last thing I needed was somebody wanting an interview.

"Hi, Sheriff. My name is Dena Bates. I think my daughter is with you."

"You're Alyssa's mom. Yes, she's at the station now. Well, in the basement." At her puzzled look, I continued explaining. "It's the only thing left so we've moved down there. She's volunteering." I looked at her shoes, which were about as practical as her daughter's original pair. "It's pretty uneven around here. Why don't I get her?" She clutched my arm.

"Is she okay?"

I smiled and patted her hand. "She's wonderful." I grabbed the walkie. "Six hundred to dispatch."

"Go ahead."

Hearing Daisy's voice gave me a sense of belonging. Even through this horrible ordeal, I knew we were going to be okay. "Daisy, can you ask Alyssa if she can meet me over by the church?"

There was a slight pause before I heard my answer. "She's on her way."

"Ten-four."

"What happened? How did she end up here?" Dena put her hands on her hips, and a part of me felt like she was scolding me, but I wasn't sure she knew the whole story.

"I think it's best that she tells you what happened. She'll be here in just a minute." The last thing I wanted was to start off on the wrong foot with Alyssa's mother. First impressions were everything, and I was usually impressive to parents. I watched as she scanned the town square.

"I'm so sorry this happened. How many miles was the tornado on the ground?"

"We don't know for sure, but I've heard that the destruction goes from just west of us to past Hodges, so at least eighteen miles."

"Was it an EF5?" she asked.

"We won't know for sure until the professionals rate it, but I believe it to be either an EF4 or EF5."

"Mom? What are you doing here?" Alyssa whizzed past me and headed straight for her mother's arms.

"Honey, I wanted to make sure you were okay. I hadn't heard from you since yesterday and I was worried."

I was used to dealing with tragedy. It came with the job. When Alyssa sobbed in her mother's arms, I realized that the last twenty-four hours was a lot for anyone to take. Even though she still had a place to go home to and would get a car sooner than later, surviving a tornado like this was a lot.

"She's been a real help." I didn't know what else to say.

"How did you end up here, baby?" Dena cupped Alyssa's face in her hands.

Alyssa sniffed and cleared her throat. "Sheriff pulled me over for speeding. The tornado kicked up out of nowhere so we ran into a diner and hid in the cooler."

I kept my face as stoic as I could when Dena looked at me.

"It's probably a good thing she pulled you over. They always say it's never good to try to outrun a tornado. Where's your car now?"

"There's nothing left of it. It's stuck in a ditch down the road. You probably passed it on the way in." She pointed behind her mother. "When things slow down here, we can get a tow truck in and have it towed back to Lee's Summit. Right now, the sheriff and almost the entire town is picking up small pieces."

"It's out of the way so whenever you want the tow truck to get it, let me know and I'll ensure they don't have a problem," I said.

"Let's get out of here so the sheriff can get back to work." Dena touched my arm. "Thank you for taking care of my daughter."

"She saved us. She's a good woman." I felt the heat on my cheeks and saw a slight flush on Alyssa's neck at my compliment. "Thank you for getting me out of the cooler. And thank you for sticking around and helping us find survivors."

She hugged me, and even though it felt awkward because it was happening in front of her mother, it felt right, too. "I'll never forget this weekend. I'm so sorry this happened to your town. If you need me for anything at all, let me know," she said.

"You have my phone number still, right?" I remembered giving her my business card yesterday even though it felt like months ago.

"Yes. Hopefully, you get phone service soon. I'll reach out."

I smiled at her softly. "For what it's worth, I'm glad I pulled you over." She looked at her feet and back up at me.

"So am I."

CHAPTER NINE

Your photographs are everywhere. Look, honey. You're even on ABC World News."

Wrapped in a giant robe after taking the longest, hottest shower I could stand, I plopped down on the couch, my sleepiness suddenly replaced with an adrenaline rush I'd never felt before. "Oh, my God." I grabbed my laptop and pulled up my emails. "Mom. They want more photos. And there's a bidding war on them. My boss has been trying to reach me. Can I borrow your phone?" Mine wasn't charging. I'd have to take it in tomorrow and get it replaced. She gave me her phone. I had to look up my boss's number. "Whitney. It's Alyssa. What's going on?"

"Are you okay? You've been tough to reach. It looks like you were in hell."

"I'm a little sore, but I'm fine. I can't say that about the town or the hundreds of people who lost everything."

"I'm sorry you had to go through that, but I'm glad you're fine. I hate to make this about business, but I've had a lot of people reaching out about your photos. The ones you sent to AP are amazing. How many more do you have?"

I grabbed my camera and looked at the SD card. "Over two thousand." Had I gone to the Luff wedding, I would have about the same. Candid photos were the best, and the last twenty-four hours were nothing but candid. Shit. The wedding. "Did the Luffs ever call you about their wedding photographer not showing up?" I cringed as I waited for her answer. I knew Hodges got hit, too, but I didn't know to what extent.

"Not a word from them," she said.

"I hope they're okay."

"I hope so, too. As far as your photos, can you watermark them and put them on the website? We can send outlets the link." I knew she was excited because this was big, but I felt dirty about making money from this horrific ordeal.

"I want to donate all the proceeds to Bayonet or Willow County. Is that possible?"

I heard a sharp intake of breath. Whitney wasn't happy with that. "This is your big break. Your photos are phenom. You're always looking for the breakaway job."

"I mean, you'll still get the company cut," I said.

"Why? You weren't on assignment. The photos are yours. Only donate a portion. You deserve to get paid for this. Everybody wins. You'll get exposure and money and so will the town."

"I don't feel right profiting from someone else's tragedy."

"That's understandable. Were you able to get any releases?"

Nothing was bigger than releases. "I got verbals from the little boy's family, the sheriff, the deputies, and the first wave of volunteers. Most of my photos were in public places, so I'm not worried about anybody suing. I mean, especially if the money goes directly to the town. I'll start a GoFundMe page today."

"Get on the photos. I'll send emails to everyone telling them one hundred percent of the money will go to rebuilding the town. You've got an hour."

"On it, boss." I hung up and downloaded my photos to my laptop. My mom sat beside me and pointed to the ones she thought were good, which was almost every one. "It was awful. I never want to be in another tornado again." My ears still popped when I swallowed or yawned.

I narrowed the list down to two hundred photos at five hundred dollars per picture. It felt outrageous, but I had the only first-on-the-scene photos. If people wanted to help, this was the way. Across the top in big, bold letters I stated that all money would go directly to the towns in Willow County for rebuilding purposes.

"You could always write a book about your story and publish your photos that way. I'm sure somebody would help you." My mother had the best ideas. While I wasn't a writer, I did know people in the business.

"That's a brilliant idea. I have a lot to say about what I went through. What Katy and I went through."

"Who's Katy?"

I shook my head. "I mean Sheriff Emerson. You go through something like that and you're on a first-name basis." I didn't tell her about how many times we held hands or how often I leaned into her for strength.

"What happens now?"

I stared at the screen intently. "Now we wait and watch the website and see how many people jump on and order photos."

"Is that normal? I mean, don't most people just send in photos and cross their fingers? I remember you said that once," she said.

"This is completely not normal, and I don't even know if it's going to work. I'm going to start the GoFundMe page and link it on the photograph site." I started explaining it, but I saw her eyes gloss over the more I tried explaining, so I gave up.

"Are you hungry? Do you want me to fix something to eat?"

One could not live on Clif Bars alone. I needed something savory. "I can DoorDash something," I said.

"How about breakfast for dinner? Pancakes, bacon, eggs."

"That sounds even better." By the time I got the GoFundMe set up and used a photo of the decimated town square, I had sold three photos. "We have fifteen hundred already!" My mom raced over to see which photos sold.

"Those are good ones."

"Oh, another four just sold." I couldn't believe it. In the span of five minutes, I sold seven photos at five hundred a pop. It was unheard of. I knew of a few lucky photographers who got thousands of dollars for celebrity photos, but this was Middle America. These were photos of a town nobody knew with people who lived small town lives.

"I'm so proud of you."

She kissed my cheek and slid a plate of food under my nose. I pushed my laptop away so I could eat. I was famished. "I need to get to the Apple store and get a new phone. Or get this one checked out." I held up my iPhone. "I'm carrying around a brick in my pocket."

"It's Sunday evening. Everything is already closed."

"Shit. Okay. I'll try in the morning." I ate while posting the

GoFundMe page to all my social media platforms. Whitney shared my post and within minutes, money started trickling in. "This is amazing. I never thought people would be so generous." Fifty dollars here, one hundred dollars there, and an anonymous person donated five hundred within an hour of the page going up. I had set a goal of ten thousand dollars, but quickly changed it to fifty thousand since it was obvious people wanted to help. "Mom, look at this. Can you believe it?"

"It's amazing what a photo can do. Good job, baby."

She kissed the top of my head and excused herself. She got about as much sleep as I did last night. Tomorrow was a busy day. I emailed my insurance company photos of the car. I hoped they would agree it was totaled and pay me a fair price, but I knew I wasn't going to get as much as I thought the car was worth. By the time I crawled into bed, over half my photos sold and I had over twenty thousand in the GoFundMe account.

❖

"What's taking so long?"

The salesclerk at Apple was transferring data to my new phone. I had walked the store twice and played with the new iPad. Life up here was business as usual while people eighty miles away were trying to salvage keepsakes from rubble. I was anxious to get back to Bayonet and tell Katy the news. I knew she was busy, but I couldn't stay away. It was the first organic relationship I'd had in a long time.

"Your messages are coming through and you have a lot. How long has it been since you've read them?"

"Almost two days."

He looked surprised. "You get this many messages a day?"

I didn't even want to explain what happened. I just wanted my phone and wanted to get out of there. "Not normally. The last two days have been crazy." After a few more minutes, he finally handed me my phone.

"Let me know if you need anything else."

I waved it at him. "Thanks. Have a nice day." I raced out of the store only to be momentarily confused because I couldn't find my car. I clicked the unlock button and realized the green Jeep right in front of me was my ride. The insurance company had instructed me to get a rental, and this seemed like the best option for driving back into a tornado disaster zone.

I slipped inside and pulled up my messages. I had over two hundred texts and direct messages on Insta and Twitter. Immediately, I pulled up bridezilla's texts. Several angry messages followed by a final text in all caps that read *YOU'RE FIRED!* That message came in right after the tornado hit and I was trapped in the cooler. Peggy had texted me, too. I didn't bother with the voice mails because I knew they were hateful.

I answered several *Are you okay?* texts and others who had congratulated me on my photographs that were now worldwide. I wanted to get on the road so I answered the important messages and headed to Bayonet to give Katy the good news.

❖

"Miss Alyssa. What brings you back down here? Are you taking care of your car today?"

I was so relieved to see Robert at the roadblock. "I'm here to talk to the sheriff. I have Gatorade in the cooler and snacks in back if you all are thirsty." I popped the trunk and he and two guardsmen grabbed apples and Gatorade.

"Thank you so much. Go on in. Sheriff is somewhere in there barking at people." He winked at me and waved me through.

I parked not far from Main Street. My heart dropped to my stomach when I found her in the crowd. Her stance was unmistakable. Today she was wearing khaki pants and a short-sleeved button-down state-issued shirt. Her hair was pulled back and she was engrossed in a conversation with somebody in a darker uniform. She did a double take when she saw me. Our eyes met across the street and the look she shot me gave me chills. There was no mistaking it. She was into me. Hunger and desire were delivered in one look that made my knees weak and chills explode down my body. I stifled the shiver. I gave her a soft smile and a shrug. I pointed to the cooler I was wheeling behind me. She held her finger up to the man she was speaking with and walked over to me and pulled me into her arms.

"What are you doing here? I mean, I'm glad you're here, but I thought I wouldn't see you for a long time."

Her fingers lingered on my arm and I tried not to smile so hard because of the monumental mess we were standing in, but it was difficult. "I had some news to share with you and I wanted to do it in person."

"Do you want to go to the station?" Her voice rose as a dump truck rolled past us.

"Too many people. Can we sit somewhere quiet?"

She nodded and gave a short, piercing whistle to the man she was talking to. He turned and she held up ten fingers. He nodded.

"Ten minutes, huh?"

"That's just for starters." She looked around and pointed at a tent with folding chairs. "Let's pull some chairs out." I followed her and waited as she grabbed two chairs and moved them away from the noise and the hustle and bustle of the tents. "You're a sight for sore eyes."

Her eyes roamed up and down and I blushed at her attention. "Thanks. It's nice to be clean and in fresh clothes."

She smoothed her hair back and nodded. "I took a shower in the portable truck, and while I couldn't shave or deep condition my hair, the hot water felt amazing." She put her hand on my knee. "What's going on?"

I handed her a cold Gatorade and pulled up my phone, praying they had service.

"Look for Wi-Fi and you'll see FEMA. The password is Bayonet."

"Got it. Okay. Hear me out." I held up my hands as though she might get upset.

She took a deep breath. "Okay. I'm listening."

"I sold photographs online from the destruction and damage of the tornado to news outlets." Her eyebrows twitched and she frowned but remained quiet. "Five hundred dollars each. I've sold one hundred and thirty-six as of right now. The money is yours to help rebuild the town. I also started a GoFundMe that right now is at eighty-eight thousand dollars. That's over one hundred and fifty thousand dollars for the county and it's only been a day. I know it'll taper off, but I can see this blowing up over the next few weeks."

She stared at me and looked away. I thought she was going to be mad at me, but she turned to face me again, cupped my face, and brought her lips to mine. My first reaction was to pull her closer to me. I hadn't been reading the signs wrong. Her full lips pressed against mine and desire ignited every cell in my body. I was hyperaware of her touch and how soft her hands were on my face. Her mouth was warm and demanding and when our tongues touched, I knew this was meant to be. We broke apart only because we heard giggling and realized we were in public.

"That's incredible. I don't even know what to say. I mean, that can be used for so much." She clutched my hands.

"There's more. I'm thinking of doing a photo journal book of when it hit, the aftermath, the cleanup, and the rebuilding of Bayonet. I'm sure you all have photos of what it looked like before the tornado. A large portion of the book could be donated as well."

"I can't believe you did all of this. Why? I mean, Bayonet is just a town people pass through."

"I tried to pass through it, but the town sheriff stopped me and wanted to get locked in a cooler with me. I mean, I've been picked up before, but never by a tornado and a woman at the same time." I smiled at my corny line.

"When all of this gets to a manageable level, I want to take you out. Obviously, where you live because the best food in this town, the Lunch Box, is under construction," she said.

I grew serious for a moment. "How are your parents doing?"

She blew out a big sigh. "Surprisingly well given they lost everything. My dad brought the generator over so we have power at my house now. It was a little banged up, but still works."

"Good. How are the insurance companies responding?"

"It's been two days but we're seeing more of them."

Her radio crackled and she was needed somewhere. "I have to go, but whatever you need, let me know. I'm sure the people here will sign releases once they know what's happening. Take photos but be careful." She pointed at my boots. "I'm glad you're wearing good shoes."

"Lesson learned. Thank you. I'll find you later."

I wanted to skip and dance around with excitement. I was right about Katy. We had chemistry and it wasn't because we were trapped in a metal box together thinking we were going to die.

I grabbed my cooler after offering the people in the tents the rest of the cold Gatorades and apples. I took photos of the workers and the townspeople who stopped in to charge their phones, grab a snack, and rest for a few minutes. I spent ten minutes listening to three old men who were at Telly's Bar and Grill and survived. The only thing standing was the counter that they were hiding behind. After the tornado passed through, one of them reached up and poured beers for the people who were crouched down with them. I wanted to believe them because we all needed something fun. I snapped a picture of them and continued my trek through town.

I saw Katy several times, and every time our eyes met, my heart fluttered. Now wasn't the time or the place, but soon. I could wait. I left with an additional seven hundred photos that I could put under the cleaning up phase. My goal over the next few days was finding a publishing company that would be interested in a photo book of the Bayonet tornado or find somebody who knew how to set one up on a self-publishing site.

Saying good-bye to Katy was awkward because she was in the middle of something, but she stopped and hugged me quickly. She brushed her thumb on the side of my face. "I'll talk to you soon."

I thought I was going to drive home, but guilt and uncertainty made me turn on Highway 57. It wasn't littered with debris, but one could tell a tornado tore across the road. My heart sank when I pulled onto the Luff property. Their beautiful house was mostly destroyed. The only thing standing was the barn. It looked solid. I was happy to see cattle still on their property. They didn't lose everything. People stopped working when they saw my car. I parked far enough away from the cleanup efforts.

A worker walked up to me. "Can I help you?"

"I'm looking for Peggy or Mandy Luff. Are either of them around?" I asked.

"Head on over to the barn. You'll find her there, ma'am." He nodded and tipped his Stetson at me. I loathed being called ma'am, but that's what they did down here. It wasn't as insulting as being called that at a perfume counter in Saks.

"Thank you. Is it okay that I'm parked here?" I pointed to the Jeep. The last thing I needed was another claim on my insurance.

"You're far enough away. It's fine."

I walked over to the barn and peeked inside. I had to know for myself that the Luffs were okay. "Hi, is Peggy or Mandy here?"

"Oh, my goodness. Alyssa, you're okay!" Peggy greeted me with a hug and tears.

"I'm so sorry I didn't make it. I tried." I couldn't believe I was tearing up in her arms. Her daughter was hateful and officially fired me, but I was still invested in their well-being.

"It's okay. Because of you, we were all in the barn. When the tornado rolled through, we were able to get to the storm shelter." She pointed to the north corner of the barn. "You saved us."

Relief washed over me as tears fell. "I got pulled over for speeding and then got stuck in a cooler during the tornado. I lost my phone in the whole ordeal. I was really hoping you all made it to safety. Is everybody okay?"

"Jason had to get stitches in his leg and one of the groomsmen broke his ankle falling down the shelter stairs, but we're all good." She squeezed my hands. "You really saved us. Thank you."

"Well, you finally made it." Mandy showed up with her hands on her hips.

I dropped Peggy's hands. "Really? You already fired me. I just came here to make sure you were okay. I'm sorry I got stuck in a tornado and couldn't make it to your wedding." I wanted to say more, but I pressed my lips together and put my hands on my hips, too.

"We're still paying you," Peggy said and immediately put up her hand when Mandy's face screwed up into a hateful scowl. "It's the least we can do since we were all here at the barn per your instruction. I don't know how many of us would've survived if we weren't already here."

"I didn't do the job, so you don't have to pay me," I said.

"At least we'll compensate you for your time."

Maybe that would cover the deductible. I nodded because I wasn't stupid and I was only there because of them. "Thank you. Just so you know, I started a GoFundMe account for Willow County and am selling my photographs of the destruction to raise money as well. All the money goes to the town."

"That's amazing, Alyssa. Thank you. I haven't left the ranch. Is it just as bad everywhere else?" Peggy asked.

"Bayonet was decimated."

She covered her mouth with both hands. "Oh, no. I heard it was bad, but I didn't know just how bad. We haven't had time or energy to look at the news. We've been trying hard to round up cattle and sheep and stay safe."

"It's a mess. I just came from there. Here, let me show you some photos." I handed her my camera and showed her how to forward to the next photo.

"This is horrible. Did everyone survive?"

I shook my head. "I don't know names, but there were fourteen fatalities in Bayonet. I don't know if Hodges had any, but you could probably get into town if you wanted to." Maybe Peggy could send one of the farmhands into town.

"Thank you for stopping by and checking on us. We'll be sure to reach out when things get better and we have a new date for the wedding," Peggy said.

"We fired her, remember?" Mandy said.

Once a bridezilla, always a bridezilla. Peggy gritted her teeth and turned to her daughter. "You're lucky Alyssa is still interested. How many people have you fired during this wedding?"

Mandy looked guilty and backed down.

"As long as I'm paying, I get final say and if Alyssa wants the job, it's hers," Peggy said.

"Thank you, Peggy. Let's see where things are when you're ready to try again. In the meantime, do you mind if I take a few photos of the ranch?"

"That's fine. Just be careful and don't get hurt."

"Thank you. I'll reach out again." I walked around the ranch and took photos of cattle roaming the property, the smashed-in roof, a photo through the kitchen window of a vase of dying flowers on the table that had somehow survived the two-hundred-mile winds, the obvious path the tornado took, and the barn that still stood. It was an emotional day, and I was anxious to get back to the comfort and safety of my house. I was fortunate, but the sadness of what people lost finally got to me and I cried most of the way home.

CHAPTER TEN

It was almost a month to the day the tornado hit that I finally took a weekend off. I slept hard from Friday night until Saturday afternoon. I wanted to sleep longer, but my mother reminded me that I had a wonderful woman waiting for me to take her to dinner.

Water and electricity were restored to the places that could handle it. I was floored by how fast houses and businesses were going up. A few families packed up and left, but most stayed. Alyssa had visited every weekend taking photos and volunteering her services where they were needed. She and her mother baked dozens of cookies, and when she pulled into town on Saturday mornings, people lined up for them. She was fast becoming the hero of the EF5 Willow County tornado. Her GoFundMe raised over two hundred thousand dollars and she sold every single photo on the site, which added an additional hundred thousand. The rest of her photos she was saving for the book she was writing. She'd found a small, local publishing company who provided an editor and layout artist. We texted daily and talked on the phone every couple of days. Starting a relationship while managing a natural disaster wasn't easy, but Alyssa was worth the wait. Tonight was my first night away from Bayonet, away from my parents, and away from the stresses of my job. I was officially off until Monday morning.

"What are you wearing?" Mom asked.

I'd forgotten what it was like to have my parents meddle in my life. Living with them again had been a blessing and a curse. I was glad they survived the tornado, but my mother needed something to do besides focus on me. According to her, I wasn't eating enough, drinking enough, or sleeping enough. I needed to cut loose but answer every call because I had a very important job.

"I don't know, but I'll find something." I knew exactly what I was going to wear, but I didn't feel like arguing with her. It was almost July and that meant the humidity and the heat were oppressive. I never felt comfortable in shorts because I thought my legs were too long, so I slipped into a pale blue summer dress and flat sandals. Heels were out of the question. I was already six feet tall. I pulled my hair back only for the drive. I planned on letting it down when I got to Alyssa's. "What do you think?"

My mom teared up. "Oh, honey. You look so beautiful. I'm so happy you are taking the weekend for yourself."

"I can't tell you how nice it is to be clean and wearing anything besides my uniform."

"You look beautiful. It doesn't matter what you wear." We both knew she was lying. She hated my uniform. It was practical and part of the job. More than anything else, it was a symbol. People trusted me when I wore it, but she thought the drab color washed me out.

"Well, don't stay up. I don't know when I'll be home."

"You should just stay there because I don't want you to drive at night. Your dad and I will be fine."

I smiled. "We'll see. I slept for almost fourteen hours. I'll be awake for a bit."

"Just be careful. Tell Alyssa we said hello."

I took a deep breath when I stepped outside. I'd ordered a basic sedan online after my personal car was a total loss. It was silver with less than twenty thousand miles on it. With everything going on, I didn't have time to think about what I really wanted. I just needed something to drive.

On my way. I sent Alyssa a quick text. The plan tonight was to eat a nice dinner out and relax at her place. I was ready for normalcy. The closer I got to Lee's Summit, the lighter my shoulders felt. The last month had aged me. My new-to-me car announced I had a new text message. I liked how everything was hands free. Maybe I'd keep this car.

Can't wait to see you finally.

I smiled when my car said the words "heart emoji." I was lucky that Alyssa was so understanding and knew I had to put any sort of dating life on hold until I had a handle on fixing the town. It was a slow process, but I was fast approaching burnout and my mental health was important. Daisy was pushing me to "take that lovely girl out on a proper date."

Alyssa and I both knew that time alone was the next level in our relationship, and I was ready for it. I wanted to lose myself in her for just one night. My heart raced when I turned onto her street. I let my hair down and pulled into her driveway. She lived in a townhouse, and I smiled when I saw a curtain flutter upstairs. I grabbed the flowers I'd impulsively stopped to buy and walked up to her door. She opened it before I even knocked and gaped at me.

"You look...I mean..." She waved her hand up and down. "You look amazing." She gave me the nicest hug. "Thank you for giving me tonight."

"I needed to get away and couldn't think of a better way to spend it than with you." I kissed her softly. I knew we had all night, but I missed her warm, full lips. Kissing her was worth the drive. It was exciting and gave me a different purpose than worrying about everything else. She made me forget about the bad and focus only on the good. "You look incredible." I let my gaze roam her body. Her taupe skirt hit right above her knee and the rose-colored sleeveless blouse showed off her toned arms. Her sandals had a slight heel so even though I towered over her, it was easier to kiss her.

She stepped away from me. "Please come in. Let me give you a quick tour. It's not much, but it's mine."

"I think it's warm and cozy," I said. She once told me that photography wasn't a profitable profession, but she had nice things and her place was inviting. It was small, but tastefully decorated. I picked up a photo on the mantel and smiled when I recognized her and her mother. "How old were you here?"

She slid next to me and took the frame from my hand. "Eighteen. Right after high school graduation. I was so young then."

I tipped her chin up so I could look into her eyes. "You're even more beautiful now." Then I kissed her. It started off as a smooth brush of my lips over hers but ignited into a feathery warmth that spread throughout my body and made me deepen the kiss. She tasted like iced tea and sugar. It was refreshing against the heat of my mouth. Her low moans mimicked my own and I had to pull back for fear of us not making it to dinner. I tucked a curl behind her ear. "We should leave now. I could use a decent meal and good company." I was running off cold fast food, energy bars, and casseroles people dropped off at the station. I also didn't want to fuck things up with Alyssa by moving too fast. Technically, this was our first date.

"I'm hungry. I could eat anything." She bit her bottom lip and looked me in the eyes. Double entendre noted.

I rubbed my thumb on her cheek and smiled softly. I was going to enjoy getting to know Alyssa. "Let's go before it's too late."

Her exhale was audible and I vowed to be worth the wait. To take my time with her, make her feel special because she was.

❖

"It's late. Why don't you stay the night?" Alyssa locked her fingers with mine and gently pulled me to the front door. I raised my eyebrows at her suggestion, and she laughed nervously.

We'd just had an amazing dinner where we talked about everything from our childhoods, the awkward teenage years where she tried to convince me she was quiet and shy with only a few friends, to the tornado that brought our lives together. Alyssa had written her account of our story and interviewed several families around town. She said she wasn't a journalist, but from what I'd read, she really captured the emotions of the moment. She interviewed people who were rebuilding and some who had scraped up what they could of their belongings and left. I was excited to see it finished. I kept her updated on the town's progress. Most of Main Street was cleared and new construction started. With the help from the world, I guessed we'd be up and running before Christmas.

"I mean, it's dark, you have to be exhausted from working nonstop for a month. You can have my bed and I will sleep on the couch," she said.

Secretly, I hoped she'd ask because I was still tired. Had I not had this date, I would be at home, in bed, listening to my mother rant about color schemes and whether she should go with white or stainless steel on all appliances.

"I think that sounds wonderful. It's nice to have a conversation without getting interrupted by people left and right." The incessant dinging of new messages from my staff disrupted our private calls in the evenings. Tonight, my phone was on silent. I wasn't risking it. Bayonet and Willow County could live without me for a night.

"Can I pour you a glass of wine?" she asked. She ran her fingertips down my arm when she walked by me.

I nodded and tried not to let her touch affect me so much. We hadn't kissed since I picked her up several hours ago, and it was the only thing on my mind every time she spoke. I stared at her lips knowing how soft they were. How perfectly they fit against mine. "Thank you." I accepted the glass and sat next to her on the couch.

"What are you thinking about?"

I played with one of her curls and smiled at her. "You."

"What about me?"

"Just our story. Pulling you over."

"During a tornado," she quickly added.

I smiled. "At the start of a tornado."

She shrugged. "Semantics."

I locked her fingers with mine. "How many couples can say they have a beginning like ours?"

She cocked her head at me and gave me a sexy, confident smile. "So, we're a couple?"

Busted. She was the only woman who occupied my waking thoughts since I pulled her over a month ago. "A bit premature, but I have to say, you're the only person I'm talking to." She leaned forward and kissed me softly. The tang of fresh strawberries from dessert still lingered on her full lips. Everything about her was delightful. I didn't want the night to end. She put her glass on the table and draped her wrists over my shoulders.

"I like everything about this. Well, not the tornado part, but I'm glad that I met you, Katy Emerson. You're exciting and I'm looking forward to being a..." She paused for effect. "To being a couple with you." She ran her fingertip along my bottom lip.

My exhaustion vanished and was quickly replaced with a jolt of excitement at the realization of being here, with her, alone without the hustle of what had recently become my life. "I'm happy I'm here. Thank you for agreeing to this date," I said.

"All because you wanted to pull me over because I'm cute," she said.

"How could I know that? You were driving so fast that I couldn't even see your face." I kissed her again playfully and quickly stood. "That reminds me. I have something for you." I went to my purse by the door.

"You, dinner, and flowers. What more could a girl want?" She looked at me with a smile that both melted my heart and hardened parts of my body I had ignored far too long.

I sat closer to her and handed her a piece of paper. "I forgot to give this to you."

She looked at it and howled with laughter. She rewarded me by straddling me on the sofa. "You're kidding me, right?"

I put my hands on her thighs. Her warm skin under my fingertips made me very aware that only a few pieces of thin clothing separated our bodies. "I mean, just because you're dating the sheriff doesn't mean you get special privileges."

"But nine thousand, nine-hundred and ninety-nine miles per hour in a thirty-five?"

She smiled harder the more she read the ticket. There was a lightness in my chest that wasn't there before I met Alyssa. I watched her cobalt blue eyes scan the ticket I'd handwritten for her before the date.

"I'm pretty sure you pulled me over in Bayonet, Missouri, not Stranded Hearts, Missouri."

"Since I'm sheriff, I officially changed the name." It was hard to keep a straight face. "Also, technically, I could haul you into jail. That kind of speeding is quite the offense."

Her eyes widened playfully. "Will there be handcuffs?"

I shook my head and frowned at her. "We don't use those that much anymore. Now we use flex-cuffs, like zip ties."

She frowned. "That's too bad." Her frown was followed by a wiggle of her right eyebrow.

"Oh, I still have my standard-issue ones."

"Oh, I like that."

I gave her thighs a playful squeeze. "If you prefer, you can pay the ticket now." I pointed to the bottom of it. "The fee is right there."

"In red ink? I don't think this is valid."

"It's definitely legit."

"A kiss for every mile over? Hmm. The fine seems pretty steep."

I was rewarded with a hot, passionate kiss that left me breathless. "I think it sounds wonderful," I said between kisses. Our bodies were finding a rhythm and it was getting harder to keep my hands to myself. Alyssa's hips were moving against mine in a way that was difficult to ignore. I pulled back and ran my fingers down her arms. Goose bumps popped up on her skin. "Are you sure about this?"

"I know this has been a whirlwind kind of romance, but I'm ready to take our relationship to the next level." She crawled off me and reached for my hand. "Let's go back to my room."

I didn't hesitate. "This is one whirlwind I don't mind getting trapped in with you."

TRAPPED TYCOON

Amanda Radley

CHAPTER ONE

Clara Foster opened her desk drawer and grabbed a handful of pens. They had the company logo on them, but she figured she could scrape it off while updating her résumé and scrolling through job advertisements. Something that she now knew she would be spending the next few days doing.

She threw the pens into her work satchel, grabbed her coat off the back of her chair, and stalked towards the lifts. Her footsteps clumped loudly on the office floor, and she was distantly aware that she sounded like someone having a tantrum. Which was quite an accurate description of how she felt.

It was early on Saturday afternoon, and the office was empty save for one other individual. Which was unusual in Clara's experience. The office was always empty on a Saturday, leaving her to work in peace. But today had been different, disastrously so.

Clara rounded the corner at exactly the same moment that the root of all her problems did exactly the same. If someone had tried to handcraft the very worst luck Clara could ever have, it would have paled in comparison to the day that she had just experienced. And it was only just after lunch.

"Didn't I fire you?" Francesca Burford asked coldly.

"You did. I'm leaving." Clara stabbed the lift call button.

"Taking your sweet time about it, Lara." Francesca sniffed.

She also pressed the call button for the lift, presumably to undermine Clara in some bullshit manner she'd once learnt at a business school. Probably the same one that taught undercutting tactics like getting employees' names wrong. Disappointment that *the* Francesca Burford was like this burned.

"Clara," she said tersely.

"If you say so." Francesca pushed the button again.

"It won't come any quicker because you continue to push the button," Clara said.

Francesca levelled a cold stare at her whilst repeatedly pushing the lift button. After a few seconds, the lift doors opened.

"We'll never know, will we?" Francesca strode into the lift.

Clara felt anger rising within her. It appeared that Francesca Burford was an entitled, opinionated, snobbish, pain in the ass. Which had come as a surprise to Clara, as she'd previously thought she knew everything there was to know about the woman.

Francesca Burford was a legend. Everyone in the investment world knew of her. She was a highly successful financial genius. Everything she touched turned to gold and she was rewarded with wealth, awards, and adoration.

The adoration mainly came from Clara. She'd looked up to Francesca for as long as she could remember. Now she'd finally met the icon, and the reality wasn't at all what she'd expected.

Clara had been working as a trainee at Burford Investments for just over five weeks and was left wondering how Francesca's flawless image had been so cleverly concocted. She never would have guessed that behind the perfect mask of the feminist business powerhouse was such a thoroughly unpleasant person.

Clara felt crushed. Her idol and her dream job had been snatched away from her. Now she was left with no idea what to think and even less idea what to do with her life. Her career path had always been set on the world of investments. Everything had now changed.

Burford Investments was the place to be if you wanted a career in the sector. The trainee scheme was second to none and Clara had moved heaven and earth to get one of the highly coveted positions. Now, just over a month in, she'd been fired. By her boss's boss's boss. Someone who, up until that very Saturday morning, she'd never even spoken with. To think she'd actually harboured a crush on this woman for years. She shivered at the thought.

She stepped into the lift and let out a sigh. As far as she was concerned, she couldn't get out of the building—and Francesca's presence—soon enough. Francesca was standing at the back of the lift, mobile phone in hand and clearly determined to ignore Clara. She noticed that the button for the ground floor hadn't been pushed, despite Francesca's previous love of pressing buttons.

Another power play. She selected the ground floor and watched the doors slide shut. *I'm going to order a curry when I get home. A big one. With every side dish they do.*

Thoughts of chutney, poppadoms, and naan vanished when the lights went out. A moment later, the lift bounced, and Clara was thrown forward into the door. For a split second, it felt as though she was falling, and then suddenly moving in the other direction. She pressed her palms against the cold metal of the lift door and waited for whatever might come next. She felt powerless and terrified. Her heartbeat deafened her. She held her breath and tensed her body, waiting for some kind of hammer to fall. Or worse, to actually fall.

The cart gently bounced. Each time, the movement was less and the gap between the bounces increased. After around a minute, which felt like much longer, an emergency light flickered to life in the ceiling.

Clara turned and looked at Francesca. The older woman looked back at her. The air of cocky indifference had vanished and fear replaced it.

"Which button did you push?" Francesca asked.

"Do you think there's a button to turn off the lift and get me stuck in here with you? And do you really think I'd ever push that kind of button?"

"Well, do something!" Francesca gestured to the control panel with a wave of her hand.

Clara sighed. Clearly, Francesca was a big shot businesswoman but absolutely no help in a crisis. She turned to look at the panel. At the bottom she saw a button with an illustration of a bell above it. She pressed it and a loud alarm sounded. When she let go, it stopped. She pressed it again and the alarm rang again.

Clara started to worry. She thought the alarm was linked to a call centre where she could speak with someone, but it appeared that all the button did was make a lot of noise.

Ordinarily, that might have been helpful. Experience told her that the office building would be largely empty on a Saturday. She knew that the security guard would be in reception; she also knew that he spent his weekends with large over-the-ear headphones on listening to Spotify. Even if he did hear the alarm, she wasn't convinced that he'd know what to do. She'd once seen him shouting at a pigeon who had flown off with a bag of crisps he'd been eating. If he couldn't protect his lunch from a pigeon, then Clara had very little hope that he could rescue her from a complicated piece of machinery.

She let go of the button and turned to Francesca. "Maybe I'm not pushing it right. You're the button expert, would you like a go?"

Francesca rolled her eyes. She held up her phone. "I have no signal, you?"

Clara pulled her phone out of her pocket. She already knew the answer. She never had a signal on her way to or from the office when she was in the lift. She'd lost a timed game of *Words with Friends* as a result once. "Nothing."

Francesca seemed to be moving away from fear and into anger. She approached the panel herself and pressed the alarm button. The bell rang out and Clara winced at the sound reverberating up and down the lift shaft.

"What good is that supposed to do?" Francesca asked.

"Someone is supposed to hear it and report it to facilities," Clara said.

"And why isn't that happening?" Francesca started to repeatedly press the button. The alarm sounded and then stopped over and over again. The echo caused a throbbing behind Clara's temple.

"Presumably because no one is here to hear it," Clara said.

"What about the security guard? Isn't this his job?"

"Could you stop pressing that? It's not doing anything other than giving me a headache."

Francesca lowered her hand and examined the panel. She pushed every button for every floor and even tried the door open and close buttons a few times.

Clara resigned herself to her fate. They would be there for a while. Maybe the lift would magically start again; it had magically stopped, after all. Or maybe the security guard would finally decide to perform his rounds and would realize one of the lifts wasn't working. Maybe the alarm had triggered at a call centre somewhere and someone was on their way.

Whatever the situation might be, right now she was stuck in a two metre by two metre box with her former boss. The woman who had quite unexpectedly fired her. The woman who Clara had spent years looking up to. Sometimes more than just looking up to.

Francesca had shaped Clara's life. If she hadn't seen Francesca being interviewed on television all those years ago, then she wouldn't have discovered her love of investments and the career of her dreams. Nor would she have realized that her romantic interests didn't reside with men. Not that she would ever give Francesca the satisfaction of knowing that. Her anger at Francesca was still fresh, and her desire to clear her name was strong.

"It wasn't me, you know." Clara put her satchel on the ground and laid her coat beside it as a makeshift blanket.

Francesca was back on her phone, holding the device aloft in the hope of getting some kind of signal. "Hmm?"

"I didn't steal your pen." Clara sat down.

"Care to explain why my five-hundred-pound Montblanc was in your possession, having strangely disappeared from my own three days ago?"

"Five hundred pounds?" Clara cried. "For that?"

"What's wrong with it?" Francesca looked down at her. "It's a perfectly good pen."

"It's okay, but it looks a bit bland for that much money. It looks like any other pen."

"It's understated," Francesca said.

"It certainly is."

"You still haven't explained how it came to be on your desk." Francesca pocketed her mobile phone and stared coldly at Clara.

"Someone put it there, but it wasn't me. Why would I steal your pen and then actively use it? Surely if I was going to steal it then I would have hidden it?"

"Maybe it's the thrill?" Francesca said.

"Of using a very understated ballpoint pen? Oh, yes, the thrill. Be still my beating heart." Clara opened her satchel and got her book out.

"What are you doing?" Francesca asked.

"Reading."

"But we're trapped," Francesca said, wildly gesticulating around the lift as if Clara were an idiot.

"Yes, I noticed. I pressed the alarm. I don't have a mobile phone signal. There's not a lot else to do but wait."

Clara opened the book, plucked out her bookmark, and started to read. If she was going to have her job snatched away from her, her career path left in tatters, and the person she looked up to turn out to be a complete and utter bitch, then she was quite happy to check out of the situation and engross herself in some fiction.

And if that annoyed Francesca, all the better.

CHAPTER TWO

Francesca watched in disbelief as the recently fired trainee investor comfortably bedded down on her coat and start to read. Apparently, she wasn't going to help at all with their predicament.

She turned around and slammed her palm over the alarm bell. Surely someone would hear the annoying din and think about investigating? Though presumably not the useless oaf who was often sitting at the reception desk at the weekend. Francesca had once seen him get a belt loop stuck on a door handle for two entire minutes.

If he was their only chance of survival, then they were sure to die.

She rang out a little tune, if only to irritate her company. Her pen was not bland. It was understated. And Clara had most definitely stolen it. Francesca hadn't quite believed her eyes when she'd walked across the office floor and not only saw someone else working at the weekend but also her missing pen in that person's hand. More accurately, in her mouth.

Clara's youthful lips had sucked on the end of the pen while she focused her attention on her laptop screen. At first, Francesca had felt a flash of attraction. The young trainee was a sight to behold with her legs gathered beneath her on an office chair and her forehead furrowed in concentration. But then Francesca spotted her missing pen and she'd seen red. She'd demanded to know who the young woman was and then told her that she was fired for theft.

Francesca didn't know any of the trainees who came through the educational program. She simply didn't have time to meet and greet every one of them. Now and then she'd turn up at their graduation ceremony and shake a few hands, but they were nothing more than a blur of faces. So, the attractive young thief reading her book on the floor behind her was an utter mystery to Francesca. And now she was stuck with her.

Francesca stopped pressing the button. The noise was starting to irritate her, and the futility of the act was beginning to dawn on her. They were trapped. It was Saturday and the building was empty except for quite possibly the worst security guard in history who had probably managed to lock himself in a toilet cubicle or something equally ridiculous by now.

The other companies in the building rarely worked on weekends. The likelihood of someone noticing one of the lifts not working was extremely slim. Which meant their chance of rescue relied on someone noticing that they were missing.

It occurred to her that no one would miss her. There was no family at home waiting for her to return. Not even a pet who would howl when dinner wasn't forthcoming. She no longer had plans for the weekend, so the only possible chance that someone would wonder where she was would come on Monday morning when she didn't turn up in the office.

She tossed her bag into the opposite corner to where Clara sat. It was a sobering thought. Now that things were over with Diana there was no one to wonder where she was. No one to notice if she didn't come home that night. Not that they had lived together. They slept over at each other's homes but had never even spoken of moving in together.

The breakup the previous evening had been a surprising disappointment. The realisation that she was completely alone again hit her harder than she thought it would. She wasn't a stranger to being alone, in fact she had always quite liked it. But as she grew older, she found she enjoyed the solitude less and less. The idea of someone expecting her home was becoming more appealing. And not just because it might help her current situation.

She kicked off her heels.

"Is anyone expecting you home?" she asked Clara.

"No." Clara placed a finger on the page of her book. "I live alone. You?"

Francesca looked at Clara's youthful features and guessed that she was around twenty-five. It was perfectly acceptable to live alone at twenty-five. In fact, at such a young age you were considered independent and successful to be living alone. Out of your parents' house, not having to share with friends. It was a badge of honour to have achieved that level of maturity.

It was different when you were fifty-three. Then people wondered why you lived alone. Was it a choice or could nobody stand to live with you? In Francesca's case it was the former, but many assumed it to be the latter.

Francesca didn't reply. She removed her Ralph Lauren trench coat and sucked in a calming breath before she placed the coat on the floor and ruined it. Sitting on the floor wasn't something she was used to, but on the rare occasion it happened, there was at least carpet. The lift had a marble floor which had been walked on by countless thousands of people and she dreaded to think what had been deposited from people's shoes and would now be indelibly imprinted into her coat.

"Is anyone expecting you?" Clara pressed.

"No." Francesca sat down with her back against the wall and adjusted her pencil dress, cursing her wardrobe decisions that morning. Most office wear was uncomfortable, but the tight dresses were the worst. Then again, she'd never predicted this turn of events. If she had, she would have never come into the office that day.

"Okay." Clara returned her attention to her book.

"Okay?" Francesca asked. "Is that all you have to say?"

Clara sighed. She placed her finger back on the page to mark her place and looked up at Francesca. "What else would you like me to say? No one is expecting me. No one is expecting you. We could be here for a while. Is there something you'd like me to say?"

Francesca didn't have an answer to that. She'd expected a snide comment about no one expecting her and when she hadn't received one, she'd acted with anger as if she had. She knew that said a lot about her and none of it was good.

"No. Nothing else. Please, go back to your book. It's not like there's anything pressing going on."

It was meant to be sarcastic, but Clara went back to her book anyway.

Francesca shook her head. She couldn't believe that Clara was going to calmly sit and read rather than attempt to brainstorm a solution to their shared problem. They may have had their differences, but they were in the same boat. Lift. Whatever.

"Are you seriously going to just sit there and read?" Francesca asked.

Clara snatched up her bookmark and shoved it into the open pages and slammed it shut. She put the book back in her bag and looked expectantly at Francesca.

"Well, clearly not. What would you like me to do?"

"We need to think about a way to get out of here," Francesca said.

Clara looked around the small space. "There is no way out. We're suspended in a box that we can't open. We have to wait for someone to rescue us."

"Is that really all you can come up with?"

"Do you have anything better?"

Francesca opened her mouth but quickly closed it again when she realized that she had nothing much to say. She wasn't used to sitting around and waiting to be rescued. She looked at the doors. "Do you think we can open them?"

"Nope."

She looked at Clara. "Is that all you have? Nope?"

Clara sighed. "No, I do not think we can open those doors. Is that better for you?"

"Marginally." Francesca stood and approached the doors. She tried to wedge her fingers into the tiny gap, but the slippery metal prevented her from getting a grip. After a few attempts she gave up and thumped the door with her palms in frustration.

"You're quite an angry person, aren't you?" Clara said in a maddeningly calm tone.

Francesca spun around. "Who wouldn't be?"

Clara held up her hand. "Me. Many people. Anger isn't the default."

A desire to argue bubbled up and then vanished just as quickly. She didn't want to prove Clara's point. She sat back down, again cursing her wardrobe decisions that morning. Why hadn't she chosen trousers? Pencil dresses were not made for sitting in general, and certainly not sitting on the floor.

Maybe that's why I'm angry. Being shoved into a fabric tube with little room to move wouldn't make anyone feel calm and relaxed under pressure. But she only had herself to blame.

She glanced at Clara, who was now looking through her bag for something. She wore smart black trousers and a casual sweater with a large C on the front. It was the weekend, so Francesca didn't expect her staff to be wearing work attire. In fact, she hadn't been expecting any of her staff to come in at all.

She personally hadn't worked a weekend in years. One of the many joys of trading was that the markets closed for business at the weekend. Quite simply, there was nothing much for her to do at the weekends. There was a time when she managed her email account, did some filing, arranged meetings, and performed general office administration. But she had a team of assistants for that kind of thing these days.

"Why were you in the office today?" Francesca asked.

"I wanted to steal your pen, obviously," Clara said without looking up.

Francesca huffed. The young woman was impossible.

"Why were you in the office today?" Clara looked up from searching for something in her bag. "You're never usually here."

That statement interested Francesca a great deal. It suggested that Clara frequently worked weekends, and that only served to increase the mystery surrounding her. What would a trainee be doing in an empty office when their mentors were not working?

Francesca had a choice. She could maintain her wall of silence towards the thief, or she could be civil and figure a little bit more out about the woman she was now caged with.

"I left my laptop here on Friday night. I thought I'd be coming back here after a meeting, but time ran away from me. I decided to catch up on some email. You?"

"I come in nearly every Saturday."

When nothing more was forthcoming Francesca asked, "Why?"

Clara sucked in a deep breath and scrunched up her face a little. It seemed that she was on the brink of maybe confessing to something. Francesca sat still and waited.

"I catch up with things at the weekend. When it's quiet. Things happen so quickly during the week." Clara returned to her bag search and retrieved a small tube of hand cream. She applied a little to her hands and the fresh scent of mango and lime filled Francesca's nostrils.

Francesca felt that there was something more to it. Something Clara seemed reluctant to say. In general, there seemed to be something else to Clara. Francesca could sense it and it nagged at her curiosity.

Clara was correct that things happened quickly during trading hours. The office was a loud hub of sound and energy. From the moment the UK market opened at eight in the morning, all the way to the last trading bells in the evening, the trading floor was full of people rushing around and the endless news cycles pouring from multiple televisions.

Burford Investments didn't trade the worldwide markets. Francesca had made the decision early on to focus on Europe and the United States. There was a possibility of spreading yourself too thin if you tried to master every market. Which meant that weekends brought silence. The televisions were off, the markets were closed, and no one bothered to come in.

Except, it seemed, for Clara.

"What do you mean? How do you catch up?" Francesca asked.

Clara mindlessly adjusted her watch strap, probably just so she didn't have to make eye contact.

"I look at trades that have happened during the week. You know, analyse the market and try to figure out what other people saw before me. Sometimes our mentors will be in the middle of teaching when something happens, and they have to go and look after their portfolio. I want to know what they saw on the data; how did they predict direction?"

"Experience," Francesca said.

"Is it? People talk of people having a knack for something. Some kind of golden touch. Or learning it by seeing patterns in the data. But the data looks random to me sometimes. Especially lately. And the others don't seem to have any problem. Just me."

Clara looked up and Francesca saw something she recognised from her early trading days: doubt. Trading was fickle. One day you were flying high and the next you'd lost everything you'd gained and then some. The feeling of frustration became more acute when you were working with someone who seemed to have an endless run of good trades.

"Some people do appear to have a knack for it, but I personally believe it comes from a mix of experience, industry knowledge, and luck."

"How do you know if you have luck?" Clara asked.

"Everyone has a degree of luck. But there's a reason I put luck at the end of that list. Experience is the most important thing you can have in your toolkit as a trader. Then comes industry knowledge. Last comes luck."

Clara shrugged. "No matter. That was the reason I came in at weekends."

Francesca could feel Clara's frustration despite her attempt to hide it. She felt it keenly, remembering her own start in investing and almost giving up several times. There were times when Francesca felt certain that she'd embarked on the wrong career path. She'd spent many evenings lying in bed and staring at the ceiling of her run-down apartment and wishing she could turn back time and exit a trade sooner, or never place the order in the first place. Sometimes she wondered what skills she had that she could apply to a different career track.

In the end she had knuckled down and learnt to take the lows with the highs, knowing that she was getting better. Eventually the crushing losses became fewer and further between. They never went away. Even today, at the top of her game, she still placed terrible trades that she regretted.

"It's a tough career choice," Francesca said. "You have to be good at selective forgetfulness."

"What do you mean?" Clara asked.

"The ability to forget the result of the mistake while retaining the knowledge of why it was a mistake. If you missed an exit point on a trade, you can't look at the monetary loss, you have to look at what signal you missed. Otherwise, you'll always be chasing a way to undo the mistakes of the past. And it's rare that you ever get a real opportunity to do that."

"Well, if I ever manage to get back into the industry that you fired me from, I'll be sure to practice that." Clara adjusted her cross-legged position and lowered her head.

Francesca rolled her eyes and leaned her head back against the wall. It seemed their brief ceasefire was at an end.

While Francesca would rather pass the time with some conversation, Clara was apparently happy to sit in silence. Any authority she had was long gone and instead she was on the receiving end of Clara's hostility.

She cursed herself for her earlier overreaction. Stealing a pen was certainly a sackable offence, but she'd not exactly given Clara any opportunity to explain herself. Her reaction had come from stress and exhaustion, never a good place to make rational decisions.

Now she was very much having to live with the results of that choice.

CHAPTER THREE

Clara felt restless. It had been forty minutes since the lift had shuddered to a stop. Thirty minutes since Francesca had last spoken. The silence was her own fault. Her sarcastic reply to Francesca's attempt at a dialogue had slammed the door closed on any topic of conversation. Now they were left painfully aware of each other's company and yet also pretending they could ignore it.

She itched to get her book out but knew she'd not be able to focus on the words. It was a good book and she wanted to enjoy it, not simply use it to pass some time while stuck in a lift. The book deserved more than that.

But while the text deserved better, she didn't feel that Francesca deserved much at all.

Francesca sat with her knees up to her chest and her forehead on her knees. She hadn't moved in some time. Clara wondered if perhaps she'd fallen asleep, which would be a blessing.

Never meet your heroes.

Francesca Burford had been an unlikely idol of Clara's for many years. While other teenagers listened to their favourite bands and coveted tickets to live performances, Clara sought out interviews with the financial genius and had completely memorised her TED talks.

Over time, she'd realized that the fascination was more than just an interest in the financial sector. While she'd denied it to any who suggested it, she'd had a crush on Francesca for years. Francesca had been the one who had opened Clara's teenage mind to the realisation that she romantically preferred women over men. That epiphany had soon led to a far deeper understanding of herself. Clara knew what she was looking for in a partner. She wanted someone older, intellectual, successful, and someone who would challenge her and support her in her goals.

Someone like Francesca.

While she had nursed a crush on Francesca for years, it had faded when she started to date women. If she'd met Francesca seven years ago, Clara would have no doubt embarrassed herself beyond belief. Thankfully, her interest in Francesca had waned to an appreciation as she'd left education and started work. She was older and wiser these days. So much so that she'd applied to join the Burford Investments trainee scheme for the scheme and not for the proximity to the woman she had looked up to for so long.

She'd understood from the start that being a trainee was the bottom rung of a very, very long ladder. There was little chance she'd ever see the impressive owner of the company while in the training scheme. She'd snagged the occasional glimpse of Francesca from across the office but nothing more. Interestingly, she'd found that she liked it that way. It enabled her to study hard and throw herself into the trainee role and soak up as much knowledge as she could.

Being interested in investments and trading with her small savings account was very different from professional trading and Clara had learnt that harsh lesson very quickly. At home in the comfort of her own bedroom, she could spend hours looking at Japanese candlestick patterns for well-known stocks and simply choose to not trade that day if she felt in any way uncertain of a trend. At the office she had seconds to make decisions with potentially very large amounts of money. Other people's money.

Thankfully, her trades were closely monitored by her mentors and she'd yet to be allowed to do anything too foolish. But there had been plenty of times when she'd been willing to risk everything on what she was sure was a great trade, just to be left watching in shock and confusion as markets slipped away. Checks and balances were the only thing stopping her from wiping out her trading account, something she had never thought was possible.

She'd been telling everyone for years that she would be the next big shot female trader, the next Francesca Burford. But five short weeks into her supposed dream job had highlighted that she wasn't as good as she thought. She didn't have the golden touch. Her instincts seemed all wrong. While her fellow trainees seemed to get better with every passing week, Clara was struggling to stay even level.

And now, on top of all of that, even Francesca Burford wasn't at all what she'd been expecting.

Clara had longed for the day when she'd be able to meet Francesca in person. She'd practiced a few lines, something casual and endearingly witty. At night she fantasised about being one of those traders who could do no wrong and possibly caught Francesca's eye in more ways than one.

Thoughts of Burford and Foster Investments being one of the top investment companies in Europe mingled with the knowledge that Francesca was single and had dated both men and women in the past. It was ridiculous to think that Francesca would even look at Clara twice, but that was what dreams were for.

Of course all of that was now in tatters as she had managed to catch Francesca's eye simply to be fired. And she'd discovered that Francesca was actually quite an unpleasant person. She felt that disappointment far more keenly than the fact she was now unemployed.

"I think we should pool our resources," Francesca said unexpectedly. She sat up and pulled her bag closer. "Food. Water. That kind of thing. We're clearly not getting out of here any time soon. We should prepare to be here until Monday morning. At least the early shift will be here at six in the morning, that's one small blessing."

Clara shivered at the thought of being stuck for so many hours.

Francesca opened her bag. "I have half a bottle of water. Some sweets I keep on hand for my niece. And I'm afraid that's it." She placed the bottle of water and colourful plastic bag of gummy sweets on her coat next to her bag.

Clara opened her bag and started to empty the contents.

"You've got to be kidding me," Francesca said.

Clara realized she'd just scooped out the massive handful of pens that she'd grabbed in a moment of anger before she'd left her desk for the final time.

"You are a pen thief. Is it an obsession? Are you seeking treatment, because you should be."

"I was angry." Clara continued to empty her bag.

"So you stole more pens. Because you were caught stealing just the one?"

Clara threw her book down onto the floor in anger. "I didn't steal your damn pen. It was on my desk, or on Meg's desk. It was a pen. An average looking, crappy pen. I'm sorry you paid hundreds of pounds for it because it really doesn't look like you did. Maybe if you'd gotten a nicer pen then people would have returned it to you rather than assuming it was a shitty ballpoint pen and allowing it to float around the office."

"You're quite an angry person, aren't you?" Francesca said, a slight smirk curling at her lip.

Clara narrowed her eyes. "Don't even."

"Anger isn't the default, you know."

"You're really dislikeable, did anyone ever tell you that?"

Francesca chuckled. "Please. You don't even know me. Don't make assumptions about me."

"Oh, I know you," Clara said.

Francesca looked at her with obvious disbelief. The smirk was maddening.

"You're fifty-three, but you've recently started changing your Wikipedia page to say you're forty-eight. Which you don't need to do, by the way," Clara said. "You started with Bercow's when you left university. Which was Cambridge, where you graduated with a degree in mathematics, one of only seven women in your year to get the full master's. At Bercow's you felt you were being underutilized and being forced into a secretarial role. You sued them and with the money they paid you from an out-of-court settlement you set up your own firm. You love dogs. You're allergic to shellfish. You speak three languages and five years ago indicated that you were going to try to learn Japanese, but you never mentioned it again so either you didn't have time, or you found it too tricky. You've got so many awards that if I started to list them, I'd probably suck all the oxygen out of the lift. And you're really mean. That last one is a recent discovery."

Francesca stared in shock.

Clara broke eye contact the moment she realized that she'd said too much. She didn't need Francesca knowing that she used to idolize her. She pulled her stainless-steel water bottle out of her bag.

"I also have water. And I have a chocolate bar which has probably melted a couple of times but it's food. And I have some cough sweets. I don't know if that's technically food but it's something."

"Did you read my bio on the company website?" Francesca asked. Clara pinched the bridge of her nose. She wished she'd never said anything. "Do you think your bio on your own company website is telling everyone that you're aging backwards on Wikipedia these days? Anyway, as I said, I have some water. Do you want to figure out a plan to distribute what we have? How long do you realistically think we might be in here?"

Francesca held up her hand. "Wait, wait. How do you know all of that about me?"

There was more than a touch of concern in her expression, not quite panic but certainly on the way towards it. Clara felt her cheeks heating up in embarrassment. She wished she had stayed quiet. The awkward silence was better.

"I just do. Anyway, we don't really have much food but we're not going to die between now and Monday morning." Clara tried a last-ditch effort to derail Francesca's line of questioning.

"Are you a stalker?"

Clara blinked. "What? No. No, of course not. I just know of you, okay? You're the most successful woman in finance, of course people know about you."

"But you seem to have some very specific knowledge." Francesca regarded her with suspicion.

Clara rolled her eyes. "Yeah, I'm a stalker. I took a job here and worked my butt off for five weeks, unpaid weekends included, so I could ultimately steal your shitty pen. You got me. Congratulations."

Clara turned around and faced the wall. She snatched her book up from the floor and pretended to start to read. Anything to avoid the look on Francesca's face. The unprepared biography was sadly only around one percent of what she knew about Francesca. She wished she could be anywhere else as she felt herself practically vibrate with embarrassment.

Being stuck in a lift with someone was one thing. Being stuck with someone who you'd admired for years and could probably write a biography on was another. Especially when that person wasn't quite what you'd expected.

"Clara, please talk to me," Francesca said, her tone surprisingly soft.

"I'd rather not," Clara said.

"Clara, one of the things you missed off your list is the stalker who tormented me for three years. So, I ask you again, how you know so much about me?"

Panic spiked in Clara. She hadn't known about a stalker. She certainly wasn't one but could see how Francesca's mind would go there. Now she had to wonder, how did she calmly explain that she'd followed Francesca's career for years but wasn't a danger to her?

CHAPTER FOUR

Francesca looked at Clara's back and tried to figure out what was going on. A shadow of fear was starting to niggle up her spine.

Francesca was used to being known. She was used to people staring at her on the train while they tried to place just where they'd seen her face before. The investment sector certainly wasn't glamourous, but being successful was. Being a woman in business meant extensive media exposure, and Francesca wasn't about to turn that down because it meant more clients and more growth for her company.

She'd been featured in newspapers and magazines for years, been invited to all kinds of events, and was frequently asked on national news shows as a commentator on financial matters.

She wasn't a celebrity by any means, but she was recognised by some people and she'd become almost comfortable with that fact. Right up until Daniel Miller came along.

At first it had seemed like a simple coincidence that he happened to be everywhere she was. Train stations, events, and even restaurants. One day she'd noticed him near her home and that had set alarm bells ringing in her mind.

What followed was the most stressful time of her life and something she had never spoken with anyone about.

Clara didn't appear to be a stalker. She didn't think a stalker would blush and turn away from the attention of their fixation. She looked at the stack of cheap company biros lying on the ground. Maybe not a stalker but still potentially unhinged.

Clara looked over her shoulder. Her face was ashen. "I'm sorry. I didn't know that."

"Not many people do," Francesca said.

Clara shuffled back around to face Francesca. She held up a calming hand. "I'm not a stalker. But I am a fan."

Francesca stiffened. "What do you mean by that?"

"I mean I admire your work and have for a long time. I've known of you for years; I've wanted to be in investments since I understood what the stock market was. I wanted to work here. Wanted to meet you, one day." Clara bit her lip. "Although, I've met you now and you're not all that."

The joke cleared the air and Francesca felt herself relax a little. "Am I not?"

"No." Clara grinned a little. "Bit of a cow, really."

"Sorry to disappoint you." Francesca couldn't help but smile in return.

"It's okay. You should never meet your heroes, right?"

Francesca couldn't help but raise an eyebrow at the admission, one which had clearly slipped past Clara's defences if the wide eyes were to be believed.

"Hero?" Francesca drawled. "Do tell me more."

Clara dropped her head into her hands. "Oh God."

"Call me Francesca."

Clara whined loudly.

Francesca chuckled. It felt good to break the stress of the confinement with some real and heartfelt laughter. Even if it was partially at Clara's expense. She hadn't expected Clara to be a fan, certainly not to think of her as some kind of hero. It felt somewhat surreal to think of herself in that way.

"Why would someone like me be a hero to you? Shouldn't you be worshipping at the feet of some reality television star?"

Clara looked up. She shuddered. "No. Yuck."

Francesca laughed again. "Some pop group?"

"Nope. I was never a normal kid. Didn't like any of the things my parents thought I would like. Didn't like dolls, didn't want a puppy, never wanted to ride a horse. As I got older, I wasn't interested in all the things my friends were. When I was twelve, I saw you being interviewed on the news, and I asked my dad who you were, and he didn't know. He read the ticker tape and said you were some tycoon.

A few months later, I saw you again. Dad was useless so that time I googled you."

Francesca chuckled at the thought of being referred to as a tycoon. That felt so Mr. Monopoly to her.

"And what did you discover when you consulted the Wild West of the internet?"

Clara splayed her fingers on each side of her head in the mime of an explosion. "It blew my mind. I found out that there was a thing called the market and it affected everything we do. And we affected it, too. Anyone could buy some shares, or some gold, or even some Japanese yen. I didn't know any of that before."

"And you were, what did you say, twelve?"

Clara nodded.

Francesca leaned her head back against the lift wall. "I'm so old."

"Is that why you changed your Wikipedia page?"

"I don't know who did that," Francesca said. She'd done it. In a moment of madness one evening, halfway through a bottle of wine. It had seemed like a good idea at the time. Being on her way to her mid-fifties had seemed thoroughly unappealing. She'd toyed with the idea of shaving a few more years off, but a look in the mirror had convinced her to keep things plausible.

"Well, you're not old," Clara said.

"Says the...how old are you?

"Twenty-six."

"Says the twenty-six-year-old." Francesca sat up straight and looked at Clara. She performed a quick calculation. "You were twelve, so that means that I was almost forty. I'd won the Women Leaders Award recently. That had led to a flurry of media interest. I was probably in my prime. Downhill after that."

Clara rolled her eyes. "That's ridiculous."

"Excuse me, I think I know when my own prime was."

"Three years ago, you turned down a position at the Treasury. Last year marked the milestone that you had given away more money to charity than the GDP of Micronesia."

"Well, Micronesia is a very small—"

"You were given a CBE by Prince William two years ago."

Francesca held up her hand. "Yes, yes. I know. I mean..." She trailed off. Suddenly, she felt very self-conscious and unsure of herself. "I meant…"

Clara frowned. "You mean?"

"Prime in another way."

"What do you mean?" Clara asked.

"I mean in myself. Body wise. I was in my prime back then. Everything went downhill after then."

"You might think so, but many would disagree." Clara's cheeks reddened. She coughed and looked away. "I'm sorry you had a stalker, by the way. That must have been scary."

Francesca itched to return to the subject before but recognised that she had to be careful with Clara. They'd only just started really talking and she had no interest in returning to the lonely silence of earlier. But she really wanted to know what Clara meant. Who would disagree? Was Clara one of them?

Knowing that Clara admired her and had even followed her career over the years was unexpected and pleasing to hear. Suspecting that Clara thought she still looked good despite her age was certainly a confidence boost. One she needed after the breakup with Diana the previous evening. She was back to being single. Old and single. Prior to Diana it had been nearly three years without a proper relationship. She had dates, but they were usually no more than a plus-one for an event.

She'd given up on the idea of a meaningful relationship, assuming that one couldn't have it all. She'd trade her wealth for someone who understood her, for someone who would miss her when she was stuck in a lift at work.

"I'm sorry, I shouldn't have brought the stalker up," Clara said at the prolonged silence.

Francesca waved away the concern. "It's fine. My mind wandered. Yes, it was pretty awful."

"Was it a man?"

Francesca nodded.

"Did they catch him?" Clara slapped her hand over her mouth. "I'm sorry. You don't need to answer that. I'm really nosey, can't control it sometimes. Sorry."

"It's okay. He was caught and charged. It's all over but that kind of thing never really goes away." Francesca straightened her legs out in front of her. "I'm lucky, he never got that close. He was just always there. Lurking around a corner. I've spoken with other victims who went through so much worse than I did."

"Doesn't make it less traumatic for you," Clara said. "Sometimes the fear of what might happen is worse than what happened."

"It left a mark," she said.

Francesca picked up her phone. There was still no signal, not that she expected anything else. But the creeping sensation of claustrophobia was starting to curl around her. She'd never suffered from such feelings before, but Daniel's actions had sometimes caused Francesca to feel trapped even in wide-open spaces. Now, just thinking of him and that time sometimes led to a shadow feeling of being stuck. And now she actually was stuck.

Clara seemed to realize that something was up. She stood up and went over to the control panel.

"I'm going to ring the bell again, just in case anyone is in the building. You never know."

Francesca nodded. Clara turned her back to her and started to tap out a little tune with the alarm button. Francesca took the chance to control her breathing and roll the stress out of her neck and shoulders.

You're safe. It's just a lift. You'll be out in a while. And she's not a threat. You're safe.

"Can you guess what it is?" Clara asked.

"Sorry?" Francesca shouted over the alarm bell.

"Can you guess the tune?" Clara asked. "I'll start again."

She couldn't help but smile at the little game Clara had inserted into an otherwise awful predicament. Presumably only to make her feel better, which was something she absolutely didn't deserve after sacking Clara just a couple of hours ago. She closed her eyes and listened to the bells ringing out.

"Is that the theme to *EastEnders*?"

"It is!" Clara released the button and the alarm bell mercifully stopped. "I'm quite proud of that. It's not an easy song."

"You clearly have impressive musicality." Francesca bit her lip, hoping that Clara would pick up on the sarcasm and hit back rather than thinking she was being rude.

"Actually, I do. You may jest, but it's not easy to be musical with an emergency alarm. You're lucky to get the chance to witness my talents."

"It's not that difficult," Francesca said, grateful that Clara was playing along.

Clara put her hands on her hips. "Fine, you try to play something recognisable on an alarm bell that echoes up and down the lift shaft. I'll wait."

Francesca got to her feet and gestured for Clara to stand back from the panel. She considered her choices for a few moments. She pressed the button three times in quick succession before pausing and doing it again.

"'Jingle Bells,'" Clara said.

"See? It's easy," Francesca said.

"Only because you picked one of the most recognisable songs in the world."

"Unlike your masterpiece?"

"Exactly."

Francesca smiled to herself. Clara wasn't at all what she expected. She was playful and yet mindful and astute. She wasn't afraid to tell Francesca exactly what she thought, and yet she knew when to stop. There could have been far worse people to be trapped with.

"If you could be trapped in a lift with anyone, who would you choose?" Francesca asked.

Clara sat and scrunched up her face, deep in thought. "That's a tricky one."

Francesca stretched her arms above her head and enjoyed the feeling of her spine softly popping with the release of tension.

"Is this one of those dead or alive things, or do I have to pick someone living?" Clara asked.

"Alive," Francesca said. "Although I'm curious about who you'd pick otherwise."

"Carrie Fisher," Clara said immediately.

"Big Star Wars fan?" Francesca asked.

"Not particularly, I just think Carrie was fascinating. She said whatever she wanted to say, had so many good points to make. I think she was ahead of her time with many things. If I'm spending a lot of time with someone then I want them to be funny and interesting. I think Carrie is both. What about you?"

"Who would I pick to be stuck in a lift with or am I a big Star Wars fan?"

"Both."

"I've watched all the films, but I wouldn't say I'm a big fan. As for this unfortunate scenario, if I could pick someone who has passed away, then I'd choose Benjamin Graham. Do you know who he is?"

Clara nodded. "The father of value investing."

Francesca appreciated that Clara knew of Graham. Not everyone in the industry had taken the time to research those who had come before. A big mistake in Francesca's mind.

"That's him. I think he'd have a lot to say about the way the markets work today. A lot of insight to cut through all the noise. His strength was simplicity. Seeing things in an extremely calm manner, despite the volatility of the marketplace."

"Who would you pick if you had to choose someone living?" Clara asked.

"I'm not sure. I'll have to think on it. You?"

Clara hesitated for a moment. "I don't know."

"You do, I can tell." Francesca pinned her with a look, interested to know who Clara would pick and why she felt the need to bury the information.

Clara lowered her head. "Before today, I would have picked you."

The breath left Francesca's lungs. She hated that Clara thought so poorly of her now, especially as it was absolutely justified. She folded her arms loosely across her chest and wondered how to fix the situation.

"I didn't steal your pen," Clara said.

Francesca lowered her head and let out a sign. She wasn't often prone to overreaction, but whenever she did, she had the luxury of being able to walk away. She was the boss. Whatever she said was gospel. She didn't ever need to explain herself; she didn't have to backtrack.

Francesca knew she wasn't perfect and knew for certain that she'd massively overreacted. And now, for the first time in a very long time, she was forced to deal with the consequences of that. It was a strange feeling, but for some reason it was not entirely unpleasant. It was probably one of the more real interactions she'd had for a while.

"I know. And I overreacted."

"Yes, you did," Clara said in the way one would speak with a naughty child who had confessed to something. "And you're…?"

Francesca tried not to smile. "I'm very sorry."

"Not the best apology I've received but I suspect you're out of practice."

"Ouch!" Francesca laughed. "True, but nonetheless. Obviously, you're not fired."

Clara chuckled. "Oh, you're going to have to do better than that."

Francesca blinked. "Sorry?"

Clara folded her arms. "Convince me to come back."

Francesca bit her lip to keep from laughing. "Convince you to come back?"

"Yes. Why should I come back to work for someone with anger management issues?"

There was a glint in Clara's eye, but Francesca couldn't read if she was joking or being serious. It didn't matter. Clara was right, she deserved better than being fired on a whim and then being offered her job back only when Francesca was forced to admit that she was in the wrong.

"Well, I promise to not fire you again," Francesca said. "Unless you really do something terrible."

"And who dictates that?" Clara asked.

"Well, someone other than me, I suppose." Francesca sat back down on her coat.

Clara looked at her expectantly. After a few moments she asked, "Is that it? Come back as I promise I won't fire you unless you do something wrong? That's not encouraging me to come back."

Francesca laughed. "Okay. Well, come back because we have one of the best trainee mentoring programs in the country?"

Clara lifted a shoulder. "It's okay. I mean, it's not quite as good as Brown's."

"Matthew Brown?" Francesca asked, her voice raising in shock. "That charlatan? Are you honestly even comparing the two programs? He—he hasn't got a clue! Lucky. That's him, in a nutshell. It will all blow up in his face one day."

"They have chocolate biscuits in the staff room."

"How do you know that?" Francesca asked. Had Clara been investigating making a move to Brown's? And why did it matter to Francesca anyway? If Clara wanted to leave the best investing training scheme, then that was her mistake to make.

"I hear things."

Clara's expression held a wisp of a grin and Francesca realized that she'd been played. She narrowed her eyes and shook her head.

"You enjoy teasing me, don't you?"

"Yep," Clara said. "But it wouldn't hurt to have a few chocolate biscuits in the staff room though, to be fair."

"Do you think you've earned chocolate biscuits?"

Clara laughed. "No. No, not me. I'm actually rethinking my career. But others might appreciate them. It's a sign of quality, a chocolate biscuit."

"Why?"

"Because plain biscuits are bor—"

"No, why are you rethinking your career? Because of me?"

"No. Because it isn't what I expected. I don't think I'm cut out for it." Clara unscrewed her water bottle and took a tiny sip. She held it towards Francesca.

She shook her head. "No, thank you. Why do you think you're not cut out for it?"

"It's just not me."

Francesca looked at the woman in front of her. She looked despondent and worn down. She remembered the feeling. Before she'd made her name, she'd made plenty of mistakes.

"I can't imagine that someone who was first interested in the sector at the age of twelve has suddenly decided that it's not for them." Francesca grabbed the bag of gummy sweets and opened the bag. She popped a red sweet into her mouth and held the bag out to Clara.

Clara peered into the open packet and reached for a green sweet.

"Is it because you discovered that you weren't instantly brilliant at it?" Francesca asked. "Because that almost never happens."

"More that I found out I'm pretty terrible at it," Clara said.

"We all are, at the start."

"I'm not at the start. I've been doing this for years. I've had an online account since I nagged my mum to set one up when I was fourteen. I told her I didn't want pocket money, I wanted money in a trading account. She reluctantly agreed and I started trading then, never quite having enough money to buy the lots I wanted." Clara chuckled to herself. "I remember the day when I'd finally accumulated enough to put money on an index, it was a minimum of two hundred dollars for an index trade. It was better than Christmas." Clara sat up a little higher as she told her story. "And it was the day that there was a big announcement at the US Treasury, and I'd read all of the papers and online analysis and I was sure it was going to go my way. But I hesitated and I wasn't sure, it had taken me months to build up that money and I could lose it, or a lot of it, in one trade. I went for a walk after lunch—it was the school holidays—and went through all of the facts again. Convinced myself that I was right. I got home, waited for the right entry point, and placed that first index trade. Boom. It skyrocketed. My two hundred dollars, with leverage, became two hundred and seventy-two dollars in the space of nine minutes."

Francesca watched as Clara became carried away with the memories. Every trader she knew could identify a moment when they went from having a passing interest in the market to utter fascination. There was the thrill of doing your research and not only being right but being rewarded for it.

"I remember so clearly placing my first thousand-dollar trade," Clara continued. "I watched it like a hawk, the spread wasn't the best, so it was a double gamble. It nudged upwards and I closed the trade with about a four-dollar profit."

Francesca laughed. "What was the trade?"

"Gold." Clara winced.

"Oh, you like gambling with commodities? You're a brave woman!"

"You started with commodities," Clara said.

"I did. I liked the action. But I lost a lot. I remember starting out and getting to the end of the year and looking back and I'd lost ten dollars over the course of the twelve months of hard work. I'd had huge wins but the same in losses. After that, I looked at currencies, and after that I stayed with stock and played the long game."

"I think my problem is that it was just me. I've never been around other investment people, just me in my bedroom at home. And then later me in my apartment. I think I built myself up to thinking I'm pretty good at it. But coming here made me realize that I'm not." Clara shuffled backwards and leaned against the wall. "I'm totally the bottom of the class. Everyone else has more experience than me. And more luck. Honestly, you should have seen Adam. He took an e-scooter to work one morning when the bus was full, then he researched a couple of companies and bought some shares in the dummy trading account.

The next day—I repeat, the next day—the company announces a major deal with train stations in nine countries."

"As you say, that was luck," Francesca said. "He took a gamble and it paid off. But it won't be long before regulators around the world start to crack down on illegal e-scooter practices. The fact that you need a driver's licence here in the UK to ride one, for example. Teenagers can press a button on the app and say they have one and then they are riding a motorised vehicle on the road. It's as volatile as commodities. He's been lucky now, but he'll suffer a loss soon if he makes his decisions like that."

"It's not just that. I'm behind the others. My trades are all over the place. Even the ones I'm really sure about. I'm not made for this."

"Are you passionate about it?" Francesca asked.

"I was."

"Do you want to succeed?"

"Yes, but—"

"Are you willing to learn? To take the hard knocks along the way?"

"Yes, but I—"

"Can you pick yourself up after you've made a mistake? Can you learn selective forgetfulness?"

"I can try."

"Then I want you to stay. Clara, we need people with a passion for this sector. Not people who enjoy the thrill, or people who treat it like gambling. If you've been trading since you were a teenager then you've wiped out your account, probably more than once, and had to start again. Am I right?"

Clara nodded. She held up three fingers and looked ashamed.

"We've all done it," Francesca said. "But the difference is doing it then when it's you alone in your bedroom and trading with your own money and learning that lesson there and then. Not doing it at work when you're cocky and playing with someone else's money. I know it's hard. Trust me. I have spent a lot of time wondering if I'm in the right career over the years. Even when I'd made my first million, I thought I was a bad fit for investing. It came naturally to others and seemed so hard for me. But I'm glad now for every mistake I made because they each taught me a lesson. And sometimes I needed to learn that lesson more than once. That's what this sector is about."

Clara gazed at her. Francesca didn't know why she was staring so intently. The cold harsh look of earlier had vanished. After she'd fired Clara, Francesca felt her stare could burn right through her. Now the look had softened. In fact, it was downright warm and bordering on appreciative. She waited for Clara to speak, unwilling to spoil the moment.

"That's the Francesca Burford who encouraged me to be a woman in business," Clara said softly.

Francesca felt her cheeks heat up in a blush. There was no chance of hiding it under the harsh fluorescent light. "I'm sorry I overreacted earlier. That's not me on a usual day, I promise. And I'll work doubly hard to meet your expectations in the future. I don't want to miss my chance to be your ideal companion to be stranded in a lift with."

Clara laughed and Francesca smiled. She was starting to enjoy making Clara laugh. It seemed such an easy thing to achieve, despite what had gone before and the obviously stressful situation.

Clara appeared to be something of an open book, or at least one that required very little convincing to open. Francesca was used to socialising with business executives who kept their cards to their chest and gave away little with their insincere smiles. Clara was honest, sometimes to a fault. It had been a while since Francesca had been with someone so candid and she was finding that she enjoyed it.

Suddenly, Clara's expression changed to one of horror.

"Oh, no! Warren!" she cried.

CHAPTER FIVE

Clara couldn't believe that she'd forgotten about Warren. She jumped to her feet and jabbed the alarm bell.

"Help!" she cried. "We're stuck! Let us out!"

She alternated between pressing the alarm bell and slamming the metal door with the palm of her hand. Panic coursed through her, mixing with utter disgust at herself for forgetting about Warren.

"Clara, Clara!"

Francesca stood beside her and eased her hand away from the alarm button.

"Breathe," Francesca said. "You have to breathe."

It was only then that Clara realized that she was panicking and her breathing was coming in short pants. Francesca took both of her hands and cupped them in her own.

"Look at me," Francesca said.

Clara looked up. She could hear her heart thudding, deafening her to almost everything else.

"Focus on your breathing."

Clara did as she was told. Trying to ignore the fact that her shaking hands were encompassed in warm, soft hands that she had dreamed of touching her. She sucked in a shaky breath and then slowly blew it out again. She repeated the process a few times before she felt better and extracted her hands from Francesca's. To stay in that position would be dangerous.

"Who is Warren?" Francesca asked.

"My cat. I only got him a couple of weeks ago. He's a rescue cat and now I'm stuck here, and he won't get his dinner." Clara felt awful, not only for not being there for her new pet but for forgetting he existed entirely.

Francesca looked relieved. "Oh, thank goodness it's only a cat. I thought he was a baby or a boyfriend."

"I'm gay," Clara said.

"Well, in any case, I'm sure your cat will be fine."

"It's taken me ages to build up his trust," Clara said. "He hated me for a week."

"I'm sure he didn't hate you."

Clara lifted her sleeves and showed off her impressive collection of scratch marks.

Francesca's eyebrows lifted. "Okay, yes, he hates you. Why did you get a cat who hates you?"

Clara lowered her sleeves. "No one else would have taken him home. He's this grumpy old man who doesn't need anyone."

"Which proves that he'll be fine having dinner a little late. If indeed that ends up happening, we may be out of here in ten minutes. We simply don't know."

"But he'd just started to trust me," Clara said, knowing that she sounded whiny. "And I'd forgotten about him. You asked if anyone was expecting me home and I said no. Warren would be expecting me home, but I'd forgotten all about him. I'm a horrible cat mum." Clara sagged against the wall and fell into a sitting position. The day could literally not get any worse. She'd had a terrible morning, been sacked from her job, was trapped with someone who she was currently experiencing a very complicated mix of emotions about, and had now forgotten about Warren. A cat who only last week she had promised to do anything for.

Francesca sat next to her. "When I asked if anyone was expecting you at home, I obviously meant a human who would notice you hadn't come home and might be of some help to us. Not a grumpy cat who clearly hates you. I wouldn't beat yourself up too badly about that."

Clara tried to control her breathing. Francesca Burford was sitting next to her. She could smell her perfume and even her shampoo. Now was not the right time for her years old crush to start to reassert itself.

"Buffet," Clara blurted out.

"Sorry?"

"I named him after Warren Buffet."

Francesca chuckled. It was a low rumble that caused a flutter in Clara's stomach. "Didn't he have a name before?"

"No, well, I don't know. They didn't have any history on him. I tried a few names, he answered to Warren."

"Must have been fate then," Francesca said.

"Do you have any pets?"

"I used to. I had a dog called Molly. She was absolutely insane. A spaniel who acted as if she'd drunk a vat of coffee every day."

"Did she pass away?"

"Oh, no, my ex took her. She had more time for Molly than I did, so it made sense. I see her now and then."

"I'm sorry. Breakups are hard." Clara looked down at her hands in her lap, anything to change her focus away from Francesca sitting next to her.

Her emotions were all over the place. She'd gone from being bitterly disappointed that her idol was in fact a bit of a monster to wondering if she was wrong. Francesca's impassioned speech to keep her in the sector had all the hallmarks of someone who really cared, someone who Clara felt she recognised.

Her heart was being pulled in multiple directions. From feeling distraught that someone she had looked up to for years wasn't what she had expected, to nervous excitement that she was now sharing a confined space with someone she'd crushed on for years. And maybe, just maybe, Francesca was the person she'd suspected her to be all along. She was certainly funny in a deadpan kind of way. Passionate, intelligent, and caring. All the things Clara had hoped for once upon a time.

"Sorry I freaked out about Warren then," Clara said.

"No need to apologise. It's a stressful situation."

Clara agreed. While she was trying to appear unaffected, nothing could be further from the truth. She was stressed and frightened. Getting stuck in the office at the weekend when no one would notice was bad, but she'd been stressed long before she'd arrived in the office that morning.

Yet another discussion with her mum about her complete lack of a social life had led to a sleepless night and a bad morning. Being distracted by the knowledge that her mum thought she was going nowhere with her life had led her to burn her toast, drop toothpaste on her top, and spill an entire cup of coffee.

She hated arguing with her mum. Hated it all the more because it highlighted that her mum thought so little of her accomplishments. Clara had worked hard to get where she was. But all her mum saw was Clara's proximity to Francesca and assumed that had always been Clara's goal. Which Clara found pretty offensive as it belittled her interests, education, and hard work and made her out to be nothing more than the holder of a childish crush. Because of that, they had been arguing more and more. Supposed motherly concern and Clara's knee-jerk reaction to any criticism collided almost weekly. So obviously this was the day that she'd first bump into Francesca, when she was at her absolute worst.

"I could have handled you firing me better," Clara said.

"I think we agree that I shouldn't have fired you."

Francesca was clearly happy to leave it there. But Clara wasn't. Now that her anger at finding out that Francesca wasn't the perfect goddess that she'd expected had worn off, she was able to see her own actions for what they were.

When Francesca had approached her, Clara had stumbled a little and then been embarrassed at her reaction. Rather than calmly explaining to Francesca that she hadn't stolen the pen, and had no idea it was her pen, she'd reacted sarcastically and defensively. The situation had quickly escalated when Clara knew that she could have just as easily turned it around and smoothed everything over. If only it had been any other day.

"I'd had a really terrible morning. You shouldn't have fired me, but I shouldn't have reacted the way I did. I'm sorry."

Francesca laughed. "We're not going to go through a series of deathbed confessions, are we? I know it's a dire situation to be stuck in here, but I think we'll be okay."

"I'm being serious."

Francesca's laughter stopped. "I'm sorry. You don't need to apologise. I'd also had a terrible morning. We were both in the wrong but we're past that now. Aren't we?"

"I just want you to know that I'm not always like that," Clara said.

"You did go off like a firecracker."

"You can talk!" Clara turned to face her. "You were all red eyes and flailing arms."

"I did flail a lot, didn't I?" Francesca chuckled. "You were more verbally devastating. I enjoyed your 'excuse me?' You got a lot of syllables into that."

"Been practicing that since high school," Clara said.

They both laughed. After a while, a comfortable silence filled the lift and Clara realized that her predicament could have been much worse. She could have been stranded with someone else. Or worse, alone.

"I'll tell you about my bad morning if you tell me about yours?" Francesca said.

"No, thanks. It's embarrassing," Clara said.

"And here I thought we were becoming friends," Francesca said. "Well, mine is embarrassing too, but I'm happy to share."

Clara smiled. "Because we're becoming friends?"

"Precisely."

"Fine, but don't expect me to reciprocate," Clara said.

"It wouldn't matter if you did, my morning was far worse." Francesca smoothed out some creases in her dress.

Clara grinned. Francesca was trying to calm her. She cared enough about Clara to want her to be comfortable despite the pretty dire situation they were in. A touch of humour, a dash of sarcasm, a pinch of competitive bravado. Maybe Francesca was the woman she'd crushed on all these years. She pushed the thought aside, rekindling those feelings now was the last thing she needed.

"I was dumped last night, in a most humiliating way," Francesca said.

Clara tried to not react. Shock that Francesca had been dating and she didn't know mixed with confusion as to why someone would dump such a woman.

"Did you accuse them of stealing your pen?" Clara said, trying to keep the mood light and deflect from the fact that her mind had quickly drifted into dangerous territory. She wondered how long she had been dating someone, who the person was, and critically if they would get back together again. Not that it should matter to her but it did.

Francesca gently elbowed her in response to her joke. "No. We were meeting at a restaurant for dinner. When I arrived, the waiter approached and we ordered drinks. Then, I could tell that something was wrong. I asked. She declined to say anything. I asked again. Then it all came out like a tidal wave. It had obviously been building for a while."

The atmosphere in the lift changed and Francesca shifted a little uneasily. Clara quickly understood that it had been an uncomfortable moment for Francesca. Any hint of a joke had vanished.

"She wasn't quiet about the whole thing," Francesca said. "The couple at the next table heard a little more than I would have liked. The waiter came with our drinks and practically ran back to the safety of the bar."

"Sounds horrible," Clara said.

"Well, it wasn't pleasant to have a public character assassination and then have a glass of wine thrown in my face."

Clara's eyes widened. "She threw a drink at you?"

"Oh, yes. The whole thing was fairly awful. I didn't have any cash on me so I had to wait for the waiter to be brave enough to return so I could pay for the drinks, that I was now wearing. The restaurant was so quiet you could hear a pin drop. Suddenly no one was eating, they were all watching to see what I'd do next. I'm also quite sure I saw someone filming, so that might well end up on the website of a gossip magazine soon."

"How long had you been dating?"

"Three months. Nothing too serious but I didn't think it was inconsequential, either. Clearly, I was in a different relationship than her, I thought things were going rather well. But from what she said, it really wasn't."

"You had no idea things had gotten to that point? Seriously?" Clara couldn't help but be surprised by that.

"None."

Clara pressed away from the wall, turned to face Francesca, and crossed her legs. "What kind of things did she say? What made her blow up like that?"

"Apparently I'm late for things, and I don't call—"

"Are you?"

"Late for things?"

Clara nodded.

Francesca looked like she was about to issue an immediate denial but stopped herself. She took in a breath, scrunched up her face, and looked to the ceiling.

"I suppose I am sometimes late."

"Why?"

Francesca looked at Clara with confusion. "I don't know. I just am."

Clara shook her head. "No. This is a time sensitive business. If you're late to a trade, that's potentially hundreds of thousands of pounds. Being timely is in your DNA if you work in the stock market. Why were you sometimes running late when it came to someone you were dating?"

Francesca swallowed. She looked lost and like she was trying to fathom a particularly difficult crossword clue. "I don't know. Why was I?"

Clara shrugged. "No idea. Only you can answer that one."

Francesca's expression turned thoughtful before she turned her head away. Clara worried her lip. She didn't know if she'd said the right thing. It wasn't her place to get involved, but she often struggled to remain silent when she had something to say.

"I suppose I wasn't very present," Francesca said.

"Why?"

Francesca looked at her lap and offered a small shrug. "It's not like it was going to last."

"Why?"

Francesca smirked. She looked up. "You like that word."

"You don't have to answer," Clara said. "But I think you know more than you're telling yourself. It sounds to me like you sabotaged yourself."

Francesca blinked. "Sabotaged myself? And why would I do that?"

"I don't know that, only you know that."

"Did you study mathematics or psychology?"

Clara sighed deeply. She'd done it again. She wished she knew when to keep her thoughts to herself.

"Sore subject?" Francesca asked.

"My mum's a therapist," Clara said.

"Oh, commiserations."

Clara laughed. "Thanks. She means well. But I do end up channelling her sometimes. I'm sorry."

"No need to apologise. I'm a big girl. I can choose not to answer."

"True. But I'm still sorry that you were dumped. And that you had wine thrown over you."

"Thank you. I'm sorry for whatever caused your bad day, despite the fact that you're reluctant to tell me. Presumably because it will pale into insignificance in light of my horrors." A wisp of a smile danced across Francesca's face.

Clara rolled her eyes. "You're competitive. But, like, compulsively so. I'll tell you, but not because of your frankly terrible stab at reverse psychology, but because it will fill the time and show you that my bad morning was far worse than yours."

Chapter Six

Francesca breathed an internal sigh of relief that Clara was willing to tell her own sequence of events that had led to her bad day. It had started out as a way for Francesca to defuse the stress after Clara's sudden panic, but it had then turned into a need to deflect from her own sob story.

She hadn't expected to ever tell anyone of the mortifying events at an upscale London dining establishment the night before. She'd sat on the Tube on the way home, aware that her makeup was ruined, she stunk of wine, and she was once again single.

Questions rang in her head. Why had she not put Diana first? Why had she frequently been late to things? And why was she convinced that the whole relationship was doomed from the start?

All good questions. None of which were appropriate for a time where she was stuck in a lift and trying to hold on to some shred of dignity and calm. Though she suspected that Clara was on to something with her assumption that she'd sabotaged herself in some way. She'd thought for a while that Diana wasn't right for her. But she'd done nothing about it. Except, apparently, push Diana away in a far more hurtful way than if she'd been honest and ended things before.

"My mum is worried that I'm a hermit," Clara said.

"Are you?" Francesca asked, happy for a new topic of conversation.

Clara laughed. "A little. But come on, what's nicer than being at home with a mug of cocoa, a good book, maybe a movie, and not having to worry about anything?"

"I'll defer to an expert. What does your mum say to that?"

"That I'm proving her point." Clara shuffled backwards and leaned her back against the wall. She picked up a pen from the stolen stash on the floor and started to roll it between her fingers. "My mum and dad really love each other. Like, it's sickening and also kinda sweet. But they want the same for me and I just don't think it's going to happen. I don't think that everyone is destined for that kind of love. So, every now and then, but with increasing frequency of late, my mum calls to complain that I don't go out and meet people."

"You're twenty-six," Francesca said. "Plenty of time. If they want to worry about someone, they should worry about me."

"Well, they've been worrying for about a decade." Clara pulled her knees up and lowered her head to hide her face.

"There are plenty of people who are single at your age. It seems overkill for them to be worried about you. Especially to worry since you were sixte—oh." Francesca felt the penny drop with a jolt. "Because of your sexuality?"

"Well, kind of. That's a part of it, I guess. It's complicated."

Francesca felt her anger build. Homophobia was a sickening weakness in some. Why people couldn't just allow others to live their own truth was beyond her. Luckily, she'd experienced precious little of it in her lifetime. Some people didn't have the same privileges she'd had. The injustice of it sat heavily with her.

"I don't see how the sexuality of your child can be that complicated," Francesca said.

"It's not quite that. It's more this crush I had as a teenager," Clara said. "This one woman. It came out of nowhere and sort of continued for a while. My mum thought it was obsession, but it wasn't." She sat up and looked at Francesca seriously, clearly wanting to make herself understood. "It wasn't an obsession then and it isn't now, but my mum doesn't get it. She always thinks there's another layer of the onion to peel away to get to the truth. But there isn't. I did have a bit of a crush, but that's faded. Now I just think they're pretty cool and interesting. But Mum thinks I need to get out and date someone so I can 'start my life,' whatever that means."

"So you argued about that and that led to a bad morning?" Francesca asked.

"Yes. We've been talking about it more and more lately. She's sort of on a mission now. It's a bit exhausting to have to justify yourself all the time. I'm happy, but she can't see that. I have my own place, which is small but it's mine and I love it. I got into this amazing training program and I'm able to work in an industry that I genuinely enjoy. She can't see that I'm living and enjoying my life."

Francesca wondered who the crush was. A crush that had faded to an interest, it wasn't unheard of. She thought back to her own idols, the ones who had guided her through the early stages of her life. To others, the interest may have looked a little like an obsession. There was Adelaide Rosemont, one of the leading female mathematicians of the time. And then Suzanna Clarence, the woman Francesca had modelled her own look after when she started to garner media attention. Neither were obsessions but certainly held more than a passing interest.

"I'm sorry," Francesca said. "It sounds tricky to navigate."

"It is." Clara leaned her head back against the wall and looked up at the ceiling. "I just wish she'd back off."

"She cares about you."

"I know, but she can care without trying to micromanage my life. She doesn't get that I'm interested in a certain type of person. I don't want to go on casual dates with people I'm not interested in. That's not fair to me or them."

"Certain type of person?" Francesca asked, her curiosity was piqued.

"Doesn't matter," Clara sighed. "Won't happen."

"Sorry, it's none of my business." Francesca raised her hand slightly in apology. "I'm incurably nosey. We share that trait."

"It's fine. It's just she keeps trying to set me up with people who I have nothing in common with. Women who I literally have nothing in common with, and then I have to say I'm not interested, and it starts a new argument. I think she thinks I'm shy and won't ever find a woman on my own. But I just know what I want and it's not easy to find that kind of person."

"You just admitted to becoming a hermit. Is the woman of your dreams likely to be found in your home?"

Clara rolled her eyes. "Hi, Mum."

Francesca laughed. "I'd take offence, but I know that I'm old enough to actually be your mum."

"Age is just a number."

"Says she in her mid-twenties."

"You don't need to lie about your age, you know."

"Don't change the subject, we're talking about your hermitdom, not my attempt to age backwards."

"I'm not really a hermit. I do go out."

"Other than work?" Francesca asked.

Clara hesitated a moment. "Well, I don't go clubbing every night, but I go out. Yes."

Francesca tilted her head. "When was the last time you went on a date?"

Clara laughed. It was full of bravado and didn't quite cover the fear of being exposed. "I don't know, a few months ago?"

It was a lie. As clear as the fact they were stuck in a lift shaft with no means to save themselves. But Francesca knew not to push. They were trapped and who knew for how long.

"You know, one of the reasons I never tried dating sites is because I don't think I have a good grasp of what I'm looking for in a person," Francesca said. "It's the same with holidays. I go onto a website, and I'm presented with options. Do I want a beach or a city? Well, both have merit. I'm not sure. Buying a house, do I want to live within three miles of the city centre? Well, possibly. Are their local shops nearby? But you seem to be an ideal candidate for a dating site, you can select whatever it is you're looking for. They'll deliver you the perfect date. I wish I could be so clear on what I want in a person."

"Is this where you sign me up on a dating site without my knowledge? I think I've seen that movie."

"If I had enough signal to do that, I'd think my first action would be ringing reception and asking them to get us out of here. No offence."

"Does my love life mean nothing to you?" Clara asked.

"Not a jot."

"Harsh."

"But maybe you could consider a dating agency? Before your mum does it for you."

Clara shuddered at the prospect. "Oh wow, I know exactly the options she'd pick. Someone fit and into healthy things, to encourage me to be the same. Probably a vegetarian or a vegan. Definitely someone who wants children, because she wants grandkids. Someone who's into culture, but like armchair culture. Will watch culture on TV but never actually get off their butt and go to a theatre."

"Would she pick a man or a woman?" Francesca asked, still curious about whether or not her family accepted her for who she was.

"A woman. I think she gets it now."

"But she didn't always?"

"No. My crush kinda came out of nowhere and I think my mum always thought it was a phase. It was a bit of a weird crush. So, she always thought it would go away and maybe I'd change my mind on being interested in women. It's not my being into women that worried her, it was that woman in particular."

"Is she a dictator? Arms dealer?"

Clara laughed. "Ish. No, she's not anything bad. She's just older than me. My mum couldn't see why sixteen-year-old me would be into fou—into her."

Francesca's eyes widened. "That's some age gap."

Clara looked at her with exasperation. "Come on, you surely know that's not the point? Surely? People find their people and if they are the same age or fifty years apart then so be it."

"But twenty-plus years, that's a lifeti—"

"I'm not interested in people my age. They bore me. Yeah, I may find the one in a thousand who uses punctuation in their text messages and doesn't want to go out drinking every weekend, but I don't want to be looking under every rock in a hundred-mile radius to find the few. And then who's to say I'd be interested in them and they me? Not to mention the fact that most people would be way happier not dating mirrors of themselves. Older women are more interesting to me, they are more likely to be in tune with me. I'm not counting years, no one should be."

Francesca opened her mouth to react, but Clara got there first and continued, "When we're young we're supposed to respect our elders. And that seems to mean never challenging convention. Never questioning anything. Respect somehow means rejecting your own individuality. We're just supposed to accept what people say is normal. Okay, many people find happiness with people of their own age. Well, congratulations. I won't. I'm not going to be happy with a man. I'm not going to be happy with a twenty-five-year-old woman. I'm just not. I know me. I know me well enough to know what I like and what I don't. Just because I discovered who I was at sixteen doesn't mean I was wrong. I liked you then, I like you now, and I—"

Clara's eyes widened in horror and her hands slapped over her mouth.

Francesca stared back. She knew she should say something, but no words were forthcoming.

"I didn't say that," Clara said from beneath her hands. "I said nothing. Okay? Nothing."

Francesca nodded. It seemed the best course of action to try to stop the panic attack that she could see building in Clara.

Clara jumped to her feet and stepped over Francesca. She pressed the alarm button again and started banging on the doors. Francesca stared at her, still putting together what she'd heard and what it all meant. Not that it mattered. Clara had made it very clear that she didn't want to talk about it. The matter was closed.

Except Francesca didn't want that. She wanted to know everything. Clara had a crush on her? Or had done? What did that even mean? She seemed very uninterested in her now and Francesca couldn't help but feel irritated at herself for not living up to whatever expectations Clara had of her.

After a few moments of slamming her fist on the lift doors and pressing the alarm button, Clara stopped and stepped away. Her face was red and she looked near tears. She looked down at Francesca.

"We're not talking about it."

Francesca nodded again.

Clara pulled her coat and belongings to the next corner, a few centimetres farther away from Francesca than she had been before. She sat on the floor—facing the wall—and picked up her book and started to read.

She scoured her memory for what Clara had said about her crush. She'd not been all that interested until she realized it was her. Now she wished she'd paid more attention. Interesting and cool popped into her mind. She smiled to herself. She supposed some people would consider her those things. Although she imagined that was all in the past now when it came to Clara.

Francesca blew out a soft breath. She picked up her phone and noted that she still had no signal. She was trapped with a woman who inexplicably liked her, or thought she did, or had at some point. She didn't know what was happening anymore. From an unknown trainee investor to someone who had followed her career for over a decade.

Whatever Clara had once thought about Francesca was irrelevant in light of her actions earlier. She was so adept at ruining relationships that she even destroyed ones she didn't know about. The previous evening played over in her head once more. Diana had called her a self-absorbed workaholic. One who apparently needed a glass of wine poured over her head. She didn't think she was self-absorbed, but maybe her lack of connection with Diana had made her appear that way.

Why were you always one step out of that relationship? Why have you always been one step out of your relationships? And how did you need a trainee investor nearly half your age to point that out to you?

CHAPTER SEVEN

Clara wasn't reading the words on the page of the book. She was chanting swear words in her head and praying that they either be rescued or fall to their death. At this point she no longer cared which as long as it happened within the next few minutes.

"We're not talking about it," she said over her shoulder for the third time since sitting down.

She could sense Francesca brimming with questions. Could feel her eyes drilling into the back of her head. And felt the cloak of her imposed silence draped heavily over them.

How they'd ended up on the topic she had so desperately wanted to avoid was beyond her. And how she'd managed to let something so important and embarrassing slip out of her mouth was even further beyond her.

Her mind was spinning so fast she could barely remember what she'd actually said. How much had she given away? The word crush floated through her mind, and she grasped her book in a grip tight enough to warp the pages.

She hoped Warren hadn't gotten too used to the apartment because the only choice she had now was to change her name and leave the country. Unless the cat heard what had transpired in the lift, then he'd probably want to disown her as well.

"You know," Francesca said.

Clara scrunched her eyes closed. She heard the splat of a tear land on her book.

"I think the reason why I knew it wouldn't last with Diana, my ex, was because I knew she wasn't right for me, or I her, however you wish to say it. Even if I didn't want to admit that to her or even to myself. So, I wasn't committing myself fully to a relationship with her. I'd not really thought of it before. I owe her an apology."

Clara bit her lip. She didn't have words. All she could think about was how stupid she'd been to let her secret out.

"I've never really known who would be a good fit for me," Francesca said. "I'd just assumed that it would be someone like me. But now I wonder if someone like me is the last thing I want in a person. Funny how you sometimes don't think about things. So, thank you for pushing me to consider it. What are you reading?"

Clara opened her eyes and winced at the tear splatters on the open pages of her book. She wiped her tears with the back of her hand and held up the book so Francesca could see the cover over her shoulder.

"Fantasy?"

"Yes," Clara whispered.

"It's nice to disappear into another world sometimes."

"I can't do this small talk," Clara said.

"I can't do the silence," Francesca said. "We either talk about it, or we talk about nothing. I'm sorry. I can't sit in silence."

Clara threw her book down and turned around. "Fine. Let's talk about it."

Francesca looked calmly at her. After a few moments of silence, she lifted a shoulder. "There's nothing for me to say. You're the one who has all the information."

Clara couldn't disagree with that. She stood, somehow talking about embarrassing things always felt better when she was standing up. Something about power, she imagined. Even though she felt woefully powerless at the moment.

"I've followed your career for years," she said. "And this is so embarrassing to say, but I've been a big fan of yours."

"Why?" Francesca looked genuinely confused.

Clara laughed. "Because you're you." She gestured to Francesca, sitting on the floor and yet still looking unfairly perfect.

"I'm sorry, I'm not being deliberately obtuse. Why?"

"Because you're successful, you're one of a kind in the financial world. And…" Clara grit her teeth and shook her head. "You're hot, okay?"

Francesca burst out laughing.

Clara tapped her leg with her foot. "Hey, don't laugh at me."

Francesca held her side and attempted to stop laughing. "I'm sorry, it's funny that you think that. Sweet, but hilarious."

"Wow, you want the ego boost of me telling you what you obviously know?" Clara folded her arms and shook her head. "It goes to show. I thought I knew you, but obviously I didn't."

Francesca's laughter died down. "Clara, let me be clear. I have never in my life looked in a mirror and liked what I saw."

Clara frowned. Francesca clearly wasn't joking.

"But you're gorgeous," Clara said, no longer worrying of her own embarrassment. Convincing Francesca of what should be one of the most obvious things in the world had now taken priority.

A blush instantly flared across Francesca's cheeks, and she looked away.

Clara opened and then closed her mouth. It felt wrong to try to convince Francesca of something she obviously didn't believe.

"I don't understand why, but I instantly felt drawn to you. I'd seen you on the TV doing interviews, and then I started to cut your picture out of the newspaper when I saw you. I kinda knew it was a bit weird. But you were fascinating to me."

Francesca continued to tilt her head away.

"I read your interviews. Watched what I could on TV or online. I started to feel like I knew you. I used your advice and started trading successfully. At first, I think I wanted to be you. But then I wanted to know you." Clara swallowed. It had gone beyond that. She'd wanted to know Francesca in every way imaginable.

"It was a crush throughout high school and in college," Clara said. She swallowed again to remove the bubble of fear that had lodged itself in her throat. "But I started to get it under control in university. I started to date a girl called Hayley and you sort of faded into the background for me."

Francesca looked back up at her. "What happened with Hayley?"

"We drifted apart. It was a real quick thing, you know? We met, we went for coffee, we were dating. All in less than a week. Then we spent four months realising we were completely wrong for each other."

Francesca smiled. "Yes, I've been there, too."

Clara paced the small space. "But dating Hayley meant I sort of got over you. A bit, at least. I still thought you were the best woman in business there was, still do. And you're still hot, by the way."

Francesca licked her lips and looked away again. Clara couldn't believe that the previously confident Francesca Burford was so uncertain about her looks.

"My mum thinks I'm obsessed. So, when I said I'd finally got into the mentoring program here, she was worried that I'd revert back to the school kid who was obsessed with you."

"Are you obsessed?" Francesca asked carefully.

Clara laughed. "No. Like, you're my childhood crush and I think you're really impressive. But I've grown up now. You're a normal person. With normal person flaws. Like the whole sacking me over a pen thing, which really puts a dent on any crush I might have had."

"I'm not going to live that down, am I?" Francesca smiled.

"No." Clara shook her head. *It's all I've got. The only defence I have left.*

"Did you apply to the trainee program to be near me, or to learn the trade?" Francesca asked.

"Learn the trade," Clara said quickly. "I was intrigued about you, of course. But my interest in trading and my interest in you were two different things." Clara let out a sigh and sat back on her coat. She crossed her legs and pinched the bridge of her nose. This was turning into the worst day ever. A fight with her mum, a terrible morning, being fired, admitting her crush to her crush, and stuck in a lift for who knew how long. Maybe days. She always tried to be truthful, but even she knew that there were times when silence was better than honesty. This would have been one of them.

"Okay," Francesca said unexpectedly.

Confusion dropped over Clara like a dark cloud. She looked up. "Okay? What do you mean?"

"I mean, okay. Thank you for explaining. I imagine it was very awkward but at least we've been honest with each other."

"You don't think I'm weird?"

Francesca laughed. "I think you're extremely weird for stealing handfuls of pens when you were fired for stealing only one. I think you're weird for adopting a cat that hates you. I don't think you're weird for having a crush on an image of a person you don't know. All teenagers do it."

"An image?"

"Yes, you saw me—a much younger me—and it triggered something you didn't understand. You realized you liked women because of a visual image of me. Nothing more substantial than that. I'm flattered."

Clara wanted to argue but knew doing so would only dig her a deeper hole than she'd already created. "You really don't think that you're attractive, do you?"

Francesca shifted a little with discomfort. "I have eyes."

"You obviously don't see what I see."

The blush on Francesca's cheeks grew brighter. "The fact remains, it was an image, probably an idyllic image, of me that your younger self had a crush on. Not me. And so, it's okay because it's between you and your imagination's conjuring of me."

"I think my imagination was pretty accurate," Clara said. "I did see interviews as well. And I read your book."

"Oh, it was you," Francesca said.

"It was a bestseller, so it wasn't only me. You have low self-esteem, that's interesting."

"You're psychoanalysing me again."

"I am. And you're doing the same to me."

"I'm not."

"You are. You're assuming that I know nothing about you other than your looks. You're assuming that I'm shallow. Your statements are designed to validate those assumptions about me. But they won't, because you're wrong."

Francesca sat up a little taller. "Well, it's not like you had a deep and meaningful connection with me. You thought I was hot—your words—and that was that."

"It was more than that. I heard you speak, I knew your ethics, saw your success. You set up financial training for girls in schools. You walked away from a lucrative deal because of suspected racism on a board of directors. I knew you. I know you. It was more than an image and you know it."

"You saw one side of things. You'd be sorely disappointed if you knew me."

Clara chuckled. "I didn't think you were perfection personified, Francesca. I knew you were a human."

Francesca opened her mouth to reply but stopped. She took a breath and closed her eyes before opening them again and holding a hand up. "Let's stop. We're getting heated about this and it's not a good idea considering that we may be stuck here for a while."

Clara inclined her head. "Agreed. I'm going to read. If you don't like the silence then feel free to hum."

Francesca rolled her eyes. Clara sat back on her coat and balled up the sleeve of her coat into a makeshift pillow and lay down. She picked up her book and forced herself to focus on the words and not all the fascinating insights she'd just gained. It wasn't any of her business that Francesca had low self-esteem. When they finally got out of the lift, she'd decided to make sure their paths never crossed again anyway.

CHAPTER EIGHT

Francesca's stomach rumbled. She placed her hand over it and shifted her position slightly to try to silence the sound. It was ten o'clock and she was beginning to genuinely worry that they were going to be stuck all night.

Neither of them had spoken since Francesca had put a stop to the dangerous line of conversation they'd been on. Instead, Clara had lain down on her coat and continued to read her book. A while later, the book fell from her hands as she fell asleep.

With little else to do, Francesca had watched the soft rise and fall of her chest. Clara was a captivating mystery to her. Different from most people that Francesca knew.

Argumentative, brave, opinionated, and yet soft and thoughtful. Francesca got the impression that she could know Clara for a long time and not get much closer to fully understanding her. Not that the thought bothered her, in fact it intrigued her.

The thought of a young Clara having a crush on her was creating a lot of internal confusion. She felt old. Knowing that Clara had admired her for the better part of a decade didn't go anywhere towards quelling that feeling.

It didn't help that Clara was very attractive. Young, certainly, but more than that. She had classically beautiful features. Francesca had tried not to notice since the moment she saw her in the office that morning. Now it was becoming impossible.

Clara had said that most people would be happier not dating mirrors of themselves. It seemed so obvious when Clara said it, but

Francesca had never considered that fact. She'd always dated people like herself. It seemed fair and balanced that way. Similar age, similar career choices, similar lifestyle. And then she'd always felt restless. Diana wasn't the first relationship she'd been simultaneously invested in and waiting for it to end. That was a common occurrence. Maybe Clara's mirror theory was the reason why.

Clara seemed convinced that she knew what she wanted in a partner. So convinced that she'd happily sit at home and socialize with a grumpy feline than actively go out to try to find someone, knowing that who she sought wouldn't be at the local bar.

Clara believed that she knew Francesca on more than just a surface level. Something which had become more and more obvious as time had passed. Which was why Francesca wanted to put an end to the conversation. For some reason, knowing that Clara valued her on more than just a superficial level was disconcerting.

Probably because she was beginning to think that they would be a good fit for one another, despite the very obvious differences between them. Clara wasn't a mirror. And it felt good to speak with someone so dissimilar to her.

Another gust of wind blew through the lift shaft. With the sun having set a long time ago, it was cold outside and that apparently was true also of the lift. Francesca automatically picked up her phone to check her weather app and the predicted temperatures that evening. She looked at the app, all data defaulting to nothing more than a line because of the lack of signal.

She held the phone a little higher, hoping for something to change. When it didn't, she let out a sigh and put it back in her bag.

"Oh, wow, it's cold," Clara murmured. She sat up and rubbed at her eyes. "What happened?"

"The sun set. There's no heat source in here so I think we're at the mercy of the elements," Francesca said.

Clara picked up her coat and wrapped it around her shoulders like a cape. "Well, this got even less fun, if that's possible."

"Don't tempt fate, dear."

"Sorry I fell asleep."

"Nothing to apologise for."

"Did I miss anything?"

Francesca nodded. "Yes. The attendant came round with the drinks trolley."

"Cool, did you get me anything?"

"Gin and tonic."

"Oh, nice." Clara shivered and pulled her coat a little tighter around her. "I'd prefer a coffee, though. Or tea. Or a mug of hot water. I'm really not fussy right now, just something warm."

Francesca didn't say anything. She knew it was likely that it would only get colder. She'd thought hunger would be their biggest issue, now she realized it would be staying warm. She wasn't about to suggest huddling for warmth, but she suspected it wouldn't be long before they were forced to do so.

Her mouth ran dry at the thought. Specifically, the thought that she'd quite like to cuddle up to Clara. It didn't feel appropriate to think that way, but she didn't seem to have much control over it.

Clara stood up. She walked over to where Francesca sat on her coat and sat next to her. "Budge up," Clara said.

Francesca did as she was told. Clara sat beside her and fanned her coat out behind her so it encompassed both of them.

"You must be cold in that dress," Clara said.

She was. But she'd pushed the thought as far out of her mind as she could. Clara pressed up against her side, seemingly not in the least bit uncomfortable with the action. Either she was a very good liar, or she had been honest when she said she'd moved on from her teenage crush.

Francesca pulled the coat over her shoulder and let out a sigh.

"Did I snore?" Clara asked.

"Yes. The lift shook." She hadn't snored. She'd made a small snuffling sound once which Francesca had found utterly adorable.

"Liar."

"I didn't hear you snore, but you weren't asleep for that long. You might have been on the brink of a giant farmyard-esque grunt. We'll never know."

"Sleeping is weird. We never know what we do when we're asleep. We rely on other people to tell us. Unless you take part in a sleep experiment, or you film yourself. Someone told me once that I talk in my sleep."

"Well, you didn't say anything this time."

"Do you talk in your sleep?"

"Not to my knowledge."

"Allegedly, I once said 'oh boy, look at all that cake' when I was asleep."

Francesca laughed. "Allegedly?"

"Well, I can't verify it," Clara said.

"Surely your partner wouldn't lie to you about that?"

"Oh, it wasn't in bed. It was on a train. I was going to the beach with a friend."

Francesca shook with laughter. "So, it was the middle of the day?"

"Yeah. Packed train, too."

"So, you had plenty of people you could have asked for verification?"

"Technically. Thought it best to just gloss over it."

"Very wise."

"I am," Clara said. "I've been told I have a wise head on young shoulders since I was about five."

Francesca smiled and said nothing. She could imagine a young Clara going toe to toe with an unsuspecting adult and telling them exactly what she thought. She was forthright but there was also a vulnerability to her that Francesca found fascinating. She was certainly wise. In the little time they'd spent together, she'd managed to give Francesca a lot to think about.

Clara looked at her watch. "We're going to be here all night, aren't we?"

"I don't know."

"What do we do when one of us needs the toilet?" Clara asked.

"Do you?"

"No, but I will at some point."

"I suggest you don't think about it."

"You're right. Things famously go away when you ignore them." Clara leaned her head on Francesca's shoulder. "Is this okay?"

"Yes." Francesca didn't think it would be okay, but it was. She'd never usually tolerate being used as a makeshift pillow by someone she hardly knew, but Clara was different.

"Poor Warren," Clara said.

"Poor us!"

"He doesn't know what's going on," Clara said. "I do. I know I'm stuck here. He doesn't know why I'm not home. Probably thinks that he's been abandoned again."

"That's rather dramatic. If he hates you as much as those scratches on your arms suggest, then he is blissfully unaware that you're not home. Probably sleeping somewhere he's not allowed."

"I was going to have an Indian takeout tonight," Clara said, suddenly switching topics.

"Don't. I'm hungry," Francesca said.

"And I'm rewatching all of the Marvel movies. I had planned to watch two tonight. And call my mum to apologise."

"Sounds to me like she's the one who should apologise." Francesca loved how easy it was to talk to Clara. They hopped between serious topics and anything to pass the time with ease.

Clara chuckled. "Yeah, she should. But someone has to do the reaching out thing, and it's my turn."

"You take it in turns?"

"Yeah, we're pretty diplomatic in our arguments. What were your plans for tonight?"

Francesca sighed. "Packing away Diana's belongings for her to pick up. I had some edits on a speech I'm giving in a couple of weeks. I wanted to research a plumber, too. I'm getting a new kitchen sink installed."

"Sounds like you're better off in here," Clara said. "That's one of the most boring Saturday evenings I've heard in a long time."

"We can't all be having Indian takeout and watching movies."

"Really? I'm hardly flying a private jet to the Maldives. As a Saturday evening goes, it's pretty standard. What's stopping you?"

Francesca hesitated for a moment. Nothing was stopping her. She'd spoken without thinking, assuming that the relaxation of an evening in with a nice meal and some entertainment was somehow beyond her reach. Which seemed ludicrous now. Had she really gotten so boring?

"Do you not like Indian food?" Clara asked.

Francesca's stomach grumbled softly at the thought of delicious warm naan being dunked into rich and creamy curry sauce. "I love Indian food," she said.

"There you go then. You can order yourself a takeout when we get out of here. Treat yourself."

Francesca was about to shake her head and say what a strange notion that was, when she caught herself. There was nothing stopping her from treating herself. Just her.

"I'll do just that," Francesca said.

"Good. Unless we freeze to death," Clara said.

"If you're that cold, then do some jumping jacks or something."

"I'm not moving any more than is absolutely necessary. I've not seen how thick the cable is that's holding us up, but I do know that I had four cheat days this week."

Francesca pointed at the sign. "We can hold eighteen people. You'll be fine. But if you'd had five cheat days then that would be a differ—"

Clara sat up. Francesca missed the pressure of her head on her shoulder. She had started imagining falling asleep like that. Thoughts of the cold, hunger, and the need to use a bathroom falling away as they slumbered.

"What was that?" Clara stood and approached the door. She put her ear to the door and closed her eyes.

"What was what?" Francesca stood up.

"Shh!"

Francesca clamped her mouth closed and tried to listen out for whatever it was that Clara had heard. She couldn't hear anything, but her heart beating faster at the prospect of being rescued.

Clara opened her eyes and pressed the alarm button.

"I heard something. I think it was the other lift."

Clara started randomly pressing the alarm button to play out a little tune. "Please hear this. Please, please, please," Clara said.

The seconds dragged by and Francesca stood uselessly by. She hoped this wouldn't be a false alarm; she didn't think she had enough strength in her for that kind of a bitter disappointment.

"Hello? Is someone down there?" a faint male voice called.

Clara let go of the alarm button. "Hello! We're stuck!"

"I'll get help! Is everyone okay?"

"Yes, just freezing cold and hungry but we're okay," Clara called back.

"I'll get you out of there soon. Hold on."

Clara spun around and wrapped her arms around Francesca's neck. "Yes! We're actually getting out of here!"

Francesca automatically caught her around the waist. "I honestly thought we'd be here until Monday morning."

"Me too! Oh, I cannot wait to get out of here. No offence."

"None taken."

Clara's eyes widened when she realized that they were standing in an embrace. The heat of blush touched the tips of her ears. "Sorry." She moved backwards, Francesca's hands falling away from her sides. "Sorry, I was just—"

"It's okay," Francesca said.

Clara lowered her head in obvious embarrassment and walked around Francesca. She crouched down and started packing away her things. Francesca did the same. She hated the awkwardness that had come between them. The atmosphere had immediately changed, and she didn't like it at all.

A few moments later, they were both standing with their coats on and their bags by their sides. Francesca thought that she'd be relieved to be finally getting out of the lift, but she found she was reluctant to part from Clara.

"You get to have that curry now," Clara said.

"You get to feed your grumpy cat."

Clara smiled. "Yes. Maybe I'll get him on my side after all."

Silence filled the lift again. It was different from the other times. It was uncomfortable and charged with something that Francesca couldn't recognise.

"I'm sorry," Clara said. "For all the weirdness."

"No weirdness," Francesca said. It had undoubtedly been weird, unexpected, and even confusing at times. On reflection, she wouldn't change a thing. Being forced to take some time out to think was probably the best thing that could have happened to her that day.

"Yeah, it was," Clara said. "I'm sorry. I should have kept things to myself. It would have been easier."

"You don't seem like the kind of person who can lie very easily."

Clara smiled. "No, I'm not. I am sorry though, I probably made things really uncomfortable for you and I didn't want to do that. I do admire you, probably always will. But I'm not weird about it. I haven't got a lock of your hair or anything."

Francesca laughed. "Well, that's pleasing to note. But you don't have anything to apologise for. I appreciate the honesty and I'm quite flattered that you admire me. And, to be honest, I admire you."

Clara looked as if she'd heard the most ridiculous thing ever. "What? Why?"

"I just do." Francesca smiled at her. "Accept it."

Anything Clara was going to say was swallowed up by the sound coming from the doors in front of them. Francesca took a hesitant step forward. She could see light from in between the doors and held her breath hoping that freedom would be moments away.

A few tense seconds passed before a gloved hand forced its way in between the doors and started to heave them apart.

Francesca was suddenly aware that she didn't want to say goodbye to Clara just yet. There was more to be said, she didn't know what, but she felt a sense of incompletion deep within her.

She turned to Clara and opened her mouth. At the same moment, the door was finally opened and the friendly face of a security guard appeared.

"Hello, ladies, let's get you out of here, shall we?"

CHAPTER NINE

Clara looked at her reflection in the bathroom mirror and attempted to tidy her hair a little. She looked as if she'd been sleeping on the floor of a stalled lift, which was accurate but still not a great look.

When they were free of the lift, the security guard had walked them down the stairs to the ground floor. Francesca and Clara had both quickly declined the offer of taking the working lift and happily walked down the four flights of stairs.

Once they reached the lobby, Clara had said goodbye to Francesca and walked into the ladies' bathroom to use the facilities that she had been needing for a while. She didn't linger on her goodbye, knowing that it would be difficult. Freedom was fantastic, but the knowledge that her time with Francesca was over was a bitter pill to swallow.

She gave up adjusting her hair. It was a mess and there was little to be done. She held her hands under the hot tap to try to get some feeling into her fingers after sitting in the cold for so long. It had been wonderful to sit next to Francesca for warmth, but it had done little to warm her.

When she stepped out of the bathroom, she was surprised to see Francesca waiting for her.

"Um. Hi?" Clara asked.

"You didn't say 'see you on Monday,'" Francesca said.

"Sorry?"

"You didn't say 'see you on Monday.' You just said goodbye."

Clara bit her lip. She'd hoped Francesca wouldn't notice that. While it was clear that she was unfired, Clara didn't see how she could possibly return to the office now that Francesca knew her secrets. And there was the very real truth that she felt like she wasn't cut out for the job. Maybe trading wasn't her future, even if she had spent all her life to date trying to get there. The reality seemed different. She didn't excel in the way she'd hoped. She'd never impress anyone, not least Francesca, with her performance so far.

"We don't see each other in the office usually," Clara said, ducking the subject once more.

"I'd like to change that," Francesca said. "And, I'd like to see you outside of the office as well."

Clara felt her eyes widen and her jaw drop. There was little that she could do to stop looking so obviously stunned by the statement. The confidence in Francesca's stance faded a tiny amount, just enough for Clara to notice. She worried that Francesca would take back what she had said.

"I'd love that," Clara said quickly. "Um. What do you mean?"

"I have no idea," Francesca said. "I just know I'd like to spend more time with you."

Clara swallowed. If she was reading the situation right, it sounded like her dreams were starting to come true. She had to check. "Like, a date?"

"Yes." Francesca looked confident, but Clara could tell that there was real fear lurking just behind the mask. "It's not because you said that you admire me. Or because you once had a crush on me. I'm not looking for the ego boost. Those things are nice, of course. But the truth is that I had a more eye-opening, honest, interesting, and fun time with you when we were both locked in that lift than I've had with anyone else for quite some time. I'd like to take you to dinner, if you'll let me?"

Clara couldn't believe her luck. She also worried that Francesca might change her mind when she wasn't cold, hungry, and reeling from nine hours stuck in a lift.

"How about curry at mine tonight? You must be hungry? You can meet Warren, explain to him that it was your fault that we got stuck in the lift—"

"My fault?" Francesca laughed. "How is that my fault?"

"I'd never have gone home at that time if you hadn't fired me. Completely your fault," Clara said, hoping to take some of the tension out of the conversation. "I always order far too much food, so you'd be doing me a favour."

Francesca smiled. "Well, I am very hungry and that does sound like an appealing offer. And I can, of course, explain to Warren that you forgot all about him."

Clara placed her hand over her chest in faux shock. "So mean."

Francesca gestured towards the exit. "Where do you call home?"

"Brixton," Clara said. "The rough end. My boss doesn't pay me much."

"Probably why she's one of the most successful women in finance," Francesca said.

They walked outside, thanking the security guard once more for his rescue. It hadn't escaped Clara's notice that this was the night security guard and the useless weekend one she usually saw was gone. She wondered if they had been rescued because of the shift change.

Outside, they momentarily walked in different directions before stopping and turning to look questioningly at one another.

"Where are you going?" Francesca asked.

"Night bus." Clara pointed towards the bus stop in the distance.

"Absolutely not." Francesca's tone that suggested Clara had proposed they travel via the sewer. "I'll drive."

Clara hadn't even thought about how Francesca arrived in the office that morning. Driving in London was a luxury that few could afford. First there was the ownership of a car, then the congestion charge, and then the little matter of where to park. It wasn't surprising that Francesca didn't have to worry about any of those issues.

She followed Francesca around the side of the building to a garage door that Clara had never noticed before. Francesca tapped a security number into the keypad and the doors automatically lifted.

Francesca unlocked a convertible sports car, a make and model that Clara couldn't identify. She could tell it was sporty and expensive, but that was the limit of her car knowledge. Clara got into the passenger seat and again wondered if she was dreaming. While it had never been this exact series of events, it had all the elements of one of her teenage fantasies. Except this felt real. It didn't have the childish gloss of an unrealistic crush. There were feelings, fears, expectations, and a fluttering of excitement.

Francesca started the car. She pressed some buttons on a panel on the dashboard and a satnav system sprang to life.

"Would you do the honours?"

Clara put her postcode into the device and then saved her address in the address book.

Francesca smirked at the action but said nothing.

"For next time," Clara said with a confidence that she didn't feel.

In a few minutes, they were on their way out of the garage and onto the quiet streets. The office was located in the financial district, far enough away from the nightlife of London that they had a clear journey back to Clara's apartment.

Clara unlocked her phone and opened a familiar food collection app.

"Poppadoms?"

"At least five," Francesca said.

Clara laughed. "Okay. How spicy do you like your curry? Personally, I can't handle more than a korma."

They spent a few minutes creating the perfect Indian banquet and Clara placed the order.

"Okay, Mr. Chakrabarti is making magic in the kitchen as we speak," Clara said. "It's around the corner from mine. He makes the best Indian food in the land."

"And it's just around the corner? Sounds dangerous."

"It is. But so worth it."

They drove over Southwark Bridge. Clara looked out the window at one of her favourite sights in the world—London at night. She saw the lights of a train crossing the river with the iconic Shard skyscraper just behind it, a triangle of random lights capped with a crown of bright white that lit up the night sky. In the distance, she saw the illuminations of Tower Bridge and beyond that the skyscrapers that made up Canary Wharf.

She was so enthralled that her nose was practically pressed to the window. Any time she crossed the Thames at night, she found herself utterly spellbound by the sight to either side of her. She realized that Francesca had slowed the car, allowing her more time to appreciate the view.

"Thank you," she said.

"It's a beautiful sight."

They cleared the bridge and Clara turned to look at Francesca. "I always think so. But it has some very strong competition tonight."

Francesca laughed. "Not from this half of the car."

Clara leaned back against the headrest and took the opportunity to really look at Francesca. Photographs and television interviews didn't do her justice. She was stunning. Clara wondered if being in the spotlight for so many years had caused Francesca to not like how she looked. Seeing yourself age in a mirror was one thing, seeing it broadcast in magazines was quite a different matter. No doubt people commented on her looks, and Clara knew that people were not always kind.

"What are you looking at?" Francesca asked, still focused on the road but no doubt aware that she was being watched.

"You. Figuring out how much time I might need to convince you that you're beautiful," Clara said. They stopped at a set of red lights. Francesca turned to her and she knew in that second that Francesca intended to issue some kind of a denial. Rather than argue, Clara leaned forward and placed a ghost of a kiss on Francesca's lips.

Clara leaned back. She hoped that she hadn't crossed any line. Francesca looked shocked but not horrified. In fact, Clara could see an internal debate being played out in her eyes. Just as Clara was wondering if she was about to be kissed, the moment was ruined by a car horn sounding from behind them. The light had turned green. Francesca slipped the car into gear, and they were on their way again.

CHAPTER TEN

Help yourself to anything from the fridge. Feel free to have a look around. There's no shrine to you, but I understand if you want to check for yourself," Clara said. "I'll only be five minutes."

"Are you sure you don't want me to come with you?" Francesca asked.

"No, you sit down and relax. Or look for the shrine. I'll be back in a bit." Clara was already heading out the front door and leaving Francesca alone in the apartment.

Francesca put her bag on the floor next to the sofa and shrugged out of her coat. The apartment was sparsely decorated and neat and clean. A large cat tree dominated one corner of the living room. It looked completely untouched.

"Warren?" Francesca called.

She entered the kitchen and looked at the cat food bowl which was overflowing with dry cat food. Clara had filled it up the moment they got back, despite the fact that Warren was nowhere to be seen and certainly not desperate for food.

She opened a few cupboard doors before discovering the plates. She decided the least she could do was lay the table in preparation for the meal they were about to have, especially considering Clara had refused to take any money for the food.

It was gone eleven o'clock and she couldn't remember the last time she ate so late. She also couldn't remember the last time her stomach had fluttered with excitement due to an unexpected kiss.

Plates, cutlery, napkins, and drinks glasses assembled, she took the opportunity to use the bathroom and then poke her head into the bedroom just in case there was a shrine to be found.

"No shrine but nice to meet you," she said to Warren, who was lounging on the bed with absolutely zero cares in the world.

Francesca remained in the doorway, not willing to cross the threshold into Clara's private domain. She crouched down and held her hand out to Warren and called him again.

He hopped down from the bed and stretched before coming to greet her. He looked old, stiff, and his fur had lost the shine it had probably once had. He was the exact picture of the oldest cat in the shelter.

Francesca stroked him gently and warily, mindful of the scratches on Clara's arms. He purred and then disappeared towards the kitchen, seemingly unfazed by the arrival of someone new.

She headed back to the living room and sat on an armchair, surveying her surroundings and wondering what she was doing. She'd been wondering ever since she'd decided to wait for Clara in the lobby.

Clara's goodbye had sent a chill down her spine. It had seemed so final, despite being said with what should have been a reassuring smile. Somehow, Francesca had seen through the smile. She felt connected to Clara in a way she had never experienced with anyone else. Conversation flowed effortlessly, they dipped in and out of complicated topics and jokes with ease.

She hadn't been ready to say goodbye. She still wasn't.

The kiss at the traffic lights had been unexpected and wonderful all at once. It had been the lightest graze of lips and yet had held so much promise. Her nerves and excitement had jangled so loudly that she felt herself waking up from a long sleep. She'd spent so long wondering if this was what a connection between two people was supposed to feel like that she'd ended up causing a small traffic jam in her haze.

Clara returned and Francesca went to greet her. The smell of the fragrant food instantly reminded her of how hungry she was. They sat at the dining table, sharing food and stories for at least an hour before they cleaned things away and retired to the living room.

"Will you come back to work?" Francesca asked the question that had been on her mind for a while.

Clara shrugged. "I don't know. I meant what I said, I'm at the bottom of the class."

"Do you have your own portfolio?"

"Sure."

"May I see it?"

Clara nodded. She leaned forward and picked up a laptop from underneath the coffee table. She placed it on her lap, unlocked the machine, and opened a trading platform.

Francesca looked over the array of stocks, indices, commodities, and EFTs. It was a diverse blend with appropriate risk management in place. There were a few things that she'd change, of course, but overall, she could see that Clara had some flair. She was trading within her limits but still pushing for maximum profits.

"Still trading gold, I see," Francesca said.

"It was nine percent down, I couldn't resist."

Francesca smiled. She'd also bought when she'd noticed the price had crashed the previous week.

"This is a competent portfolio," Francesca said. "You have spread your risk well. You've clearly not been frightened by some of the unexpected tech results last week."

"But this is mine," Clara said. "My dummy trading account in the office is a mess. I doubled down on a currency pairing last week and really messed up."

"That's what the dummy trading account is for."

"I'd still have made the same mistakes if it was the real work account."

"That's what they're for," Francesca pressed. "Most people will go into a trading environment and either overthink or underthink. It's stressful, people want to prove themselves. Some will be lucky and it will pay off. Others will struggle. Trading in the office and trading at home are vastly different worlds. The dummy trading accounts are so you can get used to the environment, not learn how to trade. You already know that. It's not like we're letting people into the trainee scheme who have never heard of the NASDAQ."

Clara lowered the lip of the laptop. "I just feel stupid. I've made some bad trades. I'm pretty sure Meg thinks I'm an idiot."

"Meg has made plenty of mistakes of her own. She knows that this is a training environment. Please, give us another try. You have the passion, and that's the whole reason I set up the scheme. I don't want get-rich-quick wannabes."

Clara worried her lip and stared down at the closed laptop. There was something else, Francesca could feel it. There was something that she hadn't caught onto yet.

"Clara?"

"Might it be a conflict of interests?"

Francesca frowned. "What do you mean?"

"I mean, if I come back, and we're whatever we might be. Might that be a conflict of interests?"

Francesca smiled at the confirmation that she wasn't the only one feeling the magnetic pull bringing them both together.

"I don't believe so," she said. "I can be interested in not losing a promising trainee investor and interested in getting to know a fascinating woman who stole my pen without it being a problem."

Clara put the laptop back, a grin on her face. "How many times do I have to tell you that I didn't steal your pen?"

"A pen thief would say that," Francesca said.

Clara rested her head on the back of the sofa and turned to look at her. They'd edged closer and Francesca knew that a kiss was on the horizon. She tried to act unfazed, but the truth was that her heart was beating hard and she could feel a slight tremble in her leg. She didn't know how Clara affected her so but was addicted to the feeling.

"I'm wondering if you left the pen on my desk as a trap," Clara said, lowering her voice to a whisper. "Maybe this was all a way to lure me in."

"It would be quite the scheme," Francesca said softly.

"I think you're capable."

"I think you're worth it." Francesca leaned in closer and moved her hand to cup Clara's cheek. Clara leaned in a little closer but waited for Francesca to close the gap, which she eagerly did.

All thoughts fluttered away from Francesca's conscious mind. All that she could think of was soft, warm lips against hers and a feeling that all was right in the world. She knew instantly that it was what a kiss was supposed to be. Her heart felt light, exhilarated, and full to bursting. The need for more pulled at her, but she knew to take things slow. The importance of the feeling was not lost on her. She wanted to savour it, to treat it well, and to ensure she kept hold of it.

Clara was the one to break the kiss and leaned back. Her cheeks were red and her eyes wide. She looked exhausted and all Francesca wanted to do was hold her as she slept. But she knew that wouldn't be possible. Rushing things at this point could be disastrous. Clara was important in ways she hadn't thought possible until recently.

"I should go," Francesca said reluctantly.

"You could stay," Clara said. Her gaze bored into Francesca but there was a shadow of doubt detectable within them.

"It's been a long and emotional day. For both of us," Francesca said. She leaned a little forward and captured another kiss. This one softer, but she hoped just as meaningful. When she pulled back, she threaded her fingers through Clara's hair, eager to keep a connection between them. "I don't want to rush things and spoil anything."

"I don't want you to change your mind," Clara said.

"I won't," she said. "Can I see you tomorrow?"

Clara smiled and nodded. "I'd like that."

"I should go. It's getting late."

Francesca didn't want to leave but she knew it was the right thing to do. She needed time to acclimatise to this new feeling that was coursing through her body and mind. Fate had dealt her the opportunity to throw out previous ideas about what she wanted from a partner and realize that someone like Clara was what she'd been hoping to find all along. But she recognised that was a lot to put to Clara in such a short space of time. Francesca had always made fast decisions; it was in her nature to analyse a situation and reach steadfast conclusions in short order.

Clara scrunched up her nose and nodded her agreement. It was adorable and Francesca resisted the urge to kiss her again. With every kiss she knew her resolve to leave would crumble.

"Thank you for today," Francesca said.

Clara chuckled. "For what? Not stealing your pen? Admitting to a really embarrassing crush when I was a teenager?"

Francesca stood. She picked her coat up from the back of the armchair where she'd left it earlier. Clara stood as well.

"For being genuine and for making me laugh." She pressed a kiss to Clara's cheek. "And for stealing my pen."

Clara rolled her eyes, but the blush on her cheeks indicated that she'd appreciated the affection.

"Have I reclaimed my crown for being someone you'd like to be stuck in a lift with?" she asked as she picked up her bag and checked she had all her belongings with her.

"No, you have a lot of work to do," Clara said, a twinkle clear in her eye.

"Good, I look forward to the challenge. I have to go. I have a hot date tomorrow."

WINGS OVER BOSTON

Emily Smith

Chapter One

Ryland Matthews's Jeep was the only car left in the hospital parking lot by the time she emerged, exhausted and dirty, from the end of another sixteen-hour shift. Technically, this particular parking lot was only for the doctors. But Ryland didn't waste a lot of time with technicalities, and when one of the neurology residents she was sleeping with forgot her key fob to the lot's gate at her place before ghosting her a couple of months ago, she decided it would make an appropriate parting gift. God, she really had to stop fucking people she worked with. But where else was a queer flight medic supposed to meet girls? The scene in Boston was pathetic at best, and that basically left Tinder. Not that Ryland was above the occasional dating app. It was a quick and easy way to find someone, and about ten percent of the time at least resulted in getting laid. As her car let out a tired *blip blip* and she yanked the driver's side handle, Ryland remembered just how much she wanted all of the one-nighters and fun flings to end. And this was never more apparent than when she had to drive home to a very empty apartment.

To be fair, the apartment wasn't entirely empty. Rodrigo, her terrier mutt mix she'd rescued from the streets of Louisiana after Katrina, came bounding to the door like he did every night. His coarse, fluffy mess of a tail whipped through the air with a ferocity you wouldn't expect from something that weighed in at only fourteen pounds, and he leapt so high he nearly collided with Ryland's chest.

"Hey, buddy!" Like most proud pet owners, Ryland's voice seemed to jump two octaves whenever she addressed Rodrigo. Rodrigo continued to wag his tail with sheer joy and followed Ryland through the entryway of her tiny studio apartment. The TV was on. She always left ESPN on for Roddy when she was at work for the day and would inevitably come home to reruns of the earlier hours' *SportsCenter*. It could have easily been CNN or even cartoons, but at some point in their years together she'd convinced herself Roddy was a big sports fan, as if he had any idea what Max Kellerman was saying about Patrick Mahomes. An overhead light was dimly shining directly above her head. Otherwise, there were no signs of life. Most nights, Ryland tolerated the loneliness—maybe even embraced it. On her shorter days, she'd order a pizza and eat it on the bed while she watched a scary movie and fed Roddy leftover pieces of her crust. Life was comfortable and easy. And she never felt like she needed more.

Her job helped. Ryland absolutely loved her job, in a way most people weren't fortunate enough to. At eighteen, she took her first EMT course after watching a five-year-old boy nearly drown at the local beach in the small Cape Cod town Ryland had grown up in. It wasn't so much the well-known feeling of helplessness people describe when they lay eyes on a tragedy. It was the paramedics. After one of the lifeguards yanked the kid from the water, two paramedics in navy blue uniforms with aviator sunglasses and radios strapped to their belts ran through the sand and scooped the boy up onto their stretcher. In what seemed like no more than seven seconds they had him hooked up to their monitors and were listening to his lungs with their stethoscopes. Ryland had never seen anyone so cool in her entire life. Of course, she was only fifteen, so the bar was pretty low. In hindsight, it was probably the lifeguard who actually saved his life. But Ryland hated water, so paramedic seemed like a more reasonable life goal.

The airborne part of Ryland's career came many years later, when she realized that saving lives was even more exciting at ten thousand feet. And every day since she stepped foot in that Boston MedFlight chopper five years earlier was the new best professional day of her life.

Ryland had her own apartment in Jamaica Plain (one of the more up-and-coming neighborhoods in Boston), a good paying job that women found undeniably attractive, and the real love of her life, Roddy. It wasn't exactly part of the plan to be a single thirty-eight-year-old, but things could have been worse. Much worse.

Roddy sat at the end of the bed, his tail wrapped around his wiry little body, as Ryland ate a bowl of Cinnamon Toast Crunch a few feet away. Eating in bed was one of her few bad habits. But she figured it was her space, and if she wanted to eat cereal in bed she damn well could. An episode of *The Simpsons* was on the small TV in the corner of the apartment, but Ryland was only half paying attention, focusing most of her energy on scrolling through Instagram to admire the lives of everyone she hardly knew.

Social media was probably one of the worst things to happen to the world. All you had to do was open an app, and in one click, the girl who hated you in high school was modeling in New York, the ex-girlfriend you were never really that into was now engaged to someone marginally better looking than you and taking stunning photos on their Maui vacation, and your coworkers were all out dancing and drinking their brains out and looking beautiful doing it. Ryland was smart enough to know most of it was bullshit. But it didn't keep the pangs of jealousy at bay as she thought about the voids in her life even sugary cereal couldn't fill. It also didn't keep her from an at least twice-daily browsing of the thrilling and perfect lives of everyone she sort of knew.

When a picture of her last failed "talking stage" popped up, decked out in a sundress with perfect long curls propped in front of a sunset with the love interest that Ryland had lost out to, it was time to shut it down for the night. Roddy let out a tiny groan, and Ryland felt judged.

"What? I know, I know. I'll stop, okay?" She shook her head. Why was it that every time she thought she was content on her own, she seemed to catch herself mid-conversation with a dog?

❖

It wasn't often that Tess Goodwin's phone pinged at midnight. At the ancient age of thirty-two, most people in her life knew Tess had downed a hefty dose of melatonin and been horizontal for at least a good few hours by then. Even with the sleeping aids on board, Tess had always been a light sleeper, so it wasn't surprising that the sound roused her awake. A moment of confusion was replaced with downright terror as her anxious mind suddenly kicked into full speed. Was it her mom? Did something happen to her? She was healthy but almost in her seventies now. Maybe she had a heart attack? Oh God. No, that didn't make much sense. Anyone trying to get ahold of her to tell her something awful had happened to her parents probably wouldn't text her. It was definitely an ex then. Tess hadn't gotten a "you up?" text in months. In fact, her date card (and her bed) had been pretty empty for the last six months or so. But that kind of thing happened to people all the time, right?

That particular muddled heap of thoughts actually only took about two-point-five seconds to blast through Tess's mind like a demolition before she fumbled with the clutter on her nightstand until she found her phone. She squinted as she held it inches from her face, nearly blind without her glasses on.

Huh, that was odd. She didn't recognize the number.

Hi Tess, this is Adam with PrideStar. We need your help. One of the pilots with Boston called out sick tomorrow and they're desperate for a fill-in. Any chance you could help? Sorry it's so late.

Tess was wide awake now, and not even a whole bottle of melatonin would help. PrideStar was the little med flight company she worked for down in Providence. They were mostly private but were affiliated with the big boys, Boston MedFlight. Any pilot who stood even a dream of a chance of running with them usually started with PrideStar and worked their way in. Tess had been waiting three years to get the chance to fly with them. If she could make some connections, it was possible she could make the switch.

She smiled and closed her eyes, already dreaming of a cute apartment in a quaint Boston neighborhood overlooking the Charles River. The fantasy was so colorful she quickly realized she had yet to actually reply to Adam's text.

Yes! Of course. Happy to help.

It was supposed to be her day off tomorrow—her first day off in twelve. But Tess didn't care. This was too good to pass up. She hit the lock button on her phone one more time to light the screen up. It was already almost one a.m., and she had to wake up at five a.m. to make it to Boston for six thirty a.m.—better make it four thirty a.m. just in case there was traffic.

Tess jostled Max, the fat, orange cat sleeping at her feet. "Max, wake up, buddy." Max didn't even open his eyes. "We're heading to the big time, baby."

❖

No one would have called Ryland a morning person. In fact, she loved everything about her job except for the daily five thirty a.m. wake-up call. Most people grew out of the majority of their morning-grumpiness by the time they left their mid-twenties. Not Ryland. Over the years, she'd found ways to make it work. Her Mr. Coffee was on a very strict timer, and there was always a fresh three cups for her to start with before she even hit the shower. The first cup or two usually did the trick, but for particularly brutal mornings (especially in the winter), Ryland actually brought her coffee with her into the shower like a college kid sneaking a beer. By six fifteen a.m., when she made her way out to her car, Ryland was usually some semblance of a human being. But she always knew by the time she made it into work, the adrenaline rush of knowing she was about to have someone's life in her hands at ten thousand feet above Boston would take over.

The med flight hangar wasn't really in Boston. The city was cramped enough for real estate without throwing in what was essentially an airfield. Instead, Ryland actually started her day in the town of Bedford, Massachusetts, every shift. The hangar was about fifteen miles north of the city, in a rural area about halfway between Boston and the New Hampshire border. Ryland usually used the thirty-minute commute to play whatever her music artist of the moment was. Today was *The 1975*. She'd probably do what she always did, which was play the album on repeat until she was so tired of it she wanted to vomit, then she'd move on to the next.

It was an absolutely perfect New England fall morning. The September sun wasn't as high as it had been a couple of weeks earlier, and the air was clear and warm without the assault of the daily humidity that had hung around through the entire month of August. It was warm enough for the top to be off Ryland's Jeep Wrangler, and her mop of hair flew everywhere. A pair of aviator sunglasses sat on her nose. It was all she ever wore. In fact, she liked to joke that Joe Biden stole the look from her. Her blue jumpsuit with the MedFlight patch on the sleeve that read "Your life. Our mission." was still one of her coolest pieces of clothing. Every time she put it on, she still felt like Tom Cruise in *Top Gun*. And it definitely didn't hurt that women absolutely loved it. Ryland's Tinder profile included at least three photos decked out in the uniform, complete with a black stethoscope around her neck and a confident grin. She wasn't insecure. And maybe in her baby-dyke days she was more than a little cocky. But she was settled—confident in herself. But something about that uniform made Ryland feel like a fucking badass.

She couldn't help but smile as she sang along (badly) to "The Sound." The station was just around the corner and Ryland was early. There was time to stop at Dunkin' for a gigantic iced coffee. This was the best kind of day.

The day was so great, and Ryland's mood so high, that she decided to pick up a dozen doughnuts too. As she headed back to her Jeep, she grinned at a little boy who was gawking at her from a corner booth. Ryland knew she had the downright coolest job in the entire world. And she also was often humbly reminded just how lucky she was to take care of people on the worst day of their lives.

Ryland's partner of the last two years, Mitch Nyland, stood outside the hangar when she pulled in. He was older than her by about ten years, and his hair had a handsome hint of gray that Ryland always envied. Mitch was an RN. And a goddamn good one at that. He'd bailed Ryland out of more than one hairy situation in their time together. Along with that, she liked him—a lot. He was much quieter than Ryland, and his humor was so dry it was easy to overlook. But if you listened closely, Mitch was one of the funniest people Ryland had ever met.

"You know each doughnut you eat takes thirty-two minutes off your life expectancy?" Mitch expertly raised one eyebrow as Ryland jostled with the box of pastries.

"Did you know the odds of a helicopter crashing are about one in one hundred thousand?"

Mitch just shook his head pensively for a while before one corner of his mouth finally curled upward a little.

"It's going to be a fucking fantastic day, my friend. Just fucking fantastic."

❖

Tess believed most pilots were probably introverts at heart, and she was no exception. She much preferred the solitude and space of the sky to the cramped, people-littered earth below. Not that a helicopter was the best place to avoid human interaction. The H145 Airbus she would be flying today was a tiny little twin engine, which didn't leave a ton of breathing room once you tossed in a sick patient, an RN, and a medic. Tess only hoped she would like the crew she was assigned to. It was going to be a long day if she got stuck with a talker, or even worse, the awkwardly silent type. Tess already had that role good and filled.

After she locked the doors to her Honda, Tess stuffed the keys in her jumpsuit pocket and let her hands follow. She meandered to the open hangar, the familiar anxiety settling as a quickening of her pulse and a tightening just beneath her chest. New jobs were like first dates, or parties with people you didn't really know—uncomfortable social pressure-cookers. And to add steam to the cooker, Tess really, really wanted to work for Boston. This was her shot, maybe her only shot, and she had to be on her game.

Standing just inside the hangar's shadow were two people, one much taller than the other and seemingly a little older, although it was hard to tell from that distance. As Tess got closer, her legs trembled a little with that expected first-meeting terror. Twenty-five feet away or so now, the trembling turned to full-blown liquidation. Her knees refused to straighten, and she was afraid if she took even one more step she would collapse on the hot pavement in an embarrassing pile. Tess knew exactly who she was looking at.

❖

"I heard Todd banged out for today?" Ryland was deftly sipping on her iced coffee as she took a seat on one of the chopper's landing skids, completely unaware of the petite redhead in a PrideStar suit walking slowly toward them.

"Yeah. Pneumonia, I think. But he's okay. They just won't let him work until he's cleared. Speak of the devil. I think this may be our fill-in headed our way," Mitch said.

Ryland tipped her chin toward the hangar entrance. She was fully expecting John Zabloski or Ace McKenna or one of the other per-diem pilots to be standing in front of her. She felt her eyes bug involuntarily and her heart skidded a little out of its usually slow rhythmic cadence. It wasn't John. It wasn't Ace either. It was Tess Goodwin—a very remote, occasionally revisited piece of Ryland's past.

Chapter Two

"Wow. I…I was not expecting this."

Tess was eternally grateful Ryland still had trouble keeping her mouth shut, easing the burden of deciding who was going to acknowledge who first.

"I guess I should have considered it, since I knew you worked here." Tess offered a cordial smile. After all, there were no hard feelings left between them. What had happened was a month or so of casual sex, a few Netflix binges, and a lot of takeout. Ryland had said she wasn't looking for anything serious, and Tess, albeit a bit wounded, took the whole thing in stride. They kept in touch for a while after, and when Ryland left to go work for Boston, Tess was fine. So maybe "fine" wasn't the word. But she sure as hell wasn't sitting up at night listening to Taylor Swift and crying her eyes out. Tess had liked Ryland. She'd wanted to see if things could go any further. And every now and then, over the few years since they'd seen each other, Ryland would cross her mind, if only for a minute or two.

"You're saying you haven't been thinking about me after all this time?" Ryland tossed Tess one of her terrible winks that always made her look more frightened than flirtatious, and Tess couldn't help but burst out laughing.

"How old are you now, Ry? Like, forty? I thought for sure you'd have at least considered adulthood by now."

Ryland feigned offense and crossed her arms, which Tess could see were just as defined as they were years ago, if not more so, even through her blue sleeves. She looked good. Really good, actually. Ryland had always joked about "aging like a fine wine" and she didn't seem to be wrong yet. Her brown hair was cut short on the sides but a little longer on top than it had been the last time Tess had seen her, and she had just a few more wrinkles at the sides of her eyes that made her look a little cleverer, and a lot sexier. There was no harm in admitting that, right? It wasn't like Tess had been pining away for her all these years, waiting for Ryland to change her mind about continuing their relationship. She'd dated plenty of people since then. There was nothing wrong with acknowledging that this woman who she'd slept with a million years ago looked damn good.

"Okay. Well, ouch? First of all, I'm thirty-eight. And don't pretend you don't know that."

Tess did know that. She knew that Ryland was a whole six years older than her, and it only took a quick second of math to know Ryland was actually only thirty-eight, not forty years old. But the jab felt playful and appropriate in the moment.

"It's been a while. I guess I forgot." Tess grinned and flicked her eyebrows quickly. Fucking hell. The flirting was already starting.

"Shit. I'm—wow. I mean, it's great to see you, Tess." Ryland shifted her feet in an uncharacteristically awkward fashion and then held her arms out. "Can I uh…can I give you a hug or something?"

Tess wasn't a hugger in general. In fact, she kind of hated people touching her. There were of course exceptions, though. On most first dates, Tess would make sure she was holding her jacket or had something conspicuous in her hands to avoid anyone trying to hug her. But she was always comfortable with Ryland—even before they'd actually slept together. Even as coworkers, Ryland had always put Tess at ease with her charm and confidence. It didn't hurt her case that Tess found her painfully attractive either.

"Duh." Tess closed the gap between them and Ryland wrapped her up tightly, and for just a little bit too long—enough for Tess to feel just the slightest pang of something ancient stirring inside her. Ryland still smelled the same as she did years ago, and Tess was surprised by the total familiarity of it. It was some mix of musk and ocean air and a little hint of coffee that wafted off the skin of Ryland's bare neck as Tess pressed her face against her. One of them finally pulled away, she wasn't sure which, and it wasn't until then that Tess remembered there was someone else standing there with them.

"Hi. Mitch Nyland, RN." The tall nurse who had been probably awkwardly waiting for Tess and Ryland to end their *L Word* reunion had a face stiller than a funeral and Tess was sure she'd been there for less than ten minutes and he already hated her.

"Oh my God, I'm so sorry. I'm Tess. Goodwin. The uh, pilot?"

"You don't sound very sure about that, Tess Goodwin. Is this your first day flying?" Mitch's tone was flat and cold, and Tess's stomach lurched. This was not a good start. Not a good start at all. Before she could think of anything to say, she automatically looked to Ryland, an old reflex, she guessed. Ryland had this presence about her that always projected strength and safety to Tess. Maybe it was their age difference, or maybe it was just part of Ryland's DNA. But even now Tess found herself turning to Ryland for help. She was glad she did. Because Ryland was smiling bigger than the sun was bright that morning, and when her eyes met Tess's, she burst out laughing.

"He's fucking with you, Tess. I'm sorry." Ryland could hardly contain herself at this point, a few tears snaking their way out both eyes. "Mitch is an asshole. It'll take you years to figure out if he's joking or not."

"Oh. Oh." Tess felt her cheeks burn and she joined in Ryland's laughter, although with not quite as much enthusiasm.

"Seriously. I'm kidding," Mitch said, still not cracking even a hint of a smile. "She's right, I'm an asshole. Welcome aboard. We're happy to have you."

With that, Mitch gracefully turned and made his way into the hallows of the hangar, presumably to somewhere indoors far away from the sexual tension that was so clearly not left behind three years earlier.

❖

Goddamn, Tess looked like a million fucking bucks and then some. She'd always been attractive, but the last few years had really done something to her. Age? Wisdom? Or was it that undeniable glow of happiness that only came from finding someone you were head over heels in love with? That had to be it. Ryland's mind immediately spun a dozen scenarios about what Tess had been up to since they last saw each other. She was probably married now—disgustingly ecstatically married to some sexy woman in the suburbs with a solid 401(k) and maybe even some foreign investments. And kids? Maybe there were even kids now. Ryland groaned internally. Why was she so resentful of the theoretical happiness of someone she slept with a handful of times a million years back? Maybe that was just human nature? Or maybe misery really did love company.

"So. Tess. Tell me, what's been going on with you?" Ryland pursed her lips and nodded in a sad attempt at some version of casual swagger that probably just made her look contrived and ridiculous.

"Not a whole lot. You know, same old, same old." Tess seemed to mirror Ryland's stab at casual, and almost as unsuccessfully too. It was several seconds before Ryland realized her eyes had drifted down to Tess's left hand, searching for a ring.

"Mmm. Good, good." Ryland nodded again and bounced up onto the balls of her feet.

"Yeah. Totally. Working a lot. I am, I mean. I'm still at PrideStar. Still living in Providence." Tess sucked in her bottom lip and Ryland's stomach tightened a little. It had been a good, long four and a half months since she'd had sex, and she was suddenly very reminded of that fact.

"How's Providence treating you? You still like it? I miss it there sometimes. I mean, Boston's great. I love it. But it's just a very different city."

"I still really like it. But I'll be honest, I was psyched to get this gig last night. I've been trying to get into MedFlight for years. I'd love to make this a more permanent thing." Tess's cheeks colored nearly immediately, and she balled her hands into loose fists that hung near her hips. "I mean, the job. I'd love to make the job a more permanent thing. Not this, this." She pointed quickly, first at Ryland's chest, then at her own.

Ryland relaxed a little, fully realizing that Tess was much more nervous than she was.

"I knew what you were getting at." She laughed coyly.

"Wow. This is—"

"Awkward?" Ryland finished.

They both chuckled a little. "Yes. Why is this so weird?"

"Hmm. I'd say it's probably because we've seen each other naked."

The color returned to Tess's cheeks, and she diverted her gaze far to the left of Ryland's. Ryland had always rattled Tess like this, and

Ryland absolutely loved it. What had gone wrong with them anyway? It wasn't even a question worth asking. Ryland knew the answer. Three years ago, Ryland was a mess. And for a thirty-five-year-old, she had a lot of growing up to do. She seemed to have gone from one failed relationship to another for far too long, and by the time she met Tess, Ryland was already done. Tess was in that uncomfortable stage of her late twenties where she was looking to get wifed-up as soon as possible while also not really seeming to know herself well enough yet to make the best choices. She was sweet, and fun, and sharp as a goddamn dagger. And the sex was undeniably some of the best of Ryland's life. It wasn't just physical either. For that month that they were together, however "casually," Tess spent the night several times a week. And Ryland had never forgotten the way she'd fall asleep with her head on Ryland's chest and wake up with it still there. More than that, though, Ryland remembered the rush she felt knowing Tess was next to her. It wasn't the kind of rush that came with easy, torrid hookups. It was the kind that came from actual feelings.

Somehow, though, Ryland had managed to convince herself that they weren't real feelings—that Tess was just filling a void in her fragile ego, or occupying the lonely nights. As Ryland looked at Tess that morning, she acknowledged without a doubt that was not it. And denial was a powerful force.

"You okay? You've been staring at me all funny for like, a solid five minutes now," Tess finally said, snapping Ryland out of what was clearly an embarrassingly long duration of reminiscence.

"Yeah." Ryland smiled. The urge to retort with a protectively flirtatious line hit strong, but she pushed it down. Tess had always been real with her, and she owed it to Tess to do the same finally. "It's just really good to see you."

Tess looked bashfully at her feet and a few strands of red hair fell perfectly over her face. Man, Ryland did not remember her being this hot.

"It's good to see you too, Ry."

"So, look. Down to business. We have to get you a new jumpsuit. That PrideStar thing isn't going to work here." Ryland was relieved to have something concrete to talk about that could distract her from Tess's green eyes that she just couldn't seem to quite stop looking into.

"Do I get to keep it?" Tess grinned.

"I won't tell if you won't." Ryland attempted her sad wink, wondering why everything they said ultimately felt like innuendo.

❖

It turned out there was an entire crew's quarters in the back of the hangar, although Tess wasn't really thinking about the architecture of the small airfield. Not when she was disconcertingly hung up on the gravel vibrato of Ryland's voice and her full, pink mouth that she still remembered kissing in excruciating detail. Ryland would always go down in Tess's book as one of the absolute best kissers ever. That kind of superlative was hard to forget.

"This should fit," Ryland said after rummaging through a closet full to the top of royal blue flight suits. She tossed one behind her, hitting Tess square in the chest.

"Thanks." Tess studied her surroundings for a minute, trying to decide what her next move was. Did she ask for a bathroom and come across like a prude? Did she strip down right there like the cool girl she always wanted to be? Ryland had turned her back and was busy folding the rest of the flight suits that she'd flung onto the floor. Tess bent over and untied the laces of her black boots. She took her time standing up, and when she did she reached for the zipper near her neck and slid it down, the suit she was currently wearing opening all the way down to her crotch. She pulled her arms out and the suit fell, gathering around her ankles. She wasn't entirely exposed, standing there in a pair of very short gym shorts and a sports bra (it was still too hot that time of year to wear anything else underneath). Besides, Ryland wasn't even paying attention.

Just as Tess picked up the new suit and started to step out of the old one, Ryland looked up from the pile of jumpsuits she'd begun to pretend to fold. Her chin dropped a little and her eyes widened, and Tess now realized she'd made the very intentional decision to undress in front of Ryland, in hopes of this very look.

"Oh. Okay. You...Uh, there's a bathroom if you want to use it?" Ryland's words came out in a machinery-like stutter that left Tess feeling unusually in control. Most things in Tess's life were about control. Hell, her job was to literally pilot helicopters. But there was always something about Ryland that melted that control into a useless puddle. And Tess liked it. She never liked the term "Pillow Princess," but she certainly didn't mind when Ryland had her way behind closed doors. That wasn't that unusual for Tess, though. She'd always been a bit of a bottom. The unusual part came outside of the bedroom. Ryland remained in control, in the least asshole-like way Tess could imagine. There was a quiet, calm strength about her that always made Tess feel like she could just let go.

"Are you blushing, Ryland? My God. I had no idea you were so bashful." Tess took full advantage of the rare glance of power she'd been gifted, her tone light and teasing.

"I have no idea what you're talking about."

They were alone in a small back closet near one of the bunks. Mitch was nowhere to be found, and the faint echoes of other crews and station workers were far enough away that Tess had to fight the very transient urge to slowly saunter up to Ryland and run a hand through her thick, wild hair, just daring Ryland to kiss her. Thankfully, the urge was just that—transient. Or, if not the urge, then at least the actual consideration of the idea. Ryland was as magnetic a force as ever, and Tess hadn't touched a woman in…God, how long had it been now? Eight, ten months? Anyway, it had at least been long enough to make her palms sweat a little at the very hint of someone else's skin against hers. Even Ryland's looks and charm, though, were no match for Tess's pride surrounding her career. She would never dream of risking chances of making it to Boston MedFlight for a quick fuck in a supply closet with a woman who'd made it very evident years earlier she wasn't interested.

"So, what happens now?" Tess asked, trying to shift her thoughts away from ideas of Ryland pinning her hands against the wall as she taunted her with that ridiculous mouth. The attempt was only marginally successful.

"What do you mean?"

"Come on. This is MedFlight. I figured we'd be wheels up by now, scraping trauma victims off the highways or whatever."

Ryland feigned a shudder. "Yikes. That's dark." She laughed.

"Sorry." Tess realized she sounded a little psychopathic and her shoulders bunched involuntarily in embarrassment. Before Ryland had a chance to answer, a loud crackle came from an overhead speaker, followed by a prolonged beep that always sent a visceral rush of adrenaline through Tess. The sound of a call coming in was pretty much the same at every station.

"MedFlight Air Unit 9, please respond to Monadnock Community Hospital in Peterborough, New Hampshire, for transport of a forty-two-year-old male status post cardiac arrest, currently intubated, pressors running, being transferred to Mass General for consideration for ECMO. Details to follow." The speaker hissed and sputtered once more and then went silent.

"There we are," Ryland said.

"Let's do it." Tess was a little surprised that their first call was a transfer from a community hospital. She always figured MedFlight did a lot more trauma response than PrideStar. But Tess didn't care what the call was. She just wanted to fly.

"We'll leave in about ten," Ryland said. "Do what you need to, and I'll go track down Mitch. He's probably reading *Good Housekeeping* on the toilet again."

Tess laughed and Ryland disappeared down the hallway. Tess hadn't been paying particularly good attention on their trip to the supply room, and for someone who made her living on her navigational skills, she wasn't entirely sure she could find her way back to the hangar. That would be humiliating—being late for her first MedFlight call because she got lost inside the station.

It wasn't an issue, though. Tess's sense of direction was always reliable, and today wasn't the day it failed her. She easily retraced a couple of turns down some dark halls, past a few closed doors and a dimly lit conference room with a few CPR dummies lying creepily on tables like possessed mannequins in a horror movie, until she arrived in the open air of the hangar. Tess hadn't had a chance to do her flight check yet, so she was glad she had a few minutes to familiarize herself with the Airbus. It was nearly identical to the bird she flew with PrideStar, but she wanted to be sure everything was in order anyway. She climbed into the cockpit and flipped the ignition switch, letting the rotors begin their slow windup. The sound of the blades cutting through the air was always immensely satisfying to Tess. Tucked inside the door panel was a binder with a laminated checklist.

"Flight controls? Free and correct." Tess always preferred to perform her checks out loud. "Throttle." She placed her hand on the handle that jutted out to her right. "Closed. Instruments? Static at zero."

"I see you still talk to yourself when you do your checks." Ryland's voice startled Tess to the point of nearly falling out of her seat.

"It works for me, okay?"

"We just about ready to go?" Mitch stood quietly a couple of feet behind Ryland.

"All ready."

"Wheels up then." Ryland jumped in the back of the chopper.

Tess rolled her eyes. "Can you stop talking like you're in *Top Gun?*"

"Not a chance, Goose."

"Wait, why am I Goose? I want to be Maverick. I'm the pilot. It only makes sense." Tess picked up the aviators that had been hanging around her neck and coolly slid them on.

"You can't be Maverick. I'm Maverick," Ryland said dryly.

"And why not?"

"Because it's my bird?"

Mitch cleared his throat from the seat next to Ryland and they both fell silent. "Whenever you two are done, I'm sure the gentleman in New Hampshire who needs a machine to keep him alive would appreciate it if we got going? But, you know, no rush." Aside from Mitch's lips, his face hardly moved. Tess's heart slid a little further toward her stomach. She'd already been mortified at least four or five times that morning.

CHAPTER THREE

Watching Tess navigate the bird's controls was always a bit of a religious experience for Ryland. Her small, delicate hands worked their way over the throttle with a strength and a certainty that seemed in opposition to her usually well-manicured nails. When they used to fly together with PrideStar, Ryland always made a point to sit in the jump seat directly behind Tess just to watch her work.

"Your takeoffs have gotten really smooth," Ryland said through the bulky headset that allowed them to speak through the whir of the rotors.

"A lot of practice," Tess said. "And are you mansplaining flying to me?" Her tone was matter-of-fact but she couldn't seem to hide the hint of a proud grin that crept onto her face.

"Jesus. Are you two going to be able to keep your clothes on for at least the rest of this call?" Ryland had almost forgotten Mitch was there too, and the radio channel on his headset was very much connected to theirs.

"We're old coworkers, Mitch. Friends." The wording felt forced even to Ryland's ears.

Mitch held up a hand. "I don't want to know, actually." He feigned a dramatic shudder and then pantomimed some epic vomiting in a performance that should have won him some kind of award, or at least red carpet appearance, and Ryland felt her face heat up.

"I get it. Details will be kept to a minimum."

"I appreciate that," Mitch said, nodding.

"Oh, and, Tess, since you can't see him back here, Mitch is joking again," Ryland shouted, as if Tess's headphones had some idea how far away she was sitting.

"No, I'm really not," Mitch snapped.

"Okay, not about the details part. But he's joking about being a total asshole."

"Noted." Tess chuckled.

Ryland took off her headset for a second and motioned for Mitch, who was sitting directly to her left, to do the same. She was pretty sure Mitch knew her well enough to know what she was about to say, but she didn't want to take any chances.

"Look, you know me. I love this job. And nothing would keep me from doing it well. I hope you know that."

"I do know that, Matthews." In a rare moment of earnestness, Mitch smiled and punched her in the shoulder. "And I'm not worried."

Ryland laughed and went to put her headset back on.

"But it is really gross!" Mitch shouted over the roar of the air between them.

A short twenty minutes later, Tess landed the chopper with a sense of ease on the helipad of the small community hospital in New Hampshire. A switch had flipped in all three of them. The friendly banter wound down with the engines, and a sense of urgency settled in around them. Now that they were there, they had a job to do, and all of their focus needed to be on that.

On the outside, that would be absolutely no problem for Ryland. But it was hard not to notice the way Tess's flight suit squeezed her ass when she walked. Not when she still remembered exactly what Tess looked like naked. Just before Tess prepared to disembark from the chopper, she reached up and gathered her long, fiery hair into a thick ponytail and pulled it to the back of her head with a grace, a confidence, that made Ryland's legs quake just a little as she tried to step out. Ryland could do her job—that was without question. But that didn't mean she was going to be able to keep herself from thinking about getting her pilot naked every now and then.

"You can wait out here, if you want," Mitch said to Tess. "The pilots don't have to come in."

"It's okay. I like to see what all these different small-town hospitals are like. I find them charming."

Ryland couldn't help but smile as she guided the cot with the attached heavy monitoring equipment to the door of the helipad and onto the elevator. Tess had a sweetness about her, a joy that most people, especially people in medicine, just didn't. It was something Ryland certainly couldn't claim for herself. And it was nice to be around. In fact, it always had been.

A security guard directed them up to the ICU, which looked like it was only big enough to hold about four patients. Two of the beds were empty. One held a very elderly man on a ventilator, the only signs of life the unnaturally rhythmic rise and fall of his frail chest. A slightly younger woman sat next to him holding his hand, seemingly having a full-on conversation as if they'd talked over breakfast like this for fifty years. They probably had. These were the kind of things that still made Ryland sad after all these years of becoming hardened and, as she sometimes worried, nearly heartless. Old people die. Hell, young people die. And a lot of the time, there's nothing anyone can do about it—even the best medics, or the best nurses, or the best doctors. It's part of the circle of life. That part hardly ever got to her anymore. What did still bother her was the people who loved the dying that got left behind. Ryland only had a few seconds to glance into this man's room before she was pulled away to pick up his neighbor, but it was enough to drum up an entire folklore of their life together.

She imagined they'd been married young—he was twenty-one, she was nineteen. They'd only known each other a few months, too. The dying man, now weak and fully dependent on machines to keep him breathing, was wild and in love, and he actually had to win the woman away from another man she was already promised to. Her parents probably didn't want her to pick this guy because he was too poor, but she loved him.

Ryland quickly realized she was basically just recapping the plot of the movie *The Notebook*. But still, it made her sad nonetheless. And something about the way the woman continued talking to him, about what Ryland couldn't make out, like nothing was wrong, nagged at Ryland's slightly brittle heart.

What was worse? To be the dying man in the bed, probably too drugged out to have any idea what was going on, but obviously loved endlessly by this woman? Or to be the wife—about to be left behind in a world she won't recognize any longer? No. There was a third possibility. And it terrified the shit out of Ryland. She didn't want to be the one in the bed, alone, with no one to miss her.

"Ry? You okay?" Tess spoke slowly, gently, as if she might wake Ryland from a night terror.

"Huh? Oh yeah. Sorry, I was just looking at those two in there. It's sad, isn't it?"

"Actually, I think it's kind of beautiful," Tess said, shifting her gaze into the man's room. "To have that kind of love? To have lived that kind of life? I bet he has no regrets."

"None? Come on. Everyone has regrets. Maybe he really wanted to go skydiving but she would never let him. Or maybe he missed an epic trip to the Arctic because he knocked her up. Everyone regrets something."

"Do you? You know, regret anything?"

Ryland's pulse doubled. She knew exactly what Tess was asking her. And although she'd thought of Tess and their time together a thousand times over the years, she wouldn't have said she regretted the way things ended. At least, not until seeing her that morning in the hangar.

"They're ready for us, guys," Mitch said.

Ryland forced out a gust of air so quickly her lips flapped together loudly. She was grateful for Mitch's interruption. There was a lot more to say about the topic—more than Tess had any idea about. Tess was probably thinking a simple "no" would have sufficed for Ryland. But that wasn't the case. Maybe "regret" wasn't the right word. But there were absolutely all kinds of second thoughts running through Ryland's head. And the hallway of the ICU was not the place to be talking about them.

Right person, wrong time. Ryland wasn't sure why the phrase suddenly jumped into her brain like an amoeba, but it did. And she couldn't get it out.

❖

The problem with Ryland Matthews was that she was addictive. Miraculously, Tess had managed to forget that for several years. And then, like a loaded shotgun aimed at her head, it came back to her. By the time Ryland told her things between them couldn't go any further, it was already far too late. Tess was addicted to nearly every part of her—the way she laughed at *The Golden Girls* reruns they'd watch late at night, the swing in her step as she sauntered through the station, the soft but absolutely certain way she'd touch her fingers to Tess's lips just before she kissed her. Yet somehow, in what had to be the most impressive case of elective amnesia in history, Tess had managed to forget all of that. The narrative she'd created in her head was something entirely different. It started off based somewhere in reality, with the thrill and shiny newness of infatuation. But the ending was altogether different. The ending Tess had crafted was something along the lines of a relatively mutual one, with both parties walking away unscathed.

She watched as Ryland carefully tucked the straps around the unconscious man who they'd just moved onto their cot, the little vertical line between Ryland's eyes sharp as her face focused. Her lips were pursed just slightly, and another incredibly awkward wave of lust crested over Tess. This was the problem with Ryland. She was like a drug. Of course, Tess had never really done drugs before, except for the few joints in college she'd smoked and the one time she accidentally rolled on Molly thinking it was a Zofran tab her roommate had left in their bathroom cabinet. But there was definitely something about Ryland that Tess just couldn't get enough of back then. Or maybe it was nearly everything about Ryland? The timing of her very juvenile fixation was entirely inappropriate in that moment, watching Ryland and Mitch package up this poor patient who needed their help. But she couldn't help it. A flood of what must have been repressed memories hit Tess square in the head. There were so many times when they'd worked together that she found herself beyond distracted by Ryland's mere existence. Nearly every shift together meant Tess quietly eavesdropping and watching out the periphery of her vision as Ryland simply was. All Ryland had to do was open that unbelievable mouth, or run a hand through her messy hair, and Tess was completely transfixed. The only exception was when she was actually flying or had to keep her focus to avoid killing them all. It was actually pathetic. No wonder her brain had shoved all of those memories into some dark little corner to, hopefully, never reemerge again. And they probably wouldn't have, either, if she hadn't shown up at the fucking hangar that morning.

"You okay?" The low growl of Ryland's voice rocked Tess out of her teenage daydream, which only embarrassed her even more.

"Absolutely. I'll head on back to the bird and get it fired up." Tess tried to keep her tone as cool as she could, terrified that Ryland would somehow have any idea what she'd been thinking for the last five minutes. She wasn't entirely sure it worked, because Ryland flashed her a coy grin that Tess had seen several times before—it was the look Ryland would give her when she caught Tess staring at her while she restocked the helicopter, or when Tess would get so flustered she'd produce just the slightest hint of a stutter, a few red patches popping up on her neck. It was the look Ryland gave her when she knew Tess was smitten. *Fuck me.*

There was nothing left to do but roll her eyes at her own internal dialogue and walk out to the helipad. *Get it together, will you, Tess?*

Tess was a skilled enough pilot at this point to think and fly at the same time. That didn't mean go into a full-blown waking dream, but it did mean she could use the time to clear out some of the garbage that had just blown its way into her brain revolving directly around Ryland.

The flight was only about twenty minutes from takeoff to touchdown, but it was enough time for Tess to get her shit together. She focused on her yoga breathing she'd mastered over the years—breathe in for a count of three, and out for a count of five. Hold. Repeat. You were a dumb kid, she told herself. It was only three years since she pined after Ryland like a lovesick puppy. But she was only twenty-nine then. To some, that's plenty of time to get married, buy a house, and even push out a handful of kids. But Tess at twenty-nine had just barely figured out who she was. Her weak sense of self and quietly deep-seated insecurities made it easy to fall for someone as big as Ryland. She was older than Tess and had vast amounts of experience with love and women in comparison. Not to mention she was well-established in her career and incredibly admired at work by just about everyone. The power dynamic was clear. Ryland was a bit of a narcissist who enjoyed the attention, and Tess had a big crush and significant daddy issues—an explosive yet ultimately toxic combination.

But now was not three years ago. Tess had grown up. She knew herself. She liked herself. And she hadn't spent much time with Ryland yet, but there was a humility about her that hadn't been there before. Maybe they'd both grown up.

After another nearly perfect landing, Tess closed her eyes, took one more deep breath, and smiled to herself, her head now as clear as the sky she'd just navigated them through.

❖

A lot of what Ryland did on the job these days was managed on autopilot. When you've been practicing the same skill set for over a decade, some things just become second nature. Stable but still critically ill patients were her most commonly encountered. And they didn't take a lot of critical thinking most of the time. The patient on the cot in front of her had a tiny portable ventilator breathing for him, a handful of IV pumps all set to automatically administer the correct medications in the correct amounts, and even his vital signs were all set to be taken without prompting. Really, most of her patients were being kept alive by machines, and much of that work, on transports at least, was already done for her by the time she arrived. Ryland was there to do what machines couldn't—divert a crisis if and when it occurred. Thankfully, the short trip to bring Mr. Reynolds to Boston was void of all crises.

Ryland often found herself wishing for a little stress on some of her transports, just to keep things extra spicy. But not that day. She was far too distracted by the free strands of Tess's fiery hair that occasionally tried to escape her ponytail under the influence of the chopper's overhead fan. Every now and then she caught the scent of her shampoo and Ryland would almost reflexively suck in her lower lip and close her eyes, thinking about how it had been months since she'd kissed a girl, and right now, all she wanted was to be kissing Tess.

She felt foolish—like some sort of infatuated kid who was about to get laid for the first time. This level of distraction couldn't continue for the rest of the shift or something bad was definitely going to happen.

CHAPTER FOUR

"How about the MGH cafeteria?" Mitch said once they had safely dropped Mr. Reynolds off in the Massachusetts General Hospital ICU. The great lunch debate had begun. Another call could come in at any minute, but it was almost noon, and there was no telling when they'd get the chance to eat again.

"Mitch, we have company. Can we do something a little more elegant?" Ryland scoffed and then turned to Tess with a look that pleaded chivalry. Tess was charmed. But she was always charmed by Ryland. She also knew better. She knew that Ryland was too good at being chivalrous. She could smile and flirt her way into a million girls' beds with her bad white-suburban-dad dance moves and veil of self-deprecation. But once she was there, you were so completely hers that it didn't matter if she walked out the next day. And she always did.

"I'm fine with the cafeteria, really," Tess said.

"How about sushi? You still like sushi, don't you?" Ryland coaxed her.

"How did you remember that?"

Ryland grinned at her and took a half a step closer so their shoulders threatened to touch, seeming to once again completely ignore Mitch awkwardly clearing his throat.

"Of course I remember that. Hey, how about that night in Newport? Remember we went to that piano bar and got so drunk that—"

"—you got up on stage and sang 'Don't Stop Believing' with the band?" Tess could hardly finish the sentence she'd started laughing so hard. It was one of the best nights she'd had in years. After a particularly long day at PrideStar, she and Ryland, along with a few others from the crew, decided to head to the bougie seaside town of Newport for the night. They'd perhaps gone a little too hard, a little too fast. But the night ended in spontaneously renting a room in a hotel by the ocean, where she proceeded to collapse into Ryland's arms sometime around three a.m., still fully dressed, maybe drooling just a little, but as content and safe as she could remember.

"I have no idea what that has to do with sushi, and I don't think I want to hear the rest of that story either," Mitch said.

"Oh, the sushi thing came from our RN puking his maki out directly next to the toilet in the bathroom of a really nice Japanese restaurant," Ryland said matter-of-factly.

Mitch's lips curled into a scowl, and he held his hand out. "What part of 'I don't want to hear the rest' did you misunderstand?"

Ryland tried to contain a giggle and apologized.

"Not really sure I'm into sushi anymore," Tess said.

"If I ever was, I'm definitely not now," Mitch said.

Ryland paused, lowering her chin in focus. A second later, her head bobbed back up excitedly. "I've got it. Deluca's."

Mitch seemed to ponder the idea for a moment, and then nodded his head in hesitant agreement.

"I'll eat anything," Tess said. "Let's just get something before we get called out again and I have to get hangry at y'all."

"This is the best deli in Boston, hands down. Let's go."

They had enough time to walk the four blocks to the deli, order their sandwiches in an impressive line of lunch-goers, and even sit down at a nearby park before the radio strapped to Ryland's belt crackled to life. Like a perfectly timed scene from a comedy, Tess actually had her turkey on rye held up to her mouth, seconds away from the first bite, when the call came in. She started eating anyway, but not without a very audible groan of frustration.

"Fastest way to get a call: pick up your fork," Tess said, her mouth still full. She was used to eating on the run, and was just happy she'd had a chance to grab something before her blood sugar plummeted and took her mood with it.

"MedFlight Air Unit 9, respond to Martha's Vineyard Hospital in…" The dispatcher paused, probably at the absurdity of her own words. "Martha's Vineyard. Patient is a thirty-eight-year-old male, polysystems trauma, fell off a roof. Intracranial hemorrhage, pelvic fracture, left femur fracture, intubated. Transfer to Brigham and Women's Hospital TSICU."

Tess felt the same surge of adrenaline she always did when a call came in. It was always five percent nerves and ninety-five percent excitement. She was glad she got the sandwich, but she also knew in a few minutes, she'd be flying to the small island off the coast of Massachusetts to help bring a man to the care he needed. And she'd undoubtedly forget all about food.

"Oh. The Vineyard. Haven't been there in a while." Ryland cooed. Everything was an adventure to her—something Tess always found just the slightest bit childish, in the most endearing way possible.

"I wish I had your youth and enthusiasm, pal," Mitch said, clapping Ryland on the back so hard she actually jolted forward.

Mitch took off in a near sprint down the street back toward the hospital where their helicopter was waiting, and Ryland tried to follow but quickly fell behind.

"Goddamn it, Mitch," Ryland said in between gasps of air. Tess kept stride next to her, slightly less winded. "Fucker was a high school track star and he never lets me forget it."

Ryland stopped and leaned forward, holding what was probably a mean stitch in her side, and then began running again. Tess knew the difference between a fast sprint and a brisk walk back to the chopper probably wasn't going to mean the difference between life and death for the man waiting for them on Martha's Vineyard. But it was sort of fun to feel like characters from a Marvel movie for a minute. She smiled to herself as she stayed on Ryland's heels—everything was a damn adventure.

"So, do you guys really run to all your calls like that?" Tess said, steadying her breath as she climbed into the pilot's seat, grateful she'd been a D1 soccer player in her younger days.

"All of them," Mitch said, a single bead of sweat dangling from his temple the only sign he'd even gotten his heart rate up.

"Mitch insists on it. He says time is always of the essence. But really, I think he just wants to show off the one skill he has—being fast as shit."

"The one skill I have? I've been putting 14-gauge IVs in since you were playing T-ball, my little sidekick."

"I have nothing to say to that other than, well, you're old as dirt. There. Argument won." Ryland did a little victory dance in her jump seat as she buckled herself in, and Tess turned to check on them just in time to see Ryland run a hand through her short hair that seemed to get wilder as the day went on and slide her sunglasses over her nose with a cocky smile. God, she hated how badly this woman could make her want.

❖

Something was wrong. Something was very wrong. One of the fuel light indicators now lit up the instrument panel in an ominous red. Tess had seen it flash on, her eyes automatically darting to the screen. This was fine. She could handle this. She was trained to troubleshoot all kinds of mechanical issues. The bird was still flying just fine, and she knew there was no way they were actually in danger of running out of fuel. They'd left the city with a full tank of gas, and Tess knew that even if there was a breach, the backup tank would take over. She took in the deepest breath she could, holding it for several seconds at the top and then blowing it out through puffed cheeks.

"Hey, guys? We have a problem." Tess tried to keep her voice even. The last thing she wanted to do was rattle the rest of the crew—especially Ryland. Whenever that chopper left the ground, they counted on Tess to get them to wherever they were going safely. And she couldn't let them down.

"What's wrong?" Mitch's tone was tense, without the usual hint of dry teasing.

"The fuel light is on. I think we're okay, but I should radio into base."

"What does that mean? It sounds bad," Mitch said.

Tess was a little surprised to find Mitch was the anxious one of the three of them.

She heard the loud smack of skin against canvas as Ryland thwacked Mitch on the shoulder. "Mitchy here is a bad flyer." Ryland laughed.

"Excuse me for not wanting to crash?"

"We're not going to crash," Ryland reassured him. But there was a tentativeness in her words that made Tess's stomach turn a little.

"We're not going to crash," Tess repeated. "It's just a precaution. These things happen all the time."

"It's never happened to me," Mitch said. "Not in twenty years of flying."

Tess tried not to take his nerves as criticism.

"One time, on a long-haul to New York, our instrument panel went totally out for like ten minutes," Ryland said excitedly. "It was scary as hell. But Tess knows how to manage this stuff. She's a great pilot and she won't let anything happen to us."

Ryland reached around Tess's seat and gently placed her hand on top of Tess's that rested uneasily by the throttle. In an instant, the rubber-band-like tension that held Tess's muscles captive released. The warmth from Ryland's skin traveled up her arm and across her chest, and settled into her head, like sitting in a patch of sun on the first perfect day of spring. With Ryland's hand on hers, any apprehension vanished into the ether.

"I'm just going to call in and let them know," Tess said, giving Ryland's hand one single squeeze before reaching for the radio.

"Air Unit 9 to base, do you copy?"

The silence before the staticky voice on the other end of the radio always triggered Tess's pulse a little, even in the weirdly drug-like hypnotic state Ryland had seemed to put her in.

"This is base. Go ahead, 9."

"We have a fuel light on. Do you want us to land?" Tess glanced at the GPS in front of her. A tiny blip flickered over Fairhaven, Massachusetts, and she knew realistically they were almost there. Another ten minutes or so and she could land them in the Vineyard like they'd planned. Then again, if the fuel tanks were going, they might not have another ten minutes.

"Do me a favor, 9, and open up your fuel log under your maintenance screen."

Tess scolded herself for not thinking of that immediately. The person on the other end was asking her the equivalent of "did you try turning it off and turning it back on again?" Thankfully, she was quite sure Ryland and Mitch had absolutely no idea just how stupid an error she'd made.

"Great idea, base. It's open. Okay, Tank One is at eighty-eight percent capacity, backup is at one hundred percent." Tess's head collapsed in relief, and she smiled to herself. They were going to be fine.

"What does that mean?" Mitch asked eagerly.

"Quit it," Ryland snapped back. "Let her work."

"Air 9, that sounds totally fine. Must just be a faulty sensor. You can keep on going to the Vineyard, but don't load that patient. I repeat, don't load that patient. Call here when you land and we'll give you more details."

Tess wasn't entirely sure what that meant, but she turned to Mitch and Ryland and smiled reassuringly like she did.

"Good news, you two. We're not going to die." Tess giggled nervously.

Mitch scowled at her. "So we heard."

"Oh, you get nasty when you're scared," Ryland said, teasing him.

"I was not scared. I had a very appropriate reaction to what could have been a potentially serious situation."

"The fuel tanks are fine, Mitch. You heard base. We have plenty of gas, and we're headed to the Vineyard as planned," Tess said. Now that the immediate terror of the moment had passed, a new worry gripped her. She hoped this little snafu wouldn't hurt her chances of joining up with MedFlight. Mitch seemed to have a lot of clout with the company, and Tess worried he might go to the captain and tell him Tess was incompetent or something. That didn't really seem like Mitch, though. He was a little shaken up when he thought they might plummet ten thousand feet to their deaths, but he wasn't mean or vindictive. Still, Tess made a mental note to talk to Ryland about it later. Just in case.

❖

Ryland had no doubt in her mind Tess could handle whatever crisis faced them in the friendly skies. That didn't mean she wasn't nearly pissing herself when she saw the flash of terror cross Tess's face. In retrospect, safe on the ground, Ryland was actually quite tickled with the fact that she still knew Tess enough to be able to gauge her feelings from one quick glance in the mirror—even over a pair of sunglasses. But she couldn't deny that she was scared. She was scared of Tess's distress. There was always something steadfast about Tess that Ryland loved. She was a rock—a rock with a soft, sexy exterior who wasn't afraid to grab you by the hips and pull you in for a kiss in the middle of the street—but a rock nonetheless. She was exactly who you wanted as your pilot. To see her rattled was, well, it was unsettling to say the least. But with Mitch having a near panic attack in the seat next to her, Ryland couldn't fall apart. Tess needed her to manifest that strength that they'd always been so good at fortifying for each other. What was even more unsettling, though, was the adrenaline that flickered through Ryland's veins when her hand met Tess's. She didn't remember feeling that years ago. And if she had, it certainly wasn't loud enough to drown out the sounds of their own mortality. This was something else entirely.

With the bird safely sitting in the field of the local high school, Mitch, Tess, and Ryland seemed to breathe one collective sigh, none of them wanting to admit just how terrified they'd really been. Flight medicine was statistically dangerous business. The Bureau of Transportation Statistics reported a total of six crashes for every hundred thousand flight hours in the last year. She flew about thirty hours every week on a normal week with overtime, which meant that based on those statistics she was likely to crash once every nine years or so. If she was better at math, she would have taken the time to figure out the odds ratio of crashing every time she came to work. But she got a B- in statistics in college, and really she only used the stat to impress people with her valor at cocktail parties and on Tinder dates. Numbers didn't scare her. In fact, a crash every ten years seemed very reasonable. Ryland had never had her helicopter threaten to malfunction while she was in it before, though. Maybe she better stop throwing fake odds ratios around just to get laid.

Her own sense of mortality now securely in check, Ryland looked around for Tess. She had hopped out of the pilot's seat a few minutes ago and Ryland just assumed she was around back neurotically checking the bird for signs of a problem. After one full lap around, Ryland spotted her standing under the shade of the field's one enormous willow tree. It was early enough in the season to still be warm enough for them to roll their uniform sleeves up and keep a light jacket stashed in the back, but the light was already beginning to fade, even at just past five thirty p.m. A soft shadow obscured half of Tess's face, the other engulfed by a brilliant red and yellow hue from the sun cascading off the trees on the perimeter of the field. She held her phone up to her ear, and even at a distance Ryland could see her forehead was wrinkled and her lips were pursed.

"You okay?" Ryland mouthed once she'd reached Tess's side. She placed a gentle hand on the lowest part of Tess's back and dared herself to leave it there.

Tess nodded, the phone still pressed to her cheek.

"I understand." She nodded again. "That's not a problem. We'll just wait to hear from you."

Ryland assumed Tess was on the phone with the MedFlight base, but she still didn't move her hand away. As she talked and nodded, and nodded and talked some more, Tess slowly inched her way closer to Ryland, making no attempt to break the touch. Just before she hung up, she looked down at Ryland and grinned. One corner of her mouth curled just a little and her eyes flashed a sultry fire that Ryland could have seen from back in Boston. By the time Ryland was able to get ahold of her breath again, the look was gone, replaced by the matter-of-fact, here-to-take-names Tess. The intensity of just how much she wanted to have Tess's back against that tree was so strong it nearly kicked Ryland's feet clear out from under her, leaving her wondering when Tess learned how to play the game better than she did.

Ryland pulled her hand away in a panic and took a step away from Tess as Tess put her phone back in her pocket, seemingly completely unfazed by whatever had just transpired between them. How was it even possible that she hadn't felt that lightning bolt? Lightning bolt wasn't right. Earthquake? Ryland was only sure it was some sort of force of nature.

"So? What's the deal?" She danced around impatiently, trying to make herself appear bored or dismissive.

"Good news, bad news?" Tess answered, her words tied together with the cutest little upward inflection.

"Good news?" Ryland hated these scenarios.

"We all get to enjoy Martha's Vineyard for the night!" Tess threw her hands up feigning enthusiasm, and it was clear she wasn't entirely sure how Ryland was going to feel about the situation.

"What do you mean?"

"They don't want us to fly the bird home. Not until they can send a mechanic over to look at it. In the meantime, we're staying here. They're sending us back on the ferry tomorrow."

Ryland thought about it for a minute. Her first question, and not unreasonably so, was what was going to happen to the patient who needed to be transferred out.

"They've already got another crew on the way to pick him up," Tess answered. "Unfortunately, they can't take all of us. So…"

Tess looked nervous all of a sudden. This was different from the nervousness of seeing her helicopter misbehave. Her cheeks were flushed with a red that rivaled the turning leaves behind them, and she stuffed her hands quickly in her pockets, bouncing on her toes like she was warming up for a road race. What was she so uneasy about all of a sudden? They'd spent the entire day together and now Tess was acting like it was their first date.

Then the possibility hit Ryland like the entire sun falling out of the sky—would they want to share a room, after all this time? Or would Tess want her own space and feel too uncomfortable with Ryland being in such close proximity? No matter how small, the prospect of sleeping near Tess again thrilled her.

CHAPTER FIVE

It wasn't to anyone's surprise that Mitch was less than thrilled about the change in plans. He had a wife and a three-year-old and valued his free time much more than Ryland did. Ryland felt bad that he was stuck on this island for the night with them when he could be home with his family. The empathy was fleeting, though, because really all Ryland was thinking about was being stuck on an island with Tess, and she wondered exactly how difficult it would be to ditch Mitch for the rest of the evening. She stifled a chuckle as she thought about it. *Operation Ditch Mitch.*

"What's so funny?" Mitch said, the same snarl from their earlier near catastrophe back like a seasonal flu.

"I was just thinking about a, um, funny cat video I saw the other day," Ryland said.

"Funny cats," Mitch grumbled.

"You are in a foul mood, sir. Can I buy you a scotch?" Ryland punched him repeatedly on the shoulder like always, but this time Mitch grabbed her arm and twisted her into an easy headlock.

"Better be a lot of scotch, you little brat." He rubbed the top of Ryland's head with his knuckles.

"Okay. Shit. Uncle. Uncle Mitch, stop." Ryland was laughing so hard tears poured out her eyes. She glanced up at Tess, who was bent over, holding her middle, laughing as hard as Ryland was.

"Uncle Mitch. I like that," Tess said once Ryland was finally standing upright again. She stood in front of Ryland and their eyes locked as she reached up and smoothed a piece of Ryland's stray hair.

"You're a mess," she said softly, her fingers slow to make their way down the side of Ryland's head, just grazing the skin of her neck as she did.

Ryland could only swallow hard and nod in full-fledged agreement.

"Look, you two. If I'm going to stay here, I need a stiff drink, a warm bed, and a cheeseburger," Mitch said, breaking the thick film of tension that had built around them.

"What are you going to do if we say no, Mitch? Swim home?" Ryland asked.

"Just shut up, will you? I'm calling an Uber. We're finding a hotel and we're getting the biggest burgers on the Vineyard." Mitch pulled out his phone and went to work.

"Is he serious? We're on Martha's Vineyard and he wants a burger?" Tess asked.

"He's dead serious. That's literally all the man eats. He's an anomaly."

"Ten minutes. Hussan will be here in his gray RAV4. We're going to the Holiday Inn and Suites and I'm going to get the nicest room they've got. And you can bet your ass the company's going to pay for it," Mitch said, bobbing his head from side to side and jutting out his hip.

"Such a diva," Ryland said. He was right, though. They did need somewhere to sleep. Wouldn't it make more sense to ask Tess to share a room? It would be the fiscally responsible thing to do. Hotel rooms were so expensive these days, especially on the Vineyard. They could get two queen beds and they could just watch movies and...

Ryland put the thought out of her head. It was too weird a subject to broach. There was too much history there. She'd get her own room, and Tess would get hers. And if one thing led to another, well then, so be it.

A few minutes later, a RAV4 pulled up to the access road just off the edge of the field, and they all got in, Mitch in the front seat, of course, and Ryland and Tess in the back. It was a fairly large SUV, but Ryland kept her hand to her side, resting close to the middle seat that lay vacant between them. Tess did the same. Ryland wasn't sure if it was intentional, but she desperately flirted with the idea of dancing her fingers closer to Tess's and weaving them together. She wanted to feel that explosion she'd felt earlier when they were flying. She wanted to see if something as small as their hands touching was enough to make her body feel like it was actually vibrating again, or if it was just a one-off.

But Ryland didn't move her hand. The car passed through winding roads and under quaint bridges, edging past the water with the vast expanse of the Atlantic Ocean out Ryland's window. The sun was a little lower now but still echoed off the glassy sea. There was something nostalgic about early fall in New England—something that made you long for a past you never actually lived. And Ryland felt it hard sitting next to Tess that evening.

Much to Ryland's chagrin, the car stopped in front of the Holiday Inn a few minutes later, neither she nor Tess seeming to have moved the entire ride. Their hands still rested about four inches apart. And Ryland felt the urge to touch her grow with every passing second.

"I'm nauseous," Mitch whispered as they walked toward the hotel entrance.

"You fly four days a week and you can't handle a ten-minute Uber ride?" Ryland asked.

"It's totally different," Tess said, defending him.

"Thank you, Tess," Mitch said. "I think we could all use that burger now."

They all nodded in agreement and passed through the automatic glass doors into the lobby of a rather high-end Holiday Inn. Overstuffed sofas that looked like they came from West Elm adorned the high-ceilinged room, a few well-dressed visitors occupying them. A family decked out in boat shoes and Nantucket-red shorts stood at the desk looking impatient. Ryland staked out a place behind them and the others followed.

"Checking in?" the woman behind the counter with a pressed white shirt and a smile fit for customer service asked them.

"We actually need some rooms for the night." Mitch took a firm step to the front.

"Hmm." The woman's face pinched tightly and she clicked her tongue a few times, then tapped some keys on the keyboard in front of her. "That's going to be a problem," she said. Ryland wasn't sure she even looked.

"What do you mean?" Mitch asked.

She looked up from her computer matter-of-factly. "How many rooms do you need?"

Panic once against crested over Ryland and she looked furiously at Tess, then back at the concierge.

"Three," Mitch said. Ryland exhaled.

"Hmm, see, now that's going to be a problem."

"I wish you'd stop saying that," Mitch said.

"There's a big regatta in town this weekend. No room on the whole island. But since you folks are in a bind," the concierge gestured to their uniforms, "and clearly in the business of helping others, I think I can help you out. I can get you two rooms. The honeymoon suite is available, and I have a smaller room with a double bed that just had a cancellation. You aren't going to get a better deal anywhere else tonight."

Before Ryland could even process what she was saying, Mitch had whipped out his Mastercard and slammed it on the counter. "We'll take them."

The concierge smiled the same practiced smile, punched a few more things into the computer, and slid three key cards to them.

"Enjoy your stay."

Mitch grabbed the keys and turned to go. With his back to them, Tess and Ryland exchanged perplexed glances, and Ryland wondered if Tess was as preoccupied with the sleeping arrangements as she was.

They followed Mitch all the way to the elevator before he said anything. "Here you are, kids. Behave yourselves, will you?"

Neither of them said anything.

"Look. The hotel is on me. But I'm old, so I get the suite. You two can take the other room." Mitch smiled and looked first at Ryland, then at Tess. Ryland wasn't sure if Mitch was trying to help or not, but somehow, she thought he was.

"We—I mean, if that's all right with Tess?" Ryland asked, her voice shaky.

The tops of Tess's ears had turned pink, like they had earlier as they stood in the field together. She bit her lower lip and nodded, not making eye contact with Ryland.

"Fine with me," she said.

"Great. I'm going to take a shower. I'll meet you two down here in an hour and we can get some dinner?" Mitch said, but the elevator doors had opened and he'd already stepped inside without waiting for them to respond, leaving Ryland and Tess standing alone.

"Are you sure this is okay with you?" Ryland asked.

"Absolutely. Why wouldn't it be?"

"I just didn't know if you'd think it was—"

"—weird? Because we've shared a bed so many times?"

They both laughed nervously and then silence fell around them again, a slew of questions left unasked.

"I can sleep on the couch if you want?" Ryland looked straight ahead at the elevator doors. A small crowd of other patrons had begun to gather behind them, and all she wanted was for everyone else to go away. Tess was taking an unbearably long time to answer Ryland's chivalrous suggestion, which, in all honesty, Ryland was hoping she'd decline.

A crisp *ding* chimed, and the elevator doors opened. Ryland waited a beat and let Tess step in first, the oblivious strangers pushing their way around them.

"That's very sweet of you to offer," Tess finally said. Ryland was still facing away from her, everyone in the elevator looking at the doors, as was the etiquette. She wasn't expecting to feel Tess's warm hand gently press against hers, Tess wrapping her pinkie around Ryland's. The same surge that had wreaked absolute havoc on Ryland when they touched earlier came back with a serious vengeance. "But also unnecessary." Tess tightened her grip on Ryland's hand as the doors opened on their floor. Ryland's legs failed her for a second, and she was forced to let other travelers around her off first. As soon as she was confident enough she wouldn't collapse, she followed Tess into the hallway.

❖

The room was of the fairly typical vacation-town chain hotel variety. A small leather love seat not big enough for anyone over five feet tall to actually sleep on sat in the corner. There was a metal-framed desk next to a big screen TV with the typical corded phone to call room service. Several fake plants adorned the window, which admittedly had a very nice view of the ocean. And in the middle of the room was a lone double bed.

Tess wanted to play it so cool when the subject came up. She wanted to be "that girl"—the go-with-the-flow, let's-just-see-what-happens girl. But that wasn't her. Ever since the possibility of spending the night with Ryland again came to light, her brain could do nothing but obsess about it. It forced her to play out every possible scenario, from mind-blowing makeup sex to a fairy-tale love story reunion to an all-out fight, about what she wasn't totally sure. And now, here they were. Ryland had offered to sleep on the couch. And Tess was sure the offer was genuine. But really, Tess knew the second she saw Ryland again that wasn't the way things were going to go. She didn't want Ryland on the couch. She wanted her in bed, next to her, holding her, kissing her bare shoulder in the middle of the night and brushing her hair back behind her ear as Tess dozed off. The consequences of wanting all that were far from silent in Tess's head. But they weren't loud enough to deter a single thing.

"Nice room," Ryland whispered, her voice hoarse. Tess could see her throat rise and fall as she swallowed hard.

"I get the impression Mitch likes the finer things in life."

Ryland laughed nervously. "You would be right."

"So I'm going to go try to clean up a little bit." Tess was the only one of the three of them who'd come prepared with a change of clothes and some toiletries. She learned a few years ago, after some bad weather stranded her in Connecticut, to always have a go-bag with her. This was the first time she'd ever had to actually use it, but she was never more grateful not to have to go out to dinner in her flight suit with the day's stink on her.

Tess closed the bathroom door and took down her hair. She shook it out a little and then brushed the ends with her fingertips, trying to bring some life back to the sad, limp strands. It had been so long since she'd packed the bag, she couldn't even remember what was in it. Whatever it was had to be better than her uniform. She pulled out a pair of black jeans and a simple striped long-sleeved T-shirt. She sure wasn't going to win any fashion awards, but it would do the job. For some stupid reason, Tess found herself hoping Ryland would be impressed. This was Ryland Matthews, who'd seen her butt-naked, in her flight suit, in her after-work spontaneous drinks attire, in her pajamas. Why did she think she could catch her attention with a little lip gloss and a fresh shirt? Why did she care?

When she opened the bathroom door, Ryland was stretched out across the bed on her stomach. She'd shed her jumpsuit and was in a pair of U-Conn basketball shorts that were just small enough to hug her ass and ride up to show off her muscled thighs, and a white T-shirt that stretched tightly across her back. Tess could see the lines of Ryland's shoulders even under the shirt sleeves, and the strong tendons of her forearms as she scrolled through the TV remote. Tess's throat tightened and then became agonizingly dry. Ryland looked good before. But it was quite clear that time had been nothing but a gift to her.

It took Ryland a beat to notice Tess had appeared, but the second she did, she averted all of her attention away from the football game that was playing on the TV and jumped to a seated position.

"Wow. You look... Shit. You're going to put Mitch and me to shame out there is all I can say." She shook her head, her eyes still wide, and Tess grinned at her. This was exactly the reaction she was hoping for—maybe even more.

"I don't know. You're managing to make a pair of gym shorts look pretty damn good."

Tess watched the color rise in Ryland's cheeks and let herself enjoy the rare moment of bashfulness she was managing to elicit. She moved to the bed and took a seat next to Ryland, close enough that their thighs touched. So much of their past left Tess feeling out of control, like she wasn't playing with a full deck. She was always chasing Ryland in a way, wanting more than she could have. But things felt different now. Ryland wanted her. And Tess was entirely in control.

She sat quietly for a moment, allowing the tension to build to a sustained hum before she reached over and placed her hand on Ryland's knee. Immediately, Tess felt the muscles in Ryland's leg tense under her exposed skin.

"You look really nice," Ryland said, her voice shaky and uncertain. She angled her body toward Tess's and placed her hand tentatively on Tess's lower back. Ryland Matthews was nervous, and it was all Tess's doing—an accomplishment Tess hadn't known she'd been striving for.

"You said that already," Tess whispered. She smiled and tilted her chin a little so her lips were just inches from Ryland's. Ryland's breath was hot against hers and they held each other's gaze, Ryland's eyes pleading for Tess to close the space between them. But Tess didn't. She wouldn't. She knew Ryland was waiting for her. She knew exactly what Ryland wanted. But she wasn't about to give it to her so easily.

Ryland parted her annoyingly inviting lips but didn't say a word.

No one broke the stare, and the only movement was the tiny stroke of Tess's thumb along the bare skin of Ryland's thigh. Tess's heart was beating so hard she thought it might shatter the bones in her chest. She was quite sure the football game was still on in the background, but her pulse in her ears and the sound of her own ragged breathing was so loud she didn't hear it. Or maybe it was Ryland's breathing. It was so hard to tell. For a split second, Tess wasn't sure she had the control to keep herself from pressing her mouth against Ryland's and exploring her tongue with her own. She couldn't remember wanting anything so badly in her entire life. But by some miracle, she channeled whatever she'd learned from flying, or from past romantic disasters, and she held on.

"We should go meet Mitch," Tess said, giving Ryland's leg one last pat and breaking her gaze.

She watched the absolute agony wreck Ryland's face, and Tess found some sick sense of satisfaction in the way she'd made Ryland want her. She knew the night wasn't going to pass without that excruciating need being met. It went against all laws of physics. But Tess was going to hold out as long as possible, trying to keep as many cards in her hand as she could.

"Oh, right." Ryland stood up and wiggled her hips a little, seemingly trying to shake off whatever had been stirring inside her.

CHAPTER SIX

Mitch was already in the lobby of the hotel when Ryland and Tess arrived exactly forty-five minutes after they'd checked in. Ryland wasn't surprised. Mitch was nothing if not aggravatingly punctual. He was still in his jumpsuit, but his hair was combed back and his face looked fresh and bright.

"I see you went with jumpsuit chic?" Ryland said, teasing him.

"Laugh all you want, but I bet you this baby gets me at least one free drink," he said, patting the MedFlight patch on his sleeve with pride.

"So where should we go?" Tess asked.

"Don't worry about that. I'm sure Mitch has spent the last twenty minutes researching and has the rest of the evening planned out," Ryland said.

Mitch rolled his eyes and looked at Tess. "Clearly we've been working together for too long. Remind me to ask for a transfer."

"Out with it. Where are you taking us?" Ryland asked. She tried to keep her eyes on Mitch, hoping it would help distract from the heat that still remained between her legs and the ever-tightening knots in her stomach. Ryland felt drunk already, like she was hearing the words Mitch was saying, and could respond somewhat appropriately, but she was somewhere else entirely, her mind stuck in a dreamland of distraction and almost disorientation. Something had shifted between her and Tess since the last time she'd seen her. Tess was confident, strong. In control. Ryland wanted her back then. But she really fucking wanted Tess now. What they had years ago was fun. Easy. But this…

this was something deeper. And all Ryland could think about was taking Tess back upstairs and kissing her until she couldn't breathe.

"There's a gastropub down the street that apparently has an epic lobster roll. I might even branch out tonight," Mitch said. "Great Yelp reviews. Then, if I haven't gotten entirely sick of you two by then, there's a whiskey bar a few miles away I want to try."

Ryland hoped they wouldn't make it past more than a couple of drinks before she could get Tess back to the hotel. But why hadn't Tess kissed her earlier? She seemed to want to as badly as Ryland did. And God knew she had every opportunity to. Something told Ryland that whatever was going to transpire between them that night had to be at Tess's hand.

The cocktail Tess had ordered, which was some fruity pineapple thing with a generous pour of vodka, was hitting hard. She'd always been a lightweight, but that might not serve her so well tonight. She'd nervously downed half the drink before her lobster roll had even arrived, and the room was starting to swim pleasantly. Her chest and belly were warm but couldn't rival the heat that had been there since her near kiss with Ryland earlier. As Ryland and Mitch bantered about the Red Sox bullpen, Tess sat quietly, more out of an effort to keep herself together than a lack of things to say about Chris Sale's fastball. She made a mental note to slow down on the alcohol, or else she'd be pulling Ryland into the nearest bathroom within the hour.

Mitch was ranting about one of the MedFlight managers, Tess only tuning in and out. She'd managed to eat some fries, although she wasn't particularly hungry, and the buzz that came on a little too strong had ebbed to a dull sense of disinhibition. She felt Ryland's hand move to her thigh, so high up that her thumb landed nearly at the ache between Tess's legs that was growing louder with every small stroke. It was just enough to send Tess entirely over the edge. She inched down in her chair, trying to bring Ryland's thumb closer to where she needed it, her hips writhing under the table. She closed her eyes involuntarily and it took every ounce of strength she had not to take Ryland's hand under the table and make her touch her.

She wasn't going to last. She was too weak.

"I have to pee." Tess flashed Ryland a quick glance and prayed she'd take her cue.

"Same," Ryland said, jumping up after her.

Mitch eyed them suspiciously, but Tess didn't care. The ache between her legs was now a physical pain. If she didn't have Ryland now, she might actually, literally die.

Tess hadn't thought about what would happen if the bathrooms were multi-stalled, but when she saw the lock on the outside, she breathed a sigh of relief. At this point, she'd take Ryland on the floor of the restaurant kitchen if she had to. She'd never needed anyone like this.

A single patron walked out of the women's room, and Tess and Ryland exchanged a knowing look. Tess took Ryland's hand, pushing the door open with her hip, and closing it swiftly behind them. Tess was a bottom if ever there was a bottom. But something was possessing her. Ryland was just a little taller than Tess, and Tess took her shoulders and pushed them hard against the closed bathroom door. She stilled herself just long enough to hold her lips close to Ryland's, letting the tension between them that had been building into a firestorm all night erupt into a full-fledged disaster. When she was satisfied she'd held out as absolutely long as she could, Tess kissed Ryland. She kissed her hard and slow, letting her tongue dart past Ryland's lips. Ryland gasped into Tess's mouth and the firestorm continued and Tess thought she might actually cum right then and there. Tess kept her hold on Ryland's shoulders, pinning her against the door. Ryland had moved her hands to Tess's waist, pulling her in closer as she kissed her with an ever-growing sense of desperation.

Ryland wasn't going to stand being topped for much longer. It wasn't in her DNA. And Tess didn't mind in the slightest when Ryland tightened her hold on Tess's hips and spun her around, never breaking the kiss, until Tess's back was now the one pressed against the bathroom door.

Tess was torn somewhere between feeling the thrill of hooking up with someone in public and the embarrassment of it being a dingy toilet stall. She was quite sure the sense of the thrill won out. Ryland's breath smelled like hot whiskey and danger, and Tess was so wet now she was over any hope of pretense. She grabbed Ryland's hand that was exploring Tess's hair and pushed it down between her legs. Ryland gasped and bit down on Tess's bare neck far harder than Tess thought she'd meant to. Tess didn't mind. The pain felt amazing, a sharp contrast to Ryland's warm tongue running down to the divot between Tess's collarbones. Ryland didn't need any more hints. She pushed her palm into the crotch of Tess's jeans with one smooth motion and Tess saw stars. Her legs shook so badly she didn't think they'd keep her up much longer and she desperately wished there was a bed or at least a clean floor nearby. But her legs held—barely. Tess bucked her hips hard against Ryland's strong hand, feeling herself agonizingly close to cumming already.

"Holy shit, Ry. Holy shit, fuck, fuck fuck." Each "fuck" Tess muttered was a little louder than the last, and Ryland shushed her, laughing in a whisper. But she never stopped touching her. Knowing she needed to keep quiet just made Tess even hotter, and she knew there was no long game being played here. She wanted Ryland too much. And in that moment, Tess's body needed her in a way she had absolutely no control over.

Tess tried to last at least a few seconds longer, wanting to draw out the mind-numbing pleasure she'd found. But when Ryland took her hand away and curled her fingers inside Tess's jeans without even bothering to unbutton them, Tess exploded. All it took was a couple of strokes against the silk of Tess's panties, and it was all over. Her throat felt like it was closing and her legs betrayed her. If Ryland hadn't been holding Tess's wrist above her head with her free hand, Tess would have absolutely collapsed. Once the waves of the near transcendent orgasm had ebbed, every muscle in her body ceased to work, and she fell in a depleted, sweaty heap into Ryland's arms.

The afterglow didn't last long. Tess's euphoria was quickly plundered by a loud knock on the door.

"Just a minute!" Ryland shouted. They giggled noiselessly and Tess kept her tight grip around Ryland's neck.

As Tess scrambled her brain trying to figure out how to get them out of there discreetly, the person on the other side of the door knocked again.

"Coming!" Tess yelled. She shrugged and turned around, unlocking the rusty hinge. A short, stout woman in her fifties with an I-want-to-talk-to-the-manager haircut and a Led Zeppelin T-shirt barely covering her large breasts stood so close Tess almost knocked her over when she opened the door.

"Sorry," Tess mumbled, avoiding all eye contact with the much shorter woman, who shot her a nasty glare.

Ryland put her hand on Tess's back and guided her quickly past the angry woman and out of the bathroom, trying to contain an amused snicker.

"Shit," Tess whispered as they made their way back to the table. "That was embarrassing." But she couldn't help but smile as she said it.

"Nah, that lady was a total Karen. I'm glad she had to see that." Ryland kept her arm around Tess until they reached their seats.

Mitch looked up from his drink, first with just a hint of suspicion and then with clear disinterest. If he had any questions, he obviously didn't care enough to ask what was going on with the two of them.

"Long line?" he asked.

"Uh, yes," Ryland said. "Another round? Come on, this one's on me."

Mitch picked his nearly empty gin and tonic up, downed the last sip, and made that same face of indifference. "Why not?"

"Great. I'll be right back."

❖

Ryland got up and walked to the bar where a handsome man with a well-trimmed beard was busy pouring tap beers for a group of cute young college students. After several minutes of his increasingly obnoxious flirting, Ryland realized she was not going to be served. This was a common problem for her. Masculine-presenting women often had trouble catching the attention of young, straight cis guys, even if it meant a hefty tip. The bartender continued to ignore Ryland, leaning over the counter to chat up the redhead who seemed less than interested in his advances. Most people as outspoken as Ryland would have said something. But for whatever reason, she could never bring herself to, usually opting to stand there with her arms crossed looking as displeased as possible, or let out a few loud sighs before walking away, drinkless and defeated.

"Need a hand?" Tess was behind her now, sliding one of her hands into the very top of the waistband of Ryland's shorts.

"How'd you guess?"

"I'm familiar with the masc-invisibility amongst straight dudes," Tess said.

"I appreciate that."

Within a half a minute, the bartender had abandoned the redhead and was smiling at Tess.

"What can I get you?" he said, never bothering to look at Ryland.

"A gin and tonic, Maker's on the rocks, and a…fuck, let's do a sex on the beach."

His smile widened and his eyes sparkled just a little. Ryland instinctively moved to Tess's side and placed a hand on her back. Now the bartender was looking at Ryland. It was a look she'd seen many times—one that said, "How is she with you?"

They collected their drinks and Ryland signed the credit card slip, leaving a measly one-dollar tip.

"I don't remember you having such a filthy mouth, by the way," Ryland said, the pink cocktail spilling a little onto her forearm.

"When the moment calls for it." Tess gently slapped Ryland's ass, making her jump just a little, a few more drops of whiskey sneaking onto the floor.

❖

Mitch hadn't even finished his third gin and tonic before he suggested a venue change. In all the years they'd worked as partners, Ryland had never actually gone out with him, and she was surprised to find he was actually a lot of fun. Not that Mitch wasn't fun. But there was work-fun and there was fun-fun. The kind of fun that wanted to keep the party going after the first rounds had finished. Ryland wasn't often fun-fun herself. But that night, with the two of them, she was more than happy to oblige. As atypical a trio as they were, they were having a great time. They were laughing and eating well into the evening, and for the first time in a while, Ryland felt relaxed and free. Of course, there was more than a little part of her that wanted to rush Tess back to the hotel and rip her clothes off. But she couldn't figure out a particularly inconspicuous way to do it, and besides, she was really liking the way Tess's hand felt on her thigh under the table. She liked that Mitch didn't know what was going on between them. She liked the passion and the imminent need and the littlest hint of "we probably shouldn't" that was flowering between her and Tess. Ryland wanted to hold on to that as long as possible, afraid that if they left, the spell would be broken. She didn't know where the night was headed, but she wasn't finding herself in any hurry to get there quickly.

"Hmm, looks like a lot of things are closing in the next hour," Mitch said, scrolling through his phone and shaking his head.

"Let's just wander out and see where we end up, then?" Tess was always so easygoing, ready for whatever adventure wanted to find them. Ryland loved that. It made her feel younger, unencumbered from the anxiety and overthinking she usually wrestled with.

"Let's do it." Mitch stood and they followed, leaving Ryland still very surprised at his spontaneity. She thought for sure he'd be headed to bed by now.

What was usually one of the busier streets that time of night in the summer looked empty and almost abandoned in early September. The cool fall air held a hint of the ocean, and a chill ran over Ryland's arm and up her neck. She shivered quickly, trying to ignore the fact she wished she'd had a jacket.

"You must be freezing," Tess whispered to her as they walked over the cobblestones. Mitch was a few steps ahead, always leading the pack.

"I'm okay," Ryland said between clenched teeth.

"Here." Tess weaved her arm around Ryland's waist and pulled Ryland's body against hers. Immediately, the heat coming from where their hips met spread up through Ryland's abdomen and into her chest, warming her core. She didn't remember liking touching Tess this much. Hell, Ryland couldn't really remember liking touching anyone this much. And Tess's confidence and willingness to hold her, even with Mitch right there, was more of a turn-on than Ryland could have imagined. As they walked a little farther, Tess dropped her grip and snaked her arm through Ryland's, which, in spite of the rather rude return of the cold around them, Ryland liked even more. She liked feeling like Tess was hers.

Ryland turned and looked at her, their stride still perfectly in sync. She smiled shyly, and an unsettling but also exhilarating vulnerability engulfed her. Tess caught her gaze and she smiled back, Ryland tilting her chin as the exposure only grew. Oh God. She liked Tess Goodwin.

She actually liked her. Not just in a "here for a good time, not a long time" way, or a "let's just get takeout and fuck" kind of way. Not like it used to be. Ryland liked her. She wanted to take her on dates. Real dates, to nice places. She wanted to show her off and call her "her girlfriend." She wanted something real with Tess.

Tess suddenly broke the stare and withdrew her arm, as if reading every thought that had just assaulted Ryland's brain. The fear that came with that same vulnerability Ryland had just accepted overwhelmed her and she began to panic. It had been so many years since they'd seen each other. Why would Tess feel the same way? Sure, they'd had a drunk quickie in the bathroom earlier, but maybe that's all Tess thought it was. And now Ryland was freaking her out.

"Well. This place looks seedy as hell," Mitch said, stopping in front of the one tavern that had its lights on and a bouncer in a black watch cap standing outside. "I'm in."

Ryland had given up trying to predict what Mitch was going to do. Besides, she desperately needed another drink.

The bouncer, who was a rough-and-tumble blue collar local clearly making a few extra bucks to help his deep-sea fishing charter, half-heartedly looked at their IDs and waved them in.

The bar was, indeed, seedy as hell. At least at first glance. It was wall to wall with straight locals drinking tallboys. A bartender in his forties with a pleasant face smiled as he spread cocktail napkins out in front of Ryland, Mitch, and Tess, who'd by some miracle found three seats left at the bar.

Ryland's buzz had worn off now, and she was looking to find the same easy vibe she'd so readily had earlier in the night. She didn't drink often, but when she did, she knew how to pace herself. The panic of realizing she actually had honest-to-God feelings for Tess was ebbing a little, but she couldn't stop thinking about the way Tess's face dropped right along with her embrace as they shared what Ryland thought was a real moment.

A few sips into her Woodford Reserve neat with an orange, Ryland's belly was warm and any worry had slowly given way to the easy hum of chatter around her and the Elton John song coming from the jukebox on the wall. She stood abruptly, the room shifting just the slightest. Ryland had an idea.

"Do you have any cash?" she asked Tess.

"Sure." Tess looked a little perplexed but didn't ask anything further. She unzipped a pocket of her tiny carryall she'd had slung around her shoulder that was just big enough for her phone and some credit cards, and pulled out a few folded dollar bills.

Ryland was gone for what felt like an hour, scrolling through the song selections on the jukebox making sure she'd gotten it exactly right. She wasn't even sure they'd have any Taylor Swift, save for maybe "Shake it Off" (easily one of her worst songs), never mind have her entire discography. Finally, she made her way back to the bar.

"What were you doing?" Tess asked, smiling suspiciously.

"Oh, just loading a few songs on the jukebox. Just wait."

No one Ryland knew loved Taylor Swift as much as Tess, save maybe for Ryland herself. Much of their earlier days together were spent driving in Ryland's Jeep listening to her own best of collection on full blast, singing at the top of their lungs out the open roof. It made for some of Ryland's favorite memories together. There were so many late evenings where she'd just wanted to keep driving, ignoring the destination, just to thrive in the energy that shouting "Fearless" out the windows always brought them.

She sat anxiously through the next couple of songs, each time shaking her head as Tess asked if this was her choice. "Trust me, you'll know," she kept saying.

Mitch was busy watching the *Monday Night Football* game that had run particularly late into overtime on the TV above them and was paying very little attention.

Then Ryland heard it—the initial bass drumbeats leading up to the intro to "The Way I Loved You." Tess's face lit up and she burst out laughing.

"Oh my God." Tess grabbed Ryland's shoulders and shook her gently. "How much Taylor did you cue up on that thing?"

"Not much. Five? Seven songs? Just enough to make the majority of the people in here want to kill me."

Tess couldn't help herself. She downed the last sip of her beer and started singing, the same joy that Ryland remembered from years ago radiating off of her. Ryland sang too. They laughed and pointed their fingers for emphasis as they sang, not caring where they were. They sang directly to each other, like they were on a Providence highway at midnight with the city lights shining like spotlights on them. And everyone else was just gone.

Mitch pretended to be absorbed in the Raiders' missed extra point, but every once in a while, when he thought Ryland wasn't looking, he glanced up at them and smiled sweetly.

One more round and an encore performance of "Red" later, and Mitch suggested they call it a night. It was almost one a.m., after all, and last call was coming. But there was something in his eyes that told Ryland he was offering it as much for Ryland and Tess as he was for himself. Ryland was relieved, simultaneously exhausted from a whirlwind of emotions she still couldn't keep straight and as amped up as if she'd taken a handful of Adderall and a few cups of coffee. The hesitation she'd sensed from Tess earlier seemed to have vanished, and Tess had long since pushed her stool closer to Ryland's, allowing herself to be draped in Ryland's lap. Ryland's panic had at least settled to a low simmer, and Tess seemed to be okay again too. They were comfortable. And they both seemed to want the same thing—to get the hell out of there.

Mitch hailed another Uber, which Ryland was grateful for since her head was swimming with too much whiskey and the knowledge she was about to be very much alone with Tess again. A few minutes later, they closed their tab and climbed into a Honda Civic, heading back to the hotel.

CHAPTER SEVEN

Ryland was nervous. Holy shit was she nervous. She'd fucked Tess a couple of dozen times before. Hell, she'd even fucked her earlier that night. But this felt different. There was a tension between them that had never been there before—a pretense? Expectation? No, that wasn't quite right either. It was the overwhelming sense that Ryland didn't want to disappoint Tess. She wanted this to be the best night she'd ever had. She wanted this to be the beginning of something—of everything.

The doors to the hotel slid open, ushering Ryland into a world of unknown. Her heart pounded harder with every footstep toward the elevator. Without a word, they got on and Mitch hit the buttons for both of their floors. There was only one other person on board—a clearly intoxicated middle-aged man in an unseasonable Vineyard Vines polo shirt and shorts with heavy bags under his eyes. Ryland wasn't dressed any more appropriately, but she was sober enough to feel the cold. When the bell dinged on the fourth floor, Mitch waved his good nights and got off, the drunk preppy man following several paces behind. Ryland and Tess were alone.

The tension between them thickened like smoke, nearly suffocating Ryland. Tess was smiling at her, her eyes calm, confident. Ryland imagined she didn't look quite so cool. They only had long enough for a look before the elevator opened again.

"This is us," Ryland said. What a stupid thing to say. Of course Tess knew this was their floor. Ryland shook her head as she stepped out, trying to clear some of the fog that had made its way into her brain. Tess had been holding the room key in her carryall the entire night, and she easily pulled it out of one of the zippered pockets and waved it in front of the door. An approving "beep" came and Tess turned the handle.

Suddenly, the quiet was deafening. The radiator hummed in the background, blowing off cool air that kept the room as frigid as a Midwest winter. Ryland was grateful for the air conditioner. She was already sweating under the collar of her T-shirt, and she knew it was only about to get worse. Tess slowly walked to the dresser and placed the key card on top, along with her bag. Her back was to Ryland, who couldn't take her eyes off Tess's perfect ass. Tess reached up a hand and pulled the clip out of her long hair, shaking it over her shoulders. The only light in the room was the glow of streetlamps and moonlight coming in through the large picture window, casting Tess's figure in a spectacular silhouette. Without turning around, Tess hooked the ends of her fingers under the hem of her shirt and pulled it over her head so agonizingly slowly Ryland let out an actual groan. Her feet were stuck to the floor, refusing to move but also offering no support for her ever-wavering legs. With her shirt cast on the floor, Tess reached down and unfastened the button on her jeans. Ryland couldn't actually see her doing it, but the mere idea of it was enough to send her over the edge. She let the pants fall to her feet and kicked them away. Ryland's entire body was going to fail her if Tess did anything else.

For a long time, Tess just stood there, letting Ryland admire the soft outline of the curves of her lower back and hips and the shape of her thighs. Finally, she turned, her ridiculous body now in full view. Ryland's nerves melted to the floor with Tess's clothes and she rushed the few feet toward her, clasping Tess's face with both hands and kissing her, taking exactly what she wanted. Tess moaned into Ryland's mouth as Ryland pushed her tongue past Tess's lips, controlling the tempo with the grip she kept on Tess's head. Just as Ryland's breath started to evade her, Tess stepped away, placing her hand on Ryland's chest.

"I want you to finish," Tess whispered. It took Ryland a second to figure out what she meant, but when she did, she smiled and leaned down to kiss Tess's neck and tease her earlobe with the end of her tongue. Ryland reached around and unhooked the clasp on Tess's bra in one smooth snap.

Tess giggled. "Good to see you've still got it," she said.

Whatever remained of Ryland's apprehension and insecurity

evaporated. She wanted Tess. And Tess wanted her. That's all there was to it.

Ryland leaned back and looked at Tess's nearly naked form, not wanting to rush a single second of what was happening between them. When she was satisfied that she would remember that image forever, she placed her hands on Tess's hips and knelt in front of her. Once she was on her knees, she looked up at Tess, completely at her mercy. Tess grabbed the back of Ryland's head as Ryland reached up and slid Tess's panties down with just her thumbs. She ran her tongue down Tess's flat stomach, dipping it in her navel and nipping gently at the skin of Tess's thighs. Tess gasped so loudly Ryland wondered if anyone walking by the room would hear. She hoped they would. She tightened her hold on Ryland's head, trying to guide her higher.

"Please, Ry. I need you." Her voice was hoarse and staggered and every word sounded like it took tremendous effort. The heat between Ryland's legs doubled and her body ached for Tess to touch her. But her mind was much stronger than that.

"Say it again," Ryland rasped, her tongue getting closer with every stroke.

"I. Need. You," Tess said again, this time stronger, more desperate.

That was enough for Ryland. She stood up abruptly, grabbing Tess's ass and lifting her until Tess's legs were wrapped around her. Ryland kissed her hard on the mouth as Tess pulled handfuls of Ryland's hair. They stumbled backward, falling into the small bed, Ryland's body now draped on top of Tess's.

She paused for a moment to look into Tess's face. Their eyes met with the same intensity they'd found earlier, maybe more so given the context. Still propped over her, Ryland lifted herself to take off her shirt. Tess dug her nails into Ryland's bare back, pulling them closer until their bodies merged at every possible intersection.

"You feel so good," Ryland said into the soft crook of Tess's neck. She once again forced herself to memorize this moment—the feel of Tess's skin against hers, the cool of the air around them, the starch of the sheets beneath them. Pieces of Tess's hair tickled Ryland's nose. Ryland knew even if this was only one night, she'd always remember it if she ever came across the fruity and floral scents of Tess's shampoo on someone else. She didn't want there to be anyone else. She didn't want this to be only one night.

"I wanted you years ago, but I really want you now," Tess said. "Please touch me, Ry."

Ryland grinned at her and slowly walked her fingers to Tess's breasts, taking one of her nipples and squeezing with an increasing amount of pressure. Tess let out a high squeak that was almost inhuman and Ryland knew she was ready. She moved her hand farther down, brushing her fingertips gently over Tess's skin as she went. When she reached the area between Tess's legs, she stopped, hovering motionless. Tess bucked her hips, trying to bring Ryland's hand closer, but Ryland kept it still until Tess began to whimper. She wasn't sure she had any more self-control than Tess did in this moment. Ryland took her middle finger and stroked softly a couple of times, Tess's fingernails now digging into Ryland's back so hard Ryland was sure she'd drawn blood.

"Oh Jesus," Tess whispered. Her hips were frozen this time, as if she were too overwhelmed to even try to move. She was completely at Ryland's mercy, and Ryland knew it. It was how Ryland liked it. It was how she knew Tess liked it.

Ryland picked up her pace, stroking faster, feeling Tess harden underneath her. She took in the cadence of Tess's ragged breathing, the ever-increasing frequency of her whimpers, and the quivering of her thighs underneath Ryland. And when she felt like Tess was about ready to lose all control, she slid two fingers inside her, and just held them there.

Tess screamed. There were no teasing moans this time. This was an actual wallpaper-peeling scream. Ryland knew anyone in a fifteen-foot radius would hear them. And she didn't mind at all.

Ryland moved her fingers faster, feeling Tess tightening around her. She was close. And Ryland wasn't far behind. Just touching Tess, hearing the noises she made and the way she writhed her hips underneath Ryland, was enough to nearly make Ryland cum. All Tess would have to do was press her knee between Ryland's legs and it was all done.

Tess let out one more scream, this one the loudest of all, and wrapped her legs around Ryland's waist as she shuddered over and over again. The aftershock seemed to just keep coming, but eventually, Ryland felt all of Tess's muscles relax and melt underneath her.

"I don't remember it being like that." Tess panted, her eyes still closed.

Ryland laughed. "I mean, it was always good—"

Tess reached up and put her hand on Ryland's cheek sweetly. "That's not what I meant. It was always amazing. But that was like, a whole new level."

Ryland smoothed Tess's hair over the pillow and leaned down, kissing her on the forehead before burrowing her head in the curve of Tess's arm and falling fast asleep.

❖

"Ry. Psst, Ry." Tess was wide-awake now, and she was hungry. She glanced at the oversized digital clock on the nightstand: 2:34 a.m.

Ryland didn't move. Tess remembered she'd always slept like a corpse. She sat up in bed for a second, trying to decide on her next move. What she wanted to do was wake Ryland up by kissing her naked body. But she knew that wouldn't work. Man, how did this girl ever wake up for a call?

"Ryland!" Tess shouted at full volume.

That one worked. Ryland shot up to attention, her eyes wide and her breathing heavy.

"Are you okay?" Ryland asked, looking at Tess with pure alarm.

"Me? Oh, I'm so fine. But hey, you're awake." Tess kissed her quickly on the lips and the distress slowly eased from Ryland's face.

"Did you yell at me?" Ryland asked, her voice still groggy.

"I don't know what you mean. You just woke up all on your own. And since you're up, I'm hungry. And I really want a brownie sundae."

Ryland erupted in laughter. "A brownie sundae?"

"Yes. A fucking brownie sundae. Is that an issue?" Tess asked, smiling.

"It's almost three in the morning."

"And?"

Ryland shook her head and laughed resolutely. "Okay. I'll try room service."

Tess clapped her hands in delight and Ryland leaned over to the side of the bed to pick up the phone.

"Hello. Is room service still available, by chance? I have a very hungry pilot here. I'm worried about my safety if I don't find her a brownie sundae ASAP."

Tess feigned a pout and then smiled, laying her head in Ryland's lap. Ryland stroked her hair as she waited, presumably on hold. Butterflies were such a cliché. But there was no other way to describe what was happening in Tess's stomach. Her body felt so light it might take off toward the ceiling. She was firmly fixed in that exact moment in time. Ryland was bad news. Or, at least, she used to be? But none of that mattered. Not that night. Not when there were brownie sundaes to be eaten in bed together. Not when everything felt so right—so safe.

"You're in luck," Ryland said after she'd put the phone back on the receiver. "The receptionist saw us come in in uniform and they're apparently suckers for heroes. The kitchen's closed, but they're going to make us one anyway."

"You are amazing." Tess sat up and put her hand on the back of Ryland's neck, pulling her in and kissing her much slower than before. The cliché fluttering in her gut was so strong now it moved all the way into her chest, climbing into her head until she thought she might actually pass out. The loudest voices in Tess's head told her she was in trouble. Big trouble. But she was able to hush them by thinking about just how good Ryland's lips felt on hers.

Not even fifteen minutes later, there was a quiet knock at the door. Tess, realizing they were still completely naked in bed, jumped up and ran to the closet, pulling out a terry cloth robe before ushering the hotel attendant in.

A tired-looking younger man who couldn't have been much older than twenty-five forced a smile and wheeled in a silver cart with a covered dish on top. Next to it was a bottle of champagne on ice.

"We didn't order the champagne," Tess said apologetically.

The man waved. "It's on the house. We really appreciate everything you guys do. My mom's a nurse. I know how hard it can be." His smile evolved into a more genuine one and Tess saw a boyishness in his face she hadn't before. He was probably just some nice kid trying to make a few extra bucks for college by working the overnight shift answering phones. Instead, he got roped into bringing ice cream to a couple of healthcare workers on an impromptu vacation at nearly three a.m.

"Wait here a second." Tess ran off to her bag, which sat in the corner near the bed.

"What are you doing?" Ryland, who was still covered only by a sheet and thankfully out of view due to the room's foyer, mouthed to her.

"Tip," Tess mouthed back. She pulled a twenty-dollar bill out of her wallet, and then thought about how bright the world had looked over the last twenty-four hours, and pulled out another. She returned to the bellhop and handed it to him.

"Thank you," Tess said. He smiled, looking more awake now, and turned to leave.

"That was very thoughtful of you," Ryland said, once they were alone.

Tess wheeled the room service cart over to the bed and climbed back in next to Ryland. She pulled the plate over and took the lid off, revealing a brick of a brownie covered with no less than four scoops of vanilla ice cream, hot fudge, whipped cream, and chocolate sprinkles.

"He was a nice kid. And probably makes minimum wage. As bad as I feel that they went out of their way to make this for us. This looks fucking amazing." Tess picked up a spoon and dug in. Once she was satisfied she had a little bit of everything, she brought it to Ryland. Ryland groaned as she engulfed the desert.

"Shit, that's good," she mumbled, her mouth still full.

Tess followed suit and took a big bite. She felt her eyes roll into the back of her head. "Oh my God."

Ryland was staring at her.

"What?" Tess said.

"You've just got a little something." Ryland reached up and dabbed the corner of Tess's lips with her thumb. "Oh, and maybe something here." She kissed the tip of Tess's nose.

"Huh, that's funny. I think you've got something on your face too," Tess said, smiling.

"No way." But before Ryland could continue her protest, Tess dipped her finger in the pile of whip cream and smeared it on Ryland's cheek, laughing.

Ryland's face was stone, the dollop of whip cream beginning to run down the side of her chin. Tess was just waiting for her to break. She finally did, the laughter spilling out of her so hard that tears followed.

"You are such a slob, you know that?" Ryland said as she picked up the spoon and traced a smudge of chocolate syrup on Tess's bottom lip.

"Hey, we better stop. We have to sleep in this bed tonight," Tess said, still laughing uncontrollably. Eventually, the laughter settled, and Ryland leaned in slowly, kissing the chocolate off Tess's lips as she ran her fingers through Tess's hair.

CHAPTER EIGHT

Ryland woke up a few hours later to the sound of her phone blasting its grating ringtone next to the bed. It wasn't even seven a.m. yet and she knew it was Mitch. Once she was done being irritated with him, she was grateful. They hadn't set an alarm, and the ferry was leaving at eight a.m. Tess barely moved from where she lay nestled against Ryland's chest. They'd been like that since they fell asleep. Ryland hated sleeping on her back, but having Tess in her arms made her feel safe and needed all at the same time. So, she lay awake for a while, stroking Tess's hair as she slept and listening to her breathe. If there was any doubt in Ryland's mind what she wanted, it completely vanished into the night as she watched Tess sleeping on her chest.

"What's going on?" Tess mumbled, her voice heavy with sleep. She sat up groggily.

"Nothing. It's just Mitch telling us the ferry leaves in an hour." Ryland wrapped her arm around Tess's waist and pulled her close, kissing her shoulder.

Immediately, she felt Tess's body tense up. Tess pulled away politely and threw back the covers, abruptly getting out of bed.

"What are you doing?" Ryland asked. "Come back to bed."

"I've got to get dressed. We should leave in a little bit if we're going to make it back to Boston." Her tone was curt and serious. Ryland's heart sank.

"Is everything all right?"

Tess stopped her frantic picking up of clothes on the floor and stood, her back to Ryland. Ryland watched her force her shoulders to relax as she took a deep breath. She turned around.

"Yeah. Fine. Why wouldn't I be?"

Ryland hadn't seen Tess in years, but she knew when something was terribly off. She racked her brain to see what it could be. They'd had an incredible night together. There was no way Tess didn't feel that too. Ryland couldn't have been wrong about that. This couldn't have been just a one-nighter brought on by circumstance.

"You just seem kind of—" Ryland stopped, choosing her words carefully. She didn't want to come off as needy or crazy. But she felt needy. And she felt absolutely crazy. "Kind of distant."

Tess zipped her bag and smiled. It wasn't the same light, enamored smile she'd offered Ryland the night before. It felt contrived and weighty. Ryland knew she wasn't fine. Tess made her way back over to the bed and got in next to Ryland, kissing her quickly.

"I had a really nice time last night," she said.

Ryland's heart continued its journey down to her feet, and an overwhelming sadness hit her like a sudden storm. She wasn't expecting to be so heartbroken at the idea that Tess might not feel the same way she did. But she was. In a matter of one night, Ryland had managed to fall for a girl who'd been right in front of her for years. And it was completely one-sided.

"Nice. Not exactly the word choice I was hoping for, but okay," Ryland said, laughing half-heartedly.

"Oh, stop it." Tess got up again and finished packing. "Come on, we should get going or we'll miss the boat."

It was a nearly perfect New England fall day. The morning chill was still very much there, especially where Tess stood at the bow of the ferry. But the sun was out enough to warm any exposed skin and the light reflected autumn hues off the water near the shore. Tess needed a minute. Hell, she needed more than a minute. Her emotions were all scrambled, tossed and tangled inside her. It felt like a war was being fought in her gut. Tess had one of the best nights of her life with Ryland. And that was exactly why she had to pull away.

"Hey." Ryland had come up behind her so quietly Tess didn't notice until she had her arms wrapped around Tess's waist. Tess's first instinct was to pull away, to self-preserve. But Ryland's body felt too good against hers.

Tess leaned into her, covering Ryland's hands with her own. "Hey."

"Are you ready to tell me what's going on yet?" Ryland asked. She pulled some of Tess's hair to the side and kissed her exposed neck. Tess melted even further into her. She knew she wasn't going to get away with just quiet evasion. Ryland was too insightful for that. She was too smart. They knew each other too well still.

Tess turned around and put her arms around Ryland's neck, locking eyes with Ryland.

"Why don't you start by telling me what you're thinking right now," Tess said.

Ryland held her closer. "Why me?"

"Because you ended it, Ry. You didn't want me. And I'm not strong enough to be the one to open up first right now."

Tess watched Ryland's face fall a little and she knew it hadn't occurred to Ryland even once just how much damage she'd done to Tess three years ago.

"Okay." Ryland took a deep breath and exhaled loudly, blowing out her cheeks. "I had an incredible night with you last night. No. Not just last night. The entire day. From the minute I saw you again something in me woke up. The way I felt with you last night, Tess…I don't know what was wrong with me years ago, but I know what we had last night? That was real."

It was exactly what Tess wanted to hear. Then again, Ryland had always been good with words. She'd also always been honest with Tess, though. She never painted their relationship to be anything other than what it was. And what Ryland said she felt the night before? Tess had felt that too. It was hard to believe that was anything but mutual.

"I never told you this. But when you cut things off, I was crushed."

"What? You were?" Ryland seemed genuinely shocked.

"Of course I was. I really liked you. I thought we had something. I honestly let myself believe we could go somewhere."

Ryland pulled her in tighter. "I'm so sorry. I had no idea. You were so cool."

Tess laughed stiffly. "I wasn't cool. I was putting on a brave face because I wanted to be cool. I wanted to be the 'cool girl' who didn't care. Because I thought that was who you wanted. But that's not me. I'm really not cool at all, actually."

"You are incredibly cool," Ryland said, grabbing her face and kissing her softly. The wind whipped through Tess's hair and the boat bobbed and up down on the nearby wake. Tess had never felt all at once safer and more vulnerable. "I'm sorry, I didn't realize. And I'm sorry I screwed everything up royally back then. I don't know what was wrong with me. But I do know it was me. You were everything. You were exactly what I wanted. I just wasn't ready for you yet, I guess."

Tess looked up at her and smiled, placing both hands on Ryland's strong chest. "Right person, wrong time?"

"Yes." Ryland nearly jumped with excitement. "That's it exactly."

"How do you know?"

"How do I know what?"

"That I'm the right person this time?" Tess wasn't sure she wanted to know the answer.

Ryland took a minute, seeming to really think about her answer, her face growing serious again. "Because you've always been the right person, Tess. I just wasn't the right me yet."

It was as good a reason as Tess could have hoped for. And she knew that she couldn't hold their past against Ryland if she wanted to attempt any kind of a future with her. It was a risk. But wasn't love always a risk?

"So." Tess bowed her head bashfully.

"So." Ryland echoed.

"What happens now?"

Ryland seemed to contemplate the question for a minute and then brushed the hair away from Tess's cheek, answering her with a soft, slow kiss that left Tess wobblier than the epic wake the ferry was battling ever could.

"Now? We go back to Boston. And then I drive to Providence. And we drive off into the sunset in my Jeep," Ryland said, matter-of-factly. "Listening to Taylor Swift, of course."

Tess laughed. "Naturally."

"I'm serious, Tess. I want this. I want you."

There were all kinds of questions tumbling through Tess's brain.

But there was time to answer all of them later. For now, she just wanted to enjoy being with Ryland.

"I want you too." Tess kissed her again and leaned her head against Ryland's neck, letting the breeze rush past them as they rocked up and down.

"And I know what you're thinking. You live in Providence. I live in Boston. But it's only like an hour. I can drive to you all the time. And I can stay with you on weekends I'm off. We can make it work."

The distance felt like a minute obstacle compared to the way Tess felt in Ryland's arms.

"That sounds really nice."

"It sounds perfect," Ryland said.

They fell silent, both watching the outline of the city come slowly into view. The whole world felt like it was in Tess's reach. Their story had ended three years earlier.

And now they would write a whole new chapter.

About the Authors

Multi-award-winning author and self-proclaimed die-hard romantic **KRIS BRYANT** lives In Kansas City, Missouri, where she is busy writing her next novel, streaming every TV show, and spending time with her family. Writing about two people stranded together who fall in love was definitely in her wheelhouse. Kris jumped at the chance to collaborate with two seasoned writers to tell these stories. She can be reached at krisbryantbooks@gmail.com.

AMANDA RADLEY had no desire to be a writer but accidentally turned into an award-winning, best-selling author. Residing in the UK with her wife and pets, she loves to travel. She gave up her marketing career in order to make stuff up for a living instead. She claims the similarities are startling.

EMILY SMITH works full-time as a physician assistant in an emergency room in Boston. When she isn't in the business of helping others, she enjoys being outside running, playing with her pups, and of course, writing. She is excited to be a part of this collaboration!

Books Available From Bold Strokes Books

Closed-Door Policy by Erin Zak. Going back to college is never easy, but Caroline Stevens is prepared to work hard and change her life for the better. What she's not prepared for is Dr. Atlanta Morris, her gorgeous new professor. (978-1-63679-181-4)

Homeworld by Gun Brooke. Headed by Captain Holly Crowe, the spaceship Velocity's crew journeys toward their alien ancestors' homeworld, and what they find is completely unexpected—and they're not safe. (978-1-63679-177-7)

Outland by Kristin Keppler & Allisa Bahney. Danielle Clark and Katelyn Turner can't seem to stay away from one another even as the war for the wastelands tests their loyalty to each other and to their people. (978-1-63679-154-8)

Royal Exposé by Jenny Frame. When they're grouped together for a class assignment, Poppy's enthusiasm for life and love may just save Casey's soul, but will she ever forgive Casey for using her to expose royal secrets? (978-1-63679-165-4)

Secret Sanctuary by Nance Sparks. US Deputy Marshal Alex Trenton specializes in protecting those awaiting trial, but when danger threatens the woman she's falling for, Alex is in for the fight of her life. (978-1-63679-148-7)

Stranded Hearts by Kris Bryant, Amanda Radley & Emily Smith. In these novellas from award-winning authors, fate intervenes on behalf of love when characters are unexpectedly stuck together. With too much time and an irresistible attraction, anything could happen. (978-1-63679-182-1)

The Last Lavender Sister by Melissa Brayden. Aster Lavender sells her gourmet doughnuts and keeps a low profile; she never plans on the town's temporary veterinarian swooping in and making her feel like anything but a wallflower. (978-1-63679-130-2)

The Probability of Love by Dena Blake. As Blair and Rachel keep ending up in the same place despite the odds, can a one-night stand turn into forever? Or will the bet Blair never intended to make ruin their happily ever after? (978-1-63679-188-3)

Worth a Fortune by Sam Ledel. After placing a want ad for a personal secretary, a New York heiress is surprised when the woman who got away is the one interested in the position. (978-1-63679-175-3)

A Fox in Shadow by Jane Fletcher. Cassie's mission is to add new territory to the Kavillian empire—murder, betrayal, war, and the clash of cultures ensue. (978-1-63679-142-5)

Embracing the Moon by Jeannie Levig. Just as Gwen and Taylor are exploring the new love they've found, the present and past collide, threatening the future they long to share. (978-1-63555-462-5)

Forever Comes in Threes by D. Jackson Leigh. Efficiency expert Perry Chandler's ordered life is upended when she inherits three busy terriers, and the woman she's referred to for help turns out to be her bitter podcast rival, the very sexy Dr. Ming Lee. (978-1-63679-169-2)

Missed Conception by Joy Argento. Maggie Walsh wants a relationship with Cassidy, the daughter she's only just discovered she has due to an in vitro mix-up. Heat kindles between Maggie and Cassidy's mother in a way neither expects. (978-1-63679-146-3)

Private Equity by Elle Spencer. Cassidy Bennett spends an unexpected evening at a lesbian nightclub with her notoriously reserved and demanding boss, Julia. After seeing a different side of Julia, Cassidy can't seem to shake her desire to know more. (978-1-63679-180-7)

Racing the Dawn by Sandra Barrett. After narrowly escaping a house fire, vampire Jade Murphy is unexpectedly intrigued by gorgeous firefighter Beth Jenssen, and her undead existence might just be perking up a bit. (978-1-63679-271-2)

Reclaiming Love by Amanda Radley. Sarah's tiny white lie means somehow convincing Pippa to pretend to be her girlfriend. Only the more time they spend faking it, the more real it feels. (978-1-63679-144-9)

Forever by Kris Bryant. When Savannah Edwards is invited to be the next bachelorette on the dating show *When Sparks Fly*, she'll show the world that finding true love on television can happen. (978-1-63679-029-9)